# Winslow: The Lost Hunters

By David Francis Curran

# Special Thanks

Special thanks goes to Patricia Curran, the love of my life, who spent so many hours reading, editing, and making vital suggestions for improvements that she deserves credit for the book itself.

Eclipse Day, August 21, 2017

# Notice:

This is a work of fiction. All characters with the exception of the late Denny Two Guns O'Loughlin, whom Denny O'London is based on, are completely fictional. (Denny appeared in my feature film, Knapid, as himself and I'm sure he'd appreciate being included here.) Any resemblance to any other persons living or dead is coincidental. There is no Garnet County. Other counties mentioned and cities like Missoula are real but any representation of said county or town is fictional.

# Adahy

## October 23: 3:03 am

In the firelight from the wood stove the dogs rose, alerted by a sound at the door. They did not bark. Instead they went over to the dog door and waited. After a moment a small Native-American boy, with long black hair braided behind his head and wide owl-like eyes, pushed open the dog door. It was a colder than normal October with snow already on the ground and a cold gust of wind blew in before the door swung shut. Mariah, the brown, long-haired, Australian Shepard, whined softly and nuzzled the boy. The boy, nine, stroked her ear. Irene, a black and white Springer Spaniel mix, not to be outdone, moved up and licked the boy's face. He giggled and pushed her away, scratching her head as he did so.

The boy stood by the door. He looked over at the bed in the center of the room where a man lay sleeping. He watched the man for a long time. On the wall was a photo of the man, Winslow, and the boy's late aunt, Lomahongva. The boy looked at the photo just visible in the fire light for a moment then turned away.

The dining room table was not far from the door. The boy took a note from his pocket and placed it on the table. He smiled to himself as he did so.

Having placed the note the boy exited the cabin via the dog door. Irene followed him outside, but Mariah did not.

# An Unexpected Visit

## October 23: 8:02 am

It was just after 8 am on an October morning a couple of days after the opening of big game season, when I heard a knock at the door. For most people this is not an uncommon thing. But for me this is more of a rarity, though slightly less so during

4

hunting season. I live in the Montana wilderness: not the official Wilderness. I don't live in the Bob Marshal or Scapegoat. But I live in the Garnet range at the top of a long dirt road that just doesn't see much traffic, much less visitors, even if you include hunters.

Since I'm in this story I'm telling, I'll describe myself. I'm 35 years old, 6'2" and broad shouldered. I basically cut firewood for a living and lifting tree parts will make anyone very strong. I have a square face with a slightly jutting jaw. One woman I deliver wood to keeps telling me I should go to Hollywood and be an actor, and so she calls me 'Hollywood.' Another said my face was like frozen granite. I guess I haven't smiled much since my wife died. I have brown hair that was blond when I was a baby, cut semi-short, and I am clean-shaven. I liked the way my late wife Lomahongva described me. She said I looked to her like a blue-eyed puma, a mountain lion. I like to think of myself in that way.

As the knock came at the door, Blu, the 4-month-old kitten I'd adopted just a week before, twisted to get loose from my hands. He is a long-haired dark grey almost black tuxedo, with the white vest and feet but no white on his face. I transferred him to the crook of my left arm as I went to the wooden door I had crafted myself quite some years before. It had layers of foot-wide planks that I'd screwed together and cut to fit the opening in the lodgepole pine walls. The door was almost two inches thick and unless you put your ear down by

5

the built-in dog door there wasn't much chance of hearing sounds through it, but I listened just in case. There was no sound. Living in the middle of nowhere has its perks in it being quiet and your life being undisturbed. On the other hand it did have its dangers. Some people when they get in the wilderness lose sight of the constraints that keep them in check in the cities of the world. They think they can do most anything, or, I should say, get away with anything. So I hesitated, considering whether I should get my Taurus Raging Bull revolver in .454 Casull before opening the door. Blu twisted to get loose. I didn't want him outside unless I could watch him. He knew nothing of birds of prey much less the other predators who made it dangerous for kittens. There was another knock. In the back of my mind I had toyed with the idea that it might be Adahy, my nephew. And almost in answer to that thought, I saw a note on the small table near the door. Adahy had apparently come in during the night and left it. The boy was the only one the dogs would not have barked at. Although he lived miles away by road his home was less than a mile from mine through the woods. His widowed mother, my sister-in-law, drank. She would not have heard him leave. I picked the note up and glanced at it. It said he'd like to go elk hunting with me today. I had promised I'd take him. The knock came again and I realized that though it was a fairly soft knock it was just a bit too heavy for Adahy's small hand.

In the back of my mind I heard my Lomahong-va whisper kiddingly, "I don't think it's an evil spir-it." She was speaking to me more and more lately. I was wondering if I should even consider the things I heard her say as something to be taken seriously in my real world when I heard a young voice say, "Maybe he's not home, Mom!"

I opened the door.

"But his Jeep is here," a petite woman, in her late thirties or early forties, with long blonde hair was saying to a boy of about six. He was the age my son would have been and had light brown hair. The boy backed up a bit on seeing me. My size makes me a bit intimidating to some people. Both mother and son had a smattering of freckles across their noses and dark brown eyes.

I looked at the boy first, "I am often not here when my Jeep is." I said. "I tend to go on very long walks." I turned to the woman and smiled, extend-ing my hand. "Winslow Doyle at your service. What may I help you with?"

I assumed that they were here in regards to a lost pet. I had a reputation of being able to find lost dogs that had vanished in the woods. Most of the pets I found had simply run off after being tired of being constrained for long periods of time in their masters' homes. The thing was that town dogs often lost their sense of direction when let loose in the wilderness for the first time.

The woman shook my hand quickly and looked into my eyes. I read pain in hers. I glanced at the boy and sensed he was not simply just ill at ease at meeting a stranger for the first time. He looked worried. I looked back at the woman who was very pretty in her way and returned her gaze.

"I'm Callie Carew. The sheriff said you might be able to help me." Her words were anxious. Some people really get upset when pets disappear, but this woman seemed more upset than I'd seen before.

"Why don't you come on in," I said and waved them into the doorway. After they had passed I shut the door and put the plastic sleeve down over the dog door. My dogs were out, and they would interrupt if they came back while I had visitors.

"This is my son, Geoff," she said introducing the boy.

I put my hand out but he did not take it. He shyly followed his mother who had spotted my couch.

My cabin is not large. There are just two rooms within its odd octagonal shape. In a blueprint the smaller utility room would look like a rectangle on the side of the handle of the war club that's the cabin. In the main cabin a boxy wood stove with an isinglass door sits in the exact center. The corner of the smaller room reaches out not quite to the stove. The walls separating the smaller room from the larger are not chinked and gaps let the heat flow through. The utility area houses the battery bank for my solar panels and for storage. I have the larger living area of the cabin roughly sectioned into four areas:

1) The kitchen which features a sink with a bucket beneath to capture grey-water, a propane cooking stove for use in the warmer months when the wood stove would make the cabin too warm, some homemade cupboards and a counter for food prep.

2) The bedroom area, which pretty much just contains my bed and a night table.

3) My work area, which consists of a computer and bookshelf.

4) And the sitting area, with a two-seat couch and two chairs facing it.

Mother and son sat themselves down on my couch. Geoff looked a lot like his mother.

I put Blu down and the kitten ran up on the couch's arm by the boy. Geoff reached out and petted Blu gently. But he had a very sad look on his young face.

I took this as another indication that these two had more to worry about than a lost pet. I looked back at the woman. "What can I do for you?"

"My husband is missing," Callie Carew said. There was fear in her voice and that struck me.

"And Cassie," the boy said.

"Yes," Callie continued, "My husband Greg and our 15-year-old daughter Cassie. They went hunting three days ago. It was supposed to be an overnight stay and then a one-day hunt on opening day. It was my daughter Cassie's first time. They were going to return that evening. They never came back."

"So they had camping gear, sleeping bags, food?"

"They had camping gear but really only had food for one day."

A tear appeared at the corner of the woman's right eye. The boy reached out and touched his mother's hand.

"I had heard my husband tell Cassie to put down 292-50 for her mule deer tag so I knew where they'd be. I told the sheriff that, and this morning he told me he has had deputies keeping an eye out in that region, but so far there has been no sign of my husband's truck or my husband and daughter."

I knew that 292-50 indicated they'd be hunting in section 292; the West Garnet Range area. It is a huge area shaped roughly like the silhouette of a dog lying with its head up. It encompasses thousands of acres and miles and miles of road. Without more information it could be impossible to find them.

Just then there was a rustling outside the door and then the sounds of claws, scraping the plastic sleeve covering the dog door.

"Sit!" I said loudly. The sound of scraping stopped.

"My dogs," I said. "But they can wait." I didn't know how Callie Carew or her son felt about dogs, but there was no problem letting Irene and Mariah cool their heels outside.

I looked into the woman's eyes. The sheriff would have asked her if there had been problems in their marriage, or if it was possible that they had just decided to stay another day. But she had al-

10

ready told me that they did not have food for a longer trip and her emotional state revealed a very loving relationship.

"Is it possible they bought more food?"

Callie shook her head. "The sheriff asked that, too. I am pretty sure my husband didn't have much cash. The sheriff checked. No money has been withdrawn from our joint checking or savings accounts, and Greg's credit card hasn't been used."

"Do you happen to know your daughter's and husband's shoe sizes?" I asked.

A distressed look appeared on Callie's face.

"I need to know what size shoe your daughter and your husband wear, just in case I can find tracks." I explained.

# 2 Days Earlier: A First Time Hunter

## October 21: One hour before sunrise.

Only Greg Carew's crew-cut blond hair peeked out as he woke to a chill that reached into his sleeping bag and touched his cheeks. He stretched his long thin legs but stayed huddled in the bag as he fought wakefulness. He had been dreaming that he and his wife Callie were already at the West Wind Inn on Sanibel Island, Florida, and when he tried to rise she had pulled him back into bed. The cold helped the dream fade. Finally, he sat up with his sleeping bag held to him, revealing his long nose and jutting jaw to any creatures that might be about, and looked out the back of the truck's camper window. He saw in the dim predawn light that it had snowed again, adding at least another inch to the five or six inches already on the ground. A covering like a layer of sugar had coated the hillside where his Chevy Silverado was parked. Before he and Callie headed to Florida for their long-awaited vacation, he meant to see their daughter Cassie get her first deer.

"Cassie," he said, softly. There was no sound from his sleeping daughter who lay curled in her sleeping bag next to him. Only a strand of her blond hair could be seen above the fabric of the twenty-below bag. "Cassie, honey, you got to wake up."

Cassie gave off a soft moan as her head poked out of her sleeping bag and a puff of white appeared by her lips. An instant later she turned as if trying to go back to sleep.

Greg reached over and grabbed her hip through her sleeping bag and shook her.

Cassie tried to twist further away, but Greg shook her again. This time her head rose, and she opened her eyes.

"It's still dark," she said.

"It's getting lighter out as we speak. And if you want to try for your deer, you'd better get moving," he said. He couldn't help but admire the beautiful young woman Callie and he had made. They were already getting phone calls where the caller would hang up as soon as he or Callie picked up the phone. It would be worse, he knew, when Cassie was allowed to date.

Lifting herself on her elbows Cassie rose and looked out. "It snowed again?"

"Yep, but not much. Lets go."

They each found private spots to answer the calls of nature, then broke out the sandwiches Callie had made. Greg discovered his PB&J sandwich had been cut into the shape of a heart. His wife, in 20 years of marriage, had not stopped letting him know she loved him. After eating, the two stood by the side of the truck with white breath clouds rising from their noses and mouths, getting their gear ready.

Cassie, at 15, stood a head shorter than her father. Her soft blonde hair extended down past her shoulders. Sky-blue eyes looked out from a face that he was sure many of the boys at Palmer High already dreamed about. It didn't ease Greg's mind that she had a body that was well past just blossoming into womanhood.

Greg shouldered his Remington pump 3600 in 30-06 and watched as Cassie shouldered her .243 Winchester. The two, decked out in new blaze orange hunting jackets and identical blaze orange knit hats, each had a pair of binoculars hanging from straps around their necks.

"Ready to get your first buck?" Greg asked in a whisper.

Cassie nodded.

Greg lifted his right index finger and licked the tip. Then he held it out in the open air, turning it about, slowly. He nodded in the direction of the fence. They were lucky. The wind was with them. The air was moving toward them so their scent would not alert any deer in front of them.

Cassie nodded, she understood.

Her father led the way up through the short grasses that peeked out through the snow covering the pine leaf debris that carpeted this wooded area on land belonging to the Bureau of Land Management. Most of the stalks were dried to a yellow-brown, but quite a few grass clumps were still a vivid green, rising from the snow-frosted ground like green heads. The area had been logged years ago so that the trees formed a sort of wooded park with wide openings between trees. The ground in the park rose in an uneven fashion with rolling hillocks, nooks and all sorts of heavy brush. They walked as quietly as they could toward the crumbling cattle fence from the days 80 years before when ranches leased the land. The fence formed the lower border of a very large open meadow. This meadow rose upward in a lazy incline for hundreds of yards to an elevation of about two hundred feet above the park they now crossed.

The year before Greg had been here alone. Back then, as he neared this same fence, three does had suddenly walked out in front of him about twenty yards away. The does had simply stopped and looked at him. It was so early in the gun-hunting season that they weren't afraid of a human who suddenly appeared in their area. He froze. The deer watched him for a while then went back to feeding on the grasses. Once their gaze was diverted Greg felt it was again safe to look about. There was a very good chance that if there were does there, there were also bucks around. Moving slowly, he turned almost 90 degrees to his right. To his surprise a young buck stood only 40 yards away. It seemed to be watching both Greg and the does. As Greg watched it, the buck seemed to become nervous. It began moving in the direction it had been heading, away from Greg. Greg had been carrying his rifle and swung it up. He had a bullet in the chamber, and as he lifted the rifle, he slipped off the safety. The buck began moving a bit faster. Aiming, almost instinctively, Greg fired. The buck suddenly vanished.

Not knowing if he had hit the deer, he racked in another round. He picked up the spent case for reloading and moved slowly in the direction he had last seen the deer.

He had not gone far, when over the taller brush he saw the deer, apparently dead, lying almost in the exact location it had been in when he shot it.

Greg had actually shot quite a few deer over the past few years in this area. And he knew on opening day that the chance of seeing a buck before all the deer became really spooked by hunters was at its best. The rut, where male deer were reckless in their pursuit of females, was a few weeks away. So for opening day he had brought Cassie here.

He had shown Cassie how to walk quietly. The trick was not to try and walk tiptoe, but rather to look down at where you were putting your feet and put your heel down first. Once down, in an area free of sticks and other noisy debris, you put your weight on your heel as you eased forward.

He listened as Cassie walked next to him. He was only a few feet away and could barely hear her. Of course, deer could hear far better than either of them, still he was proud of Cassie.

They reached the fence at the edge of the park. They could now see out into the open meadow before them. There were no deer in sight.

Cassie looked at him. They had agreed to keep talking to a minimum. Greg nodded in the direction of the huge rising meadow bordered on either side by trees. Together they both stepped across the strands of barbed wire that now hung only inches above the ground from rotting posts.

They climbed to the top of the meadow, which was in fact a ridge. As they stood on this ridge and faced away from the meadow fence, far below, the ground plummeted sharply into a narrow canyon hundreds of feet in depth. Here they turned right and followed the ridge to the bordering treed area. They found neither tracks nor deer. They turned and were soon descending the meadow again at an angle that would take them to the spot where they had crossed the fence. Suddenly, Cassie stopped and pointed. She lifted her own binoculars as Greg glanced down. Far below them, walking along the fence line heading away from them, were two deer.

"An older doe and a younger doe," Cassie said, quietly, and then covered her mouth, realizing her mistake in talking.

Greg said nothing.

The two deer had seen them now. Both stared upward at them. The deer did not watch for long. Unlike the deer Greg had seen the year before who showed no fear of him, these two seemed to become almost instantly uncomfortable. They did not run, but began walking quickly away along the fence line.

"Should we follow them?" Cassie whispered.

Greg watched the deer hurry away. Unlike whitetail, which raised their white tails like flags when alarmed, these mule deer whose dark tails were hard to make out at this distance, simply walked away at a fast pace. Greg watched them cross the fence at a spot where a tree limb had fallen on the barbed wire and flattened it. As the deer vanished behind some trees, Greg spoke.

"Thanks to the snow we can just follow their tracks."

Cassie nodded enthusiastically.

Greg and Cassie took their time walking back down toward the fence line. There was always the chance that the deer had stopped and were watching them right now.

"When you want to follow a deer," Greg had told Cassie, "its best to pretend you aren't trying to follow it."

Near the fence where they had last seen the deer, they began to search the ground.

"Dad!" Cassie said quietly. She pointed to a spot on the ground not far in front of her.

Greg walked over and looked down, then took in the snow surrounding the small tracks Cassie had found. It took him only a moment to spot the larger set of tracks, just a few feet away.

"Let's follow them," he whispered.

Cassie nodded. Together they followed the tracks. After crossing the fence the deer had gone more or less in a straight line for a while, which twisted around brush and trees, but once the deer felt safe their tracks seemed to meander.

"They think they've lost us, or at least are safe," Greg said.

"So they are feeding?" Cassie asked.

"I think so." Greg looked at the ground. Though the tracks meandered quite a bit, they were more or less going in the same direction.

"Let's take a shortcut that way," Greg said pointing off away at a 90-degree angle. "There's a large open area that way. Maybe we can see something."

Cassie nodded. Together they made their way toward a thick stand of trees. They did not walk fast, but went as quickly as they could without making noise.

They had been walking for about five minutes, when they stepped through a line of trees into the open area where the dirt road they had driven up ran through a very large grassy meadow.

Cassie pointed far off in the direction they were now moving. Greg followed her finger. There at the other end of the field, off to the right of the road they had come in on, stood a deer. Greg raised his binoculars.

"It has antlers. It's a four-point." The deer had brownish grey hair on its torso with white hair beneath. The coat outlined a body well muscled and made for fleeing from threats. The horns were a protective halo of bone. In the spring they grew covered in velvet. And if you touched them they would be hot. By fall, as the mating season began, the velvet had fallen off, giving the buck a many-pointed weapon to protect him from predators and to do battle in competition for a mate.

Cassie was already lowering herself to the ground. Her favorite shooting position was prone. She got down on the ground and stretched out.

"Can't see it from this position," she said.

"Try kneeling."

Cassie slowly rose and knelt on one leg. The other leg, positioned forward, she used as a rest for her elbow with her rifle resting on the palm of her hand above it. Greg watched her hands shake as she adjusted the scope. She turned the magnification to 4 and sighted in the deer. As Greg looked down the field the deer raised its head. It looked at them as if wondering if they were a danger. It was a relatively young deer. It had not yet learned to be wary of people. Looking down at Carrie, Greg wanted to advise her. In his head he was saying 'sight him in and squeeze slowly' but this was not the time to be speaking or giving lessons. He did not want to distract her.

20

"Varoom," the report pushed out so loudly, Greg startled. He looked back toward the deer and saw it jump, then run to its left toward a wall of brush. It jumped into a small cluster of aspen and in a moment was out of sight.

"Did I hit it?" Cassie asked. There was a hint of disappointment in her voice that made Greg smile.

"I do believe you did," Greg replied. "Come on, let's go down there and see."

Greg counted the paces from their position to where he remembered the deer standing. On the way, above where they had made the turn toward the dead end, they crossed the tracks of a vehicle with a narrower wheelbase that had driven in that very morning and gone up toward the ridge. Greg had paced off 223 yards, a long shot, when he stood in the general area where the young buck had been standing. They walked the brush line first, looking down, looking for tracks and blood.

"I don't see any tracks or blood," Cassie said, the disappointment apparent in her voice.

"The deer was a little closer to the road when you shot," Greg said. "Let's look over here."

Cassie looked over at the road almost 40 feet away. She was sure the deer had not been standing near the road at all.

Greg took a few steps away from the brush line into an area where some weeds poked above the snow-covered ground. Then he saw it, a single track. "Found a track, but no blood by it," he said.

Cassie rushed over, scanning the ground as she did so. "Blood!" She cried excitedly after a moment, pointing at a spot a few steps away.

Greg walked over. There was a dug-in track, deeper than the hoof print he had just seen. The deer's hoof had dug into the snow as the deer pushed hard against the ground in an effort to escape. Next to the print was a small droplet of blood.

"I hit it."

"Yes, you hit it," Greg said.

"Why didn't it drop?"

"They rarely do, unless it's a headshot, or one in the spine."

Cassie was looking at him with a puzzled expression.

"Even with shots that take out the heart or lungs, they can run for a bit. What we have to do now is track it."

They followed the tracks into the brush. As soon as the tracks had entered the brush, the blood drops seemed to stop. Greg knew this didn't mean that the deer wasn't dying. Although, he had tracked a deer he shot some years before for miles before the blood stopped and the deer's tracks became lost in a highway of other deer tracks.

"I don't see any more blood," Cassie said, her voice troubled. "Does this mean he wasn't hurt bad?"

"I don't know," Greg said. "We have to just keep following his tracks and hope he doesn't lead us into a maze of other deer's tracks."

"Couldn't you tell which tracks are his?"

"I'm not that good," Greg said.

The tracks seemed to go on in a wild random way, which made it obvious the deer was trying to lose anything following. Greg had his head down, a step behind Cassie, watching the deer's trail, when he heard Cassie gasp. He looked up. The buck lay on its side about ten feet away. It lay still. There was no obvious sign of breathing.

Cassie ran toward it.

"Whoa," Greg yelled. "Stay well back and poke it with your rifle first. If it is not dead, it could charge you, and those antlers could hurt you."

He watched Cassie gently poke the buck with the muzzle of her Winchester. The buck did not move. Greg stepped up. The deer's eyes were clouded. The tongue hung out limp. It was clearly dead.

The bullet hole had to be under a small patch of bloodstained hair no bigger than a fifty-cent piece high up on the front part of the body.

"Okay," Greg said, "now comes the fun part. We have to gut it."

"I know that, Dad!" Cassie said in that tone that mimicked her Mom's voice when she disagreed with Greg about something.

From one of her large hunting jacket pockets, she pulled out a pair of rubber dishwashing gloves. Greg smiled. Callie had given him a set, too, but had not mentioned giving a set to Cassie. He'd found he had a reaction to the latex gloves they sold hunters in sets. For years he thought it was deer blood on his skin that made him itchy after a kill, but realized one time when he'd put the gloves on for a cleaning job, that it was the gloves or the powder they used to coat them that he was allergic to.

Though he offered to help, Cassie insisted she make the incision to open the deer up.

"Okay, but don't cut too deep or you'll spill its stomach contents and we don't want that." He'd done that himself when he was a teen and could remember the smell to this day.

But Cassie, using her own Wyoming knife, a small knife with a short curved blade on one side and a razor inside a small hook-like cover on the other, opened a small incision with the blade beneath the deer's breastbone, then slit the deer's skin open easily with the razor. She let her Dad pull the stomach, liver, and intestines out, but got blood all over her gloves and sleeves while severing the trachea. Her Dad had insisted she do that to remove the lungs and heart. He did do the cutting around the anus and penis because she asked him to. The deer's nether regions where something she did not want to think about or touch.

Greg looked around. "We're only about twenty yards from the main road. Why don't you stay here, and I'll go back and get the truck and bring it around?"

Twenty minutes later, each taking a front leg, they dragged it to the truck, lifted it onto the hood, and Cassie held it in place while Greg tied it on with paracord.

"Ideally it would be better if we could put this deer in back, but we've got all our camping stuff in there, and Mom will kill us if we get blood all over everything. "

"Won't the heat from the engine cook it?"

"It's cold and we aren't going too far. But it is best not to put the deer on the hood."

"Well," she said, as he stood by the tied on deer. "Do you want to try to find one, too?"

Greg laughed. "I think we'd better take this one home and get it skinned and cut up, first."

"Okay," Cassie said, smiling.

"One thing we have to do first," Greg said. He inserted his right index finger into the open cavity of the deer and brought it out covered with a gob of blood. Cassie just looked at him, puzzled as he approached her. He took his finger and marked the center of her forehead with a spot of blood.

"Ewwwww," she cried. "Why the hell did you do that?"

"A right of passage," Greg said. "My father did it to me, and I'm passing it on. You are now marked as a hunter."

Cassie stared at him for a moment, then smiled.

"A successful hunter," she said.


"I'm going to take my hunting jacket off," Cassie said twenty minutes later, "I'm getting too warm." She unbuckled her seat belt and began unzipping her coat. They were going around a very sharp curve on the single lane road leading back to town when a red truck came speeding around the curve toward them. There was an open area on his left so Greg swerved toward it to avoid a head-on crash. As the oncoming vehicle clipped the back end of the Chevy, jarring Greg, his foot hit the accelerator instead of the brake.

# Tracks and Blood

## October 23: 11 am

I couldn't waste any time. The hunter and his daughter had been missing for two days. Callie told me that the sheriff had told her that no accidents at all had been reported in the 292 hunting district. The 292 hunting district encompasses three counties: Missoula, Garnet, and Powell. And although the Carews lived in Missoula County near Potomac, she had been shunted somehow to the Garnet Sheriff's department who had put her in touch with me.

The good news was that it had only snowed very lightly since they had gone missing, and it had gotten colder on each of the days since. I might still be able to find their tracks.

Callie had known her daughter wore a size-eight boot because she had purchased them. But she wasn't that sure about her husband's. She thought he wore a 10-1/2 or 11. She had cried when she told me the sheriff had also asked if she could be more specific about where her husband and daughter had gone hunting, but she had no idea.

"Murky Gulph," the boy had said then.

I looked down at the boy and asked a corrected name, "Do you mean Murkey Gulch, Geoff?"

Geoff had nodded, as his mother looked at him in surprise.

"And how do you know that?" I asked, eagerly.

"I wanted to hunt too. But Dad said that Murkey Gulch was too hard a place for me to go hunting. I had to wait until I was older."

"He had pneumonia over the summer. He tires easily. Otherwise Greg would probably let him tag along even if he couldn't legally hunt."

I nodded my head. You needed to be 12 and had to take a hunting safety course to hunt in Montana.

I had looked at Callie. "You didn't have him with you when you went to the sheriff?"

She shook her head, no.

I told her to call the sheriff when she got home and tell him that Murkey Gulch was the probable area where her husband had been hunting. And in the meantime I would go out there and take a look around.

A gulch is a narrow canyon with a stream running through it. But to most people Murkey Gulch referred to all the land surrounding the stream: gullies, hills, meadows, and mountains. I had hunted Murkey Gulch many times, and it was a good place to find game, especially on opening day. Callie told me her husband had been hunting for years and had brought back a buck each year for many years. This told me he was a knowledgeable hunter. What the boy had said about his father not believing he'd be able to handle the walking around, told me that Greg Carew was not a road hunter--that is someone who drove around hoping to see a deer without ever really getting out of his car.

This meant that he would have parked somewhere in the Murkey Gulch area and walked. If I could not find the Blue Chevy Silverado in this area there were two choices. One: he had hunted here, but he or someone else had moved his truck. Or two: he had changed his mind and hunted somewhere else within the 292-50 hunting district they had mule deer tags for. But I thought that it was unlikely he had gone somewhere else. If he had gotten deer in this area for years, it made sense he'd come back. Based on the vibe Callie Carew had given me, I did not think her husband ran away. I had decided that I'd satisfy myself whether he'd been in the area before considering anything else. But I had to hurry. A new snow system was predicted to be coming in from Washington the next day. I had about 24 hours to find them or some sign of where they'd been.

The road to the areas surrounding Murkey Gulch climbed a mountain called Midas Mountain. I don't know why it was so-called. There were many mines in the area, but I had never heard this mountain being associated with much gold. Near the shoulder of the mountain this road circled around a steep area where the road itself had been cut into the rock. As I drove it, on my right, a steep slope dotted with snow-covered tree stumps dropped hundreds of feet to Rocker Creek, the next creek over from Murkey. On my left the land that rose above me had not been logged and conifers, mostly subalpine fir, rose with snow-dusted branches. By instinct or habit I kept my eyes on the areas between the trees. It was still elk season, and I had not filled my own tag.

I had left Adahy a note apologizing and explaining that I had to look for a lost hunter and would go elk hunting with him at my next opportunity.

Almost as if in answer to that thought, a young voice from the back of the Jeep said, "If you see an elk, will you stop to shoot it?"

I braked so hard Adahy, who must have been hiding in the cargo compartment all this time, fell over the back of the back seat on top of Mariah. Mariah whined.

"Serves you right for not letting me know he was back there," I said, scolding the girls.

To Adahy I said, sternly, "How long have you been there?"

He climbed in-between the two front seats and sat in the passenger seat. He put his seatbelt on. The Jeep was too old for airbags.

"I came while you were talking to the two who visited your cabin. I heard what they said. So I got in your Jeep so I could help you."

Just then my cellphone rang. I hoped it was Callie calling to say her husband and daughter had turned up. It was Yona, Adahy's mother. I assured her he was with me and safe. After the loss of her sister and then her husband she may have become a drinker but she cared about her son. Adahy was shaking his head, no, over and over.

"He is answering a call of nature right now. Did you want to wait to speak to him."

"No," Yona said. "Tell him I hope you two get an elk."

After his mother had hung up, I turned to Adahy, "I would feel guilty if I stopped my search for that lady's family to shoot an elk."

I depend on hunting for meat but I had already gotten an eight-point mule deer during early gun season in the Scapegoat with my new crossbow.

"Besides," I added, "Irene and Mariah are with us, and we can't hunt elk with dogs."

I was driving slowly looking for places where vehicles had pulled off and the drivers had gotten out. I found the first such spot on a corner of the mountain where a little spur dotted with lodgepole shot off.

I stopped my Jeep Cherokee and got out after gesturing for Adahy to stay put. A bloody drag-trail, deer sized, snaked back in among the trees. The tracks along the drag-trail all belonged to men with big boots. No size-eight boots had left tracks in the snow. I got back in the Jeep, shook my head to let Adahy know it was not the right spot, and drove on.

But I quickly got lucky. The next turn off went into a road that split further in: one fork climbing to a high ridge and the other dead-ending about a half-mile in. The entry was by a bend in Murkey Gulch road where an area had been cleared and leveled by bull-dozers so a long ago logging operation had a place to store logs for their logging trucks. The turn onto the side road was so sharp you could only reach it from the opposite direction.

As I turned around in the leveled area, I saw someone had built a campfire off to the side. I stopped and we both checked around the fire. There were no size-eight tracks. When we were both back in the Jeep I drove up to the entrance to the side road.

I knew about this turn up to the ridge and, the dead-end road, because I'd been here many times over the years. But it was partly hidden and few knew about it. I got out of the Jeep, again telling the dogs and Adahy to wait, and looked down at the tracks going in. There were only two sets of ruts. One set was definitely wide enough for vehicles the size of a Chevy Silverado. How many vehicles that size had driven in or out I could not tell.

The area the road traversed was wide open for a bit. It was a large logged field dotted with widely-spaced stumps. I got back in the Jeep. Adahy was standing on the seat looking down at the ruts in front of us.

"They are the right size for a Silverado," Adahy said. He was one of the smartest kids I'd ever met. His grandfather, William Longbear, my father-in-law, who had a Ph.D. in Philosophy from Harvard home-schooled the boy. But during hunting season school was closed. William Longbear always hunted alone.

We drove in slowly; looking for sign that showed hunters had stopped and gotten out. Across the white snow deer tracks crisscrossed everywhere. At one point, not far in, someone with man-sized boots had walked to the ruts and then, as his tracks vanished I assume he'd walked in them. I decided to check that out later. At a spot about 300 yards from the entrance to the road, the vehicle tracks split. One set headed up to the ridge and the other toward the dead end.

Adahy and I got out this time, leaving the dogs in the Jeep and examined the tracks.

Adahy pointed to the set of tracks going up to the ridge. "Those tracks are too narrow for a Chevy Silverado"

I nodded and looked at the tracks that were wide enough that headed toward the dead end. We walked along the wider tracks for a bit. At a spot just past the turnoff two separate sets of ruts where clear. Either two vehicles had gone in or the one that had gone in had come back out again.

Back in the Jeep, we drove along the road slowly, scanning the snow on both sides. Bare larch, which had shed its needles, and green lodgepole closed in, though not too thickly. The woods on the edges of the road were more park like.

As we neared the dead end I slowed. This was a spot where huge old trees stretched out their branches overhead. The land sloped down on my right and rose on my left. When the tracks ahead indicated the vehicle had made a K-turn, I parked. We were twenty yards from where that truck had turned. Leaving the dogs in the Jeep, Adahy and I got out. Adahy stood and watched as I walked ahead. After a few steps I saw a large boot print heading toward where that truck had been parked. A man, returning to the truck, had most likely walked back to his truck in his truck's ruts then driven over his own tracks. I thought back to the man-sized tracks I had seen earlier. Was this the same man? Unfortunately, the tracks leading back to where the man had walked from had now been driven over twice.

"I would have turned the truck around when I arrived," Adahy said.

I nodded in agreement. Where the truck had been parked, two sets of tracks led off from either side. If Adahy was correct about their turning the truck around the larger hunter's tracks led off and back from the driver's side and a smaller set of tracks from the passenger side. My heart raced. There were also tracks where the back of the turned around truck would have been.

"What do you make of these?" I asked.

Adahy looked the tracks over. "I think they were camping in the back of the truck. They got out here."

I nodded.

The tracks leading away from the truck as they, I assumed, went hunting were the clearest. One set were definitely from man-sized boots and the other from a set of size-eight boots. I didn't know for sure if we'd found Cassie and Greg or not, but in my gut I was sure. The only thing I could do was follow.

I let the dogs out of the Jeep. Unless I gave them the signal to run they would follow us. I wear Muck Wetland boots in the snow and have always been comfortable walking around, even for hours in fairly deep snow. Adahy wore Minnetonka laced boots that William Longbear bought and waterproofed for him.

We went slowly following in the truck's occupant's footsteps. After an hour we were headed back toward the open area and the fork where we'd both turned onto the dead end road.

The trees got thinner. The tracks led through low brush covered with snow and the occasional tree, followed by the wide clearing I had just driven through before turning onto the dead end road, which was now below us to my left.

The tracks led to a spot where the person with the smaller shoe size had taken a prone shooting position, apparently changed their mind, and then knelt in the same spot in the snow.

Adahy laid down on the snow next to the impression the hunter had left. "I cannot see above the grass like this," he said. He rose and got down on one knee. "I can see fine from here."

He pointed to a disturbance in the snow a foot away from where the kneeler must have been. "I think this person picked up an ejected shell."

Adahy had good eyes.

I looked down across the clearing. A gust of wind threw snow devils into the air. There were no animals in sight now. How far away had the shot been?

I paced it off as we followed the tracks of the big hunter and the small hunter. They actually crossed the tracks of the smaller vehicle that had gone up to the ridge. The tracks were far enough away from the place where we'd turned off for the dead end, that we had not seen them.

Irene and Mariah ran far ahead, stopped, and began sniffing the ground. I found deer tracks where they were sniffing. I found spots of blood by the tracks soon after and before Adahy saw them. I pointed them out to him. My pacing set the distance as 227 yards from where the shooter had knelt. The dogs kept sniffing the blood excitedly. From the tracks we could tell the hunters had apparently not seen the deer tracks at first. But then it was clear they had found and followed them. We followed their tracks. The gut pile was not that far from the spot where I had first seen the deer tracks and the blood. Drag marks showed me they had eventually dragged the deer to Murkey Gulch Road, which was closer than the road to the dead end. If I had a deer fall where this one did I would have loaded the deer there, too.

I studied the tracks by the gut pile.

"I think the girl sat her for a time," Adahy observed. He pointed to a spot where snow had been compressed on top of a flat stump as if someone had sat there. Tracks suggested small boots had moved her feet about as she sat there. Another set of tracks showed large boots had walked back toward the road. My guess was she'd waited here while her father got the truck.

I told Adahy to keep looking around as I ran back along the road to my Jeep. The dogs, as if understanding the urgency of the situation, were right behind me and jumped right in when I opened the driver's door.

Luckily, my cell phone worked. I called the sheriff's office. A woman, Nadine, answered. She told me that the sheriff was out of the office. When I gave her my name there was a pause. "Hold a second," she said. I looked off into the snow-covered pines below me. While I watched a doe peeked out, looked up at me, then backed back into the trees.

"Mr. Doyle, sorry to keep you waiting," Nadine said. "I knew the sheriff was actually looking for you, and I wanted to make sure…" She paused. And I realized what she meant.

"That I wouldn't run," I said and laughed.

"Yes," she laughed too.

I explained what I'd found, and then said, "I'm in the Murkey Gulch area now, so if you can get him on the radio?"

"Mrs. Carew called, so he was headed that way," Nadine said.

"Well, if you can get him, I'm back in a ways at the moment, but I'll walk out to the Murkey Gulch road and wait."

# A Surprise

## October 23: Early Afternoon

I drove the Jeep over to where I'd first found the blood, and honked the horn. Adahy appeared and got in. I asked him to wait, as I didn't want the sheriff to know I had a young brave with me. He understood. I got out and headed for the gut pile intending to follow the hunter's drag path to the road.

I had just found where big tracks and small tracks had dragged their deer to Murkey Gulch Road to load it up, when the sheriff's 4-wheel-drive SUV pulled up alongside me. He was driving in the opposite direction from where I had come which meant he had come the back way from I-90. Paul Goldstone is a heavy man in his 40's with close-cropped red hair beneath a brown Stetson with sharp creases. He wears gold-framed glasses, has blue eyes, and he seems to always have a smile, which is why he was reelected over and over by voters. This time, though, he looked flustered. "Can you come around this side," Paul asked through the open passenger side window, titling his head to indicate the driver's side window.

I walked around quickly. as he powered closed the passenger side window and opened his driver's side window. That he did not want to get out of his vehicle meant he was pressed for time. He obviously wanted to show me something.

As I looked in the driver's side window he seemed to be evaluating me. "Just heard from Nadine that you found out they got a deer," he said.

I nodded, and pointed into the brush on the side of the road. "Just about 20 yards in," I said.

Paul nodded. "I've been thinking on this," he said, "and my staff is just a bit..." he paused, "... hell, we're so damn busy I haven't got enough personal to do all we have to, and I just got a call that I have to go back to town for."

He looked me up and down. "Raise your right hand," he demanded.

I raised my hand.

"Do you, Winslow Doyle, swear to uphold the laws of the State of Montana?"

This was a surprise. "I am not sure I want to be a deputy. I just want to find these missing people," I said.

"That's all I'm going to ask you to do. You'll be part-time."

I still had my hand raised. "I do," I said.

Paul fished in his shirt pocket and pulled out a badge. He handed it to me through the window. "Well, now you are official. See what you can do as far as locating these missing people. I think we both know that if they didn't just take off, it's likely they went off the road somewhere on their way home. I'll pay you for your time, just keep track of it."

I looked down at the badge I held in my hand, thinking Paul was probably right.

"If you find them…" Paul hesitated. "Wait," he fished around the seat next to him and handed me a small two-way. "If they're alive call for help. I'd try your cell phone first but if that doesn't work this might."

I nodded my understanding.

"If they are not alive, get ahold of me. I can make the notification."

"I can do it," I said.

Paul shook his head. "No, it has to be me."

"I'll go with you if it comes to that," I said.

Paul nodded. He paused, then said, "One more thing." He reached into the glove compartment and pulled out a pair of rubber gloves and then some glassine envelopes. "Just in case you find any evidence."

Goldstone didn't explain as I quickly pondered the implications the word 'evidence' brought to mind.

I took the gloves and evidence bags and divided them between my pockets. Then I stepped back from the cruiser, and he began backing up. When he reached a wide part of the road he did a K-turn and drove off, going back the way he had come.

I stood there thinking about Callie Carew and Geoff. I really hoped I wouldn't have to share telling them bad news. But the likelihood of there not being bad news was now very remote.

# A Road Hunt

## October 23: Mid Afternoon

We drove slowly. There are about 25 miles of dirt roads between the spot where Greg and Cassie Carew had put their deer into their truck and the highway. There are many twisting curves and the roads, snow packed by the wheels of vehicles, can be icy and treacherous.

Adahy had been studying the badge the sheriff had given me. "Now that you are a sheriff I suppose I have to be good."

"You should be good whether or not I'm a sheriff. And I'm a deputy not a sheriff."

"I suppose if you are only a deputy I don't have to be that good," he said with a smile.

I knew that only certain parts of the road have spots where a vehicle could slide off an embankment and vanish. I was almost done checking the first and most likely area. This was a steep climb up a mountainside where almost any spot along that stretch had a sharp drop-off to the side where a vehicle could slip off and fall quite a distance before any trees might stop the fall. As we drove I carefully scanned the cliff side for any sign of disturbance in the snow and there hadn't been anything to see.

However, as we drove the last leg to the top, which curved to the right, I saw up ahead on the mountainside visible on my left, the unmistakable reddish white of a newly broken tree. I felt a little sick to my stomach as I pulled over as far as possible to the right, hugging the mountain so other vehicles, which might come along, could pass. Leaving the dogs and Adahy in the Jeep, I walked along the right of the road without looking down the slope to my left until I was just opposite where I had seen that broken tree. I heard in the distance a vehicle coming. There were no tracks indicating a vehicle had gone off. Still I had a bad feeling about my search.

This was not a well-traveled road. The few hunters driving by drove in the ruts of others. Even with a covering of snow, the ruts could be slick and to walk in them would risk a fall. I stepped over the icy ruts, keeping my feet in the snow and eased close to the edge and looked down. The broken tree I had spotted was indeed below me. But the large broken subalpine fir was the only sign of disturbance in the area. It was just an old tree broken by the weight of the latest snow. No vehicle had gone off the road here.

In a way it was strange. This mountainside was the most dangerous section of the entire drive back to Potomac. There are spots along the rest of the drive where a vehicle could go off. But the embankments did not involve deep drops. The steepest I guessed was no more than fifteen or twenty feet. I wasn't an expert on truck crashes but I could only imagine that it would take both the driver and passenger not wearing seat belts and going fairly fast for such a drop to prove fatal to both. I wished I had asked Callie Carew if her husband and daughter regularly wore seat belts. I wouldn't call now. Such a call would only alarm her.

I was turning to get back into my Jeep and continue the search, when a horn blasted from above me. The rusty Ford pickup was twenty yards away. It was the vehicle I'd heard. I crossed the road to the mountainside and waited. The truck slowed by me.

"See any elk?" a barrel-shaped, bewhiskered man with prune-like features asked through the open window. His words were slurred. He held a Pabst Blue Ribbon can in his left hand as his right held the steering wheel at 12 o'clock. His passenger, with a dirty black ponytail and an acne-scarred face, also had a can in his hand, but his was lifted to his lips.

Through the open window I smelled rancid sweat and stale beer.

"No, sorry," I said. They were coming from the direction I was heading. "I'm looking for my friends," I added. "Have you seen a blue Chevy truck with a man and a young girl in it today on your way here?"

The driver shook his head. The passenger said, "Haven't seen but one truck today, and that one had three guys in it."

If the passenger had sounded any more sober than the driver, I might have suggested, in my new role as deputy, that he drive. But he seemed as drunk as the driver if not drunker.

"Thanks," I said, hitting the roof of the cab with my hand. "Good luck to you."

They waved and drove off. I wondered for a moment if my responsibilities as a deputy included stopping drunk drivers. Or if I'd be responsible if something happened to them now that I had witnessed their drunkenness.

As I got in my Jeep Adahy said, "The lost hunters are more important than drunk drivers."

I nodded and drove on, looking every foot of the way over as carefully as I could, even if the spot was not one where a car could go over a cliff or embankment. My encounter with the drunks had reminded me that going over a cliff in a single vehicle accident was not the only possible thing that might befall a hunter on this road. I had met quite a few drunken hunters on these roads over the years, narrowly avoiding getting hit by them more than once. A drunken driver might have run into them. But if that was the case, and no one had reported it, then the prospects became even more sinister.

I had driven for another 36 minutes and was about midway through the route I suspected the father and daughter had gone on, when I saw something that made me stop my Jeep.

I was traversing an almost circular curve in the road that had its own name: Octopus Tree Curve. I was at four o'clock on this curve, driving counter-clockwise toward three. Off to my left, was a now snow-covered parking spot made by a man who had mined a claim there years back. He had removed what remained of the Octopus Tree and cleared the approximately twenty by twelve spot so he had a place to park where vehicles coming around the curve on this single lane dirt road wouldn't hit him. The parking spot angled into the woods much like a clock hand at 4 o'clock if you followed the hand back to the clock's center.

About three years ago, at the far end of this 'parking spot,' a fairly large multi-branched tree, dead for many years, had fallen almost perpendicu-lar to the spot on top a little hillock that formed a backstop for the parking area. This old larch was probably as old as the tree that the curve had been named after. One huge lower branch twisted out from the tree's trunk and pointed toward the road. Because its tip had been broken sharply, most likely when the tree fell, the extended branch resembled a giant's lance held high above the ground.

It wasn't just that I had a tendency to remember details of topography when traveling in the wild, but that I had trained myself to after getting lost a few times when I first moved way off the grid. Some Native Americans, like my wife Lomahongva, believe that the wilderness contains spirits. I don't only mean ghosts of people or animals, but of trees, rocks, everything. I remembered this tree, because Lo had always loved it. And although Lo died before it fell, I had heard her whisper to me the first time I saw it lying on its side like a fallen giant, that now the giant's lance was pointing down at me.

The branch had not in anyway blocked the road, but it had taken up over two-thirds of the length of the parking spot. The thing that made it stand out this time as I dove by was that it had been cut. Beneath the snow that covered its top, a flat surface of newly cut wood just over three inches thick faced me. That the cut had not been made to recover the parking spot was apparent as something like a bare four feet of the branch's length had been removed.

Adahy just looked at me. I think he sensed something too, but didn't know how to put it into words.

I knew I needed to search the area and did not want to park in the middle of it. So I backed up my Jeep about 30 yards to a wide area where at least one other vehicle had turned around. This spot was past the beginning of the curve and where other

46

driver's could see it. Leaving the dogs and asking Adahy to wait in the Jeep, I got out.

# An Unsettling Discovery

## October 23: Late Afternoon

I have been asked to find quite a few pets and have located a number of missing people. Two of the pets and one of the persons I found were dead when I found them. The fact that someone had cut the branch I now walked toward made me think that it had gone through someone's front windshield. I hoped that, whoever, had simply backed away after cutting the limb and then driven home. But I now had a familiar bad feeling in my gut.

Fallen logs perpendicular to the road made the area surrounding the sawed-off branch a tight parking-space-sized rectangle. The tree, the branch extended from, formed the back end of that space.

Vehicles had obliterated any foot tracks on the road itself. But a tale was told by the tracks in that rectangular space. It was clear a vehicle with the same wheelbase as my Chevy Silverado had gone off the road here. So that I would not disturb the tracks, I examined the tracks by walking only between the two wheel ruts of the vehicle where the snow had not been disturbed. The tracks went straight in and apparently the truck had been removed by backing it straight out. Two distinct sets of man-sized tracks went to where the driver's door would have been. The smaller of those two sets made the trip to the door more than once and had also gone to the front of the vehicle. This smaller set apparently had also entered the truck. Moving as close as I could to where this person appeared to have climbed onto the hood of the truck, I carefully brushed a small section of the snow from one track with my hunting knife. As I suspected sawdust was mixed in the track. This led me to believe that this person had climbed on the hood of the vehicle and had cut the tree limb with some kind of saw, most likely a chainsaw. I took out my iPhone and took photos.

On the opposite side of the vehicle's ruts, footprints, larger than both the other tracks, showed someone had walked over to where the hood of the vehicle would have been. Deep red globs of what looked like blood around these tracks puzzled me, until I figured out that someone must have removed a recently taken deer from the hood of the vehicle. I had assumed Cassie and her Dad had put her deer in the back of their truck, but they might have put it on the hood. That this person had apparently moved a dead deer alone indicated it was most likely a very strong man. I took photos of the tracks and the blobs of blood.

I began trying to imagine what might have gone on. If another vehicle had come along, perhaps they had stopped to help the person involved. Not knowing, really, what I was looking at, I left the rectangle between the ruts and examined the roadway.

In the tire-packed snow I saw a piece of glass. I took a photo of it then I took the hunting mittens I usually wore off and put the rubber gloves the sheriff had given on. I did not want to chance threads from my mittens getting stuck to the glass. Then I bent down and picked up the small piece of glass. It looked to be from a headlight.

I carefully put the piece of glass into one of the glassine bags and put it in my pocket. I unsheathed my hunting knife and scraped the snow where I'd found the piece of headlight. I was rewarded with more pieces of clear glass and some pieces of reddish-orange glass, the kind you find in turn and parking lights. I took a few photos and then took a sample of the reddish glass and put the piece in a new glassine bag. I took the rubber gloves off and put my mittens back on.

My gut kept nagging me. Was it possible that this wasn't a serious accident? There hadn't been any accidents reported. Could it have just been someone without auto insurance who had simply not wanted to report it?

I gave the road one final look and saw nothing else of interest. I was about to head back to my Jeep when Adahy said, "I left the dogs in your Jeep. Did something bad happen here?" He was standing a few yards back from the tracks I'd been examining.

"I think so."

He began walking forward and I was about to stop him when he stopped and pointed at something just off the road peeking out from a covering of snow.

It was not anything of the natural world as the part of it that was visible was a sliver of neon lime green. I took a photo of its position in the snow, and then I put the rubber gloves back on, thinking as I did so, I was wasting time, and whatever this was, was probably nothing. Yet, my heart beat wildly as I pulled it out and recognition hit me. I was looking down at Cassie Carew's Montana deer license. There were red stains that I assumed were deer blood. On Montana licenses the hunter must notch out the triangle drawn on the back of the license for the month and day the deer was taken. The triangles ran around the rectangular license. The current month and the date that Cassie and her father had chosen to hunt were notched out: October 21. This was Cassie's license and she had gotten a deer.

50

There was also a hole punched through the center in which a string hung. The string had most likely been used to secure the license to the deer. This license had not fallen off. The string had been cut. I took photos of the front and back of the license and made sure I had a good shot of the cut string.

# Crime Scenes

## October 23: Late Afternoon — Early Evening

The snow-covered road was actually easier to see after dark as I drove Adahy and myself home after a very long day, because my headlights lit up the ruts. Often, during the day, the sun was so bright in open areas that the glare made the road invisible in a field of white. But because I could easily see where I was driving I was able to think about all that had transpired after finding Cassie Carew's notched hunting tag.

Assuming the worst, I tried to call the sheriff but could not get a signal. I could get nothing on the little radio the sheriff had given me but static. I drove slowly toward the highway searching for a signal and checking every possible spot the truck could have been hidden. The first drop-off I checked was just a half-mile from where I'd found the tag. By drop-off I mean a place on the road where a vehicle could have gone down out of sight.

We got out of my Jeep and walked along the edge. The drop-off was actually on a curve. Over the edge of the road there was a 7-foot drop down to Wisdom's Creek, named for a miner who discovered gold in it in the early 1860s. I kicked snow off the edge of the drop. No Chevy truck sat in the spring. I had already begun to wonder if whoever had hit the truck had even gone in this direction. Someone who caused a fatal accident, who intended to cover it up, would have wanted to dump it as soon as possible. They would be less likely to run into someone, I assumed, if they drove further into the wilderness than if they drove out. In my experience once you were off the main access roads it was possible to never run into any other hunters at all.

We did check every other likely spot on my way to the highway where I finally got a cell signal. We saw no sign of the Silverado.

The sheriff was not happy. He was not unhappy with me but with what I had found.

"It's good for us they threw her tag away right there," the sheriff said. But I could tell he did not feel good about it.

The county did not have a crime lab and use of the state crime team was charged to his budget.

We had to wait by the highway exit for the crime lab team. They came from Missoula so they were not that far away. By the time I got them to the crime scene it was dark. With Adahy waiting in the Jeep, I spent only 15 minutes with them, pointing out where I'd found the headlight and other light glass and where the tag had been laying in the snow. The one woman on the team, who was the team leader, had the two men laying out crime scene tape as we spoke. I drove Adahy and myself home the back way, away from the highway. I had decided to return to the crime scene early the next morning to continue my search in the opposite direction. Adahy seemed to accept my decision to go alone. Neither of us said that it was because I was expecting to find dead bodies. That grim belief had fallen over me. I did not now think it mattered if I found the vehicle tonight or sometime the next morning.

# A Morning Search

## October 24: Morning

I found it hard to sleep. I could not get Callie Carew's face out of my thoughts. I did not believe that her husband and daughter could both still be alive. But I could not tell her that, for I knew nothing for sure. So I was awake well before the kitten gave me his usual morning greeting by walking over my face then sitting on my head and purring. Thus, I got up before daylight, ate a mountain man's breakfast of elk steak and eggs, and was out by the Jeep before the first rays of sunlight peeked over the mountains on the other side of the creek.

I found Adahy sleeping in the cargo compartment. I would have to talk to his mother. I lifted him out somehow without waking him and put him on my bed. I wasn't taking the dogs so they'd watch out for him. I locked them in. They could all use the dog door. I was on the road a few minutes later.

My starting point was the area where I had found Cassie's deer tag and where I had taken the crime scene team. They were gone, but orange crime scene tape still clung to the trees. One bit, torn in the middle, was rising and falling on the snow, teased by a slight breeze, as it dangled from the branch of a skinny, five-foot subalpine fir. It was too early to call Nadine at the Sheriff's office.

From the crime scene, I drove into the Garnet Range. At first I stopped often, at places where there were drops where a vehicle could be pushed off the road. But there were no giveaways by any of them, and by that I mean broken branches, knocked over trees, etc. And after awhile I didn't bother checking if there were no hints at all that something had gone through.

I tried to think as if I were someone trying to hide a vehicle that had a huge hole in the wind-shield, and perhaps even two bodies. Where would I try to hide them? The sprinkling of snow on the pine leaves overhanging the road seemed to say any-where under the snow would be fine, but there wasn't enough snow yet. The fact that whoever did this, did not, simply, cover the vehicle with snow and branches just off the road, spoke to their cun-ning. I'd seen three sets of footprints so, of course, they had the two people to drive the two vehicles.

The first likely place I checked was a dead end road running by a mountain peak where elk were known to be from time to time. The area was most-ly open having been logged sometime before. The new growth was only just coming up and waist high. Only subalpine firs, having not been worth the logger's time, and a few large patches of ten-years-old lodgepole, probably planted, stood. The white ruts in the snow covering the road indicated that many hunters had driven through. The sun, getting higher, faced me and I had to concentrate on the ruts that were becoming almost invisible in the white glare on the snow. Only the fact that there were low banks at the edge indicated that nothing had passed over the edges. Before long I reached the end of the road. For the moment the sky hung blue and cloudless. That hunters had turned their vehicles around here was clear. An almost circular crisscrossing of tracks like a railroad turntable made turning around easy. I had imagined that perhaps the Chevy could have been driven off the edge here and covered with brush. But now I realized there wasn't enough brush for that. I thought again about what these people would need to hide a vehicle as large as a Chevy Silverado.

Next I drove out the long dead end road that reached out from Murkey Gulch in the direction of Missoula. This was a twisting snake of a road that was heavily wooded with mostly lodgepole on either side. Springs in more than one place made the ruts muddy and wet despite the cold. Along the road there were a few spots I wanted to check out.

The first was a wide-open track that was defined enough to look like a logging road. But, except for some of the dead lodgepole along it that had been harvested for firewood, there seemed to be no logging here. I drove in to the end making my own ruts as few hunters had driven in, in the past day or so.

Exiting the Jeep, binoculars in hand, the cold air washed my face and chilled me. I reached back in the Jeep and put on my heavy, orange, hunting jacket, which I had taken off while driving.

The air smelled of pine needles and coming snow. I stood by the Jeep at the head of a T of sorts. There wasn't any real road on either side of me. Ahead over the top of the T the land sloped down and snow covered trees and brush spread out before me. I had been here some summers before when a fire had raged in this area. I had parked on the main road and walked out to this spot to see the tongues of flames far below. A fire-fighting plane had zoomed over my head and let out a thick, ongoing cloud of reddish-purple fire retardant. The smoke had been rolling up, and I soon left for a safer spot.

From the joint of the T, I moved west along the right arm of the T. Crossing a deep dip in the snowy landscape, I climbed past some lone trees and had a clear view of the valley below, C road which snaked through it, and C mountain just beyond. It was a beautiful view, the kind that gave Montana the Big Sky name, and it gave me quite a range of landscape. I scanned carefully until I was sure that in the field of my vision, the Chevy had not been hidden.

As I continued down the dead end road, there were quite a few places along it where a vehicle could have been rolled off. But all such hills leveled off before long into flat areas. I saw a beautiful Mule Deer buck with a six by six rack with a lone doe but no sign of the Carew's Silverado.

There was one offshoot-logging road going down toward C road far below. At the top trees surrounded it, but I knew those trees soon opened to a clearcut area. Ruts told me someone had driven in a short way but then the ruts stopped. I parked and walked through the snow far enough down so that I could see all the land below. There were no vehicles down there.

I parked in a short turnoff where I could see others had parked before me. The end was only a little over 100 yards away on a hook of a road that circled a rocky nob. There was nowhere to turn on that hook of road and it was easier to park and walk. The ground sloped away from the road along the edge of the hook.

A level open area about 60 feet below formed a belt between the road and a thick stand of trees. There was nothing like a vehicle at the bottom of the slope, covered or uncovered. I saw a movement in the trees past the open area and saw the bulk of an elk moving away. Blocked by trees I could not tell if it was a bull or a cow but it set my heart racing.

I went back to the Jeep and drove back down the dead end to the next juncture. It was getting late, and I had not found anything. I was beginning to have doubts about my theory, but decided I'd check it out to the end.

The next turnoff I checked out was far down below the one I had just checked. It was a short road that snaked around a wooded peak that faced C road. It stood like an island in an ocean of open ground. Two roads circled the peak actually. One goes close to the front of the peak and connects back to the main road a ways down. The other forks off and runs around the back of the peak. At the fork there was some indication that that fork had been driven on just recently; one set of ruts beneath the new snow. Hunters may have skipped it because it led to the steep side of the peak, and the peak, though wooded, was so lightly wooded, its slopes could easily be glassed.

In all the years I had hunted the area, I don't think I had ever seen an animal there.

I drove carefully once I was around the side of the mountain. This mountainside was close to vertical next to the road, and the road was often littered with stones of varying size that had fallen. I did not want to run over a good-sized stone covered with snow and damage the Jeep. I was getting tired.

The road came to an abrupt end soon after I got close to the mountain. A long thin dead lodgepole, with a light covering of snow, which made it look thicker, blocked the end of the road. One end of the fallen tree was leaning against the mountain and the other hugged the far side of the road by the drop-off, like a natural gate. I had walked this area once and knew there was a steep drop not much further on, which went down to a rocky ledge. There was little forage there for deer to hang about, so it was of little interest to hunters.

I had turned in my seat, about to back up when I stopped. I was so tired I'd almost missed it. I felt my heart begin to race, and this time not because of game I had seen. The single set of ruts on the road before me went under the tree.

I got out of my Jeep and again the cold hit me. But I was too excited to grab my hunting jacket. I walked toward the tree, looking up as I did.

My eyes scanned the steep side of the peak. Stone rose some hundreds of feet to where the peaked sloped and I could see sky. Stone. No trees, just stone. Where had this tree come from? There was no way it could have just fallen to where it was now.

I looked down at the single set of ruts in the snow. They seemed to drive under the tree. I scanned the ground outside the ruts. On my left side as I faced the tree there were boot tracks under the shallow new snow. There was a confusion of these tracks by the tree, and then sign that whoever had left them had walked away back toward the main road. The size of these tracks was the same as that of the person, who with smaller boots, had apparently climbed onto the hood of the vehicle impaled by the tree limb.

I knew the mountain dropped off just a few feet from where the tree leaned in front of me. It seemed easier to duck under the tree than maneuver around. I stopped before looking down and looked up at the sky.

Clouds hung now in the previously all blue sky. In the white froth I saw the image of what looked like a charging horse.

"Lo," I whispered to myself. Lo was Lomahongva, who had been my wife. She had been part Cheyenne and part Hopi, her parents having met at an AIM rally. Her name in Hopi meant "Beautiful Clouds Arising," and together we looked to clouds for inspiration.

I took a careful step forward, watching where I placed my foot, then looked down. About twelve feet below me the Chevy Silverado hung on some rocks more or less upright. I was looking down at the back window of the camper. The rest of the vehicle was covered with a light coating of snow.

Regretting not grabbing my hunting jacket, and the gloves in its pocket, I made my way down carefully on slippery white rocks to the bottom. I glanced in the back window of the camper. Neither Greg, nor Cassie were there.

I circled to the driver's side window. I saw the obscene hole in the windshield first. As I shifted my gaze, I saw Greg Carew. His body was curled over toward the passenger door on the bench-style seat. The sawed-off tip of the tree limb protruded from his upper chest. Another piece of sawed tree limb rested on the body. His skin looked grey in the indirect sunlight. Blood and sawdust mingled everywhere. I fought the urge to check him for a pulse. There was no way he could possibly be alive, and I did not want to disturb any evidence. From where I stood I could not see Cassie, but realized she could be on the floor hidden by Greg's body.

As I moved around the front of the Chevy, I brushed a line of snow off the hood. Smears of blood on the hood indicated I had been right about their deer being tied there.

I went around the vehicle and fully expected to see Cassie. But she was not under Greg. The rest of the passenger side floor and seat were empty but for a pair of woman's hunting gloves.

My ungloved hands were already starting to sting from the cold as I took my iPhone out and took photos before even checking for a signal. To my surprise I had cell phone coverage.


While I waited for the sheriff I tried following the footprints that lead away from the truck. But, I soon found, whoever, had made sure to walk in the Chevy's tracks as he or she had left the area.

Less than an hour later the whumphing of a helicopter grew slowly to a roar as it sailed under an increasing mass of white cumulus clouds. The sheriff had given me instructions to lay out a landing area and I had found one between the two roads near where they forked. Fortunately I carried road flares with me for emergency purposes. As the helicopter approached I lit them one by one, placing them at the corners of the flat area I had found. The Bell the department used settled down between my flares. The snowstorm the blades created forced me to turn my head away. By the time I was able to look back the sheriff was walking up to me stooped over, and the Bell was rising back into the air.

"Heat imaging cameras," Paul said loudly next to me. "I know after three days her body might be frozen but it's worth the effort, and the money." He turned and looked at me. "Crime lab is on its way. The helicopter will send them the exact location. Meanwhile show me what we have."

"Best leave it for the crime scene team," Paul said after I showed him where the Chevy was, and pointed out how I had gotten down myself.

After the crime scene team had arrived, Paul and I decided to get our next unpleasant task over with. Paul arranged for a ride home to be waiting for him at the Carew's house. As I drove I felt a terrible sense of Déjà vu. There was nothing to see but snow and trees in all directions. There had been snow the last time I had found a body, too. Now I wondered if somewhere, out there, covered with snow, lay Cassie Carew.

# Notification

## October 24: Evening

Paul Goldstone looked me directly in the eyes and asked, "Have you ever done this before?"

"No," I answered honestly. I had had it done to me. I had answered a knock at my door, which had turned my entire world upside down.

I don't think I will ever get the image of William Longbear, my father-in-law, and my sister-in-law, Yona, standing in my doorway. My father-in-law is a handsome man with long black hair and penetrating eyes. Yona is still a young beautiful woman with long dark hair and the face of an angel.

That day the expressions on their faces were dark. The looks on their faces alone told me something life changing had happened before they said a word.

Callie Carew, I consoled myself, had had time to prepare herself for the worst possible news. And the news we were bringing her was not, at least not yet, the worst possible. Cassie Carew might still be alive no matter how unlikely that possibility might be.

The family lived in Potomac area. When Callie Carew saw us in her doorway, her expression might have been much like mine was when William and Yona informed me that my Lomahongva had died saving Adahy. Adahy had been a toddler at the time. He had seen a bear cub walk into what amounted to the back yard at Yona's where Lomahongva was visiting. The sisters had been hanging clothing on the clothesline that stretched across the yard. The cub had wandered into the yard and Adahy had apparently gone to look at the "doggy." Lomahongva, coming around the hanging clothes, I imagine smelling of fresh soap as she always did when she did laundry, had been the first to see the boy approaching the cub and the mother bear on a dead run to protect her cub.

Callie began crying before either could say a word. She seemed about to collapse and I rushed forward and grabbed her before she fell. I held her in my arms as she sobbed.

When we left some time later, I don't know how long it was that we were with the newly widowed woman, Goldstone had promised that both of us would not stop looking until we had found her daughter. We had waited to leave until Callie's sister and an FBI agent had arrived. The agent would monitor phone calls. But neither Paul, nor I believed there would be any ransom demands.

# FWP

## October 25:

I called Goldstone at 9 am when his office officially opened, suspecting that the heat imaging would not have located Cassie's body. I wanted to suggest search and rescue dogs. The sheriff was way ahead of me.

Dogs had been on site since dawn. The only thing they had found was an untagged dead elk, with the backstrap cut out.

Both the sheriff and I knew I was not up to date on crime scene processing; in fact, what little experience I did have was during my short nine-month stint as an MP. So, when he told me that the headlight and turn light glass I found looked to have been from a 1990 to 1996 Ford at what was now being called the crime scene, I volunteered to go to Missoula and ask some questions at the Department of Fish and Wildlife.

"They found windshield glass from a Chevy Silverado, where you discovered the vehicle went off the road. I got no pleasure out of being right. At my suggestion he agreed to hold off announcing the finding of Greg's body to the media for one more day.

In Montana the FWP, as it was called, set up stations along major routes into cities like Missoula. They always set up in a small fishing access parking area by the Bonner Mill. The check station was only open on weekends. What I needed to know was if the people who manned the station could tell me if they remembered a 1990 or slightly older Ford truck with a recently broken headlight.

The FWP offices are on Spurgin Road in Missoula and there are quite a few places with FWP signs. And although I'd been there some years before with a bear I had killed and needed checked, I did not remember the correct turn.

Finally, I found it. The office was empty but for a woman behind a desk in a gated off area who gave me a friendly smile. The name on her tag was Phyllis.

"How can I help you?" she asked.

I took out my badge and showed it to her, "I'm a part-time deputy and I'm afraid that I'm investigating a suspicious hunting death."

"Oh, no," she said.

"You are aware of the father and daughter reported missing a few days ago?"

"They're dead?" she asked.

"We found the father. But the daughter is missing. So it is essential we find out what we can as soon as possible."

"How can I help?" she asked.

"I need to contact the men stationed at the check station in Bonner this past weekend. That's when we think the father died."

"But how can they help?" she asked, concerned but confused.

"There was an accident that we believe led up to the death. Do you have video of the check-ins?"

Phyllis shook her head no. "We only have the budget to man the stations on weekends. If we had video there wouldn't be enough manpower to check it."

"Then I need to ask the people who manned the station some questions about hunters who checked in."

"I tell you what," she said, "since you're not at the sheriff's office right now, I'll call them for you. If they see it's my phone, they might be more inclined to answer than if they get a call from a unknown number."

I gave her a quizzical look.

"This is their day off since they worked the weekend."

I nodded my understanding.

In just minutes I had the first of the men who manned the station over the weekend on the line.

"Jim Bridges," she said as she handed me her handset.

"Mr. Bridges," I said, "this is temporary deputy sheriff, Winslow Doyle."

"Jim, please," Bridges said. "How can I help Deputy Doyle?"

Phyllis had told him about Greg Carew being found, and that I was calling in reference to that, before handing me the phone. It made my job easier.

"First, were you there at the check station the whole time or did you take breaks during the day?"

"No, we were so busy all of us ate lunch while working. No one got to take a break."

"Do you remember any check-ins where there was an older Ford truck with a newly damaged headlight. It's likely there was more than one man and at least one deer in the vehicle.

There was a moment of silence on the line. Then Bridges spoke hesitantly. "There may have been but I didn't check the vehicle I'm thinking of in myself, so I didn't pay that much attention to it.

"You'd have to ask Shawna Edwards, or Tim Bobbins about it. They were the other checkers with me that day."

I thanked him, got his contact information in case I had to get back to him, and hung up.

"I've got Shawna on line 2," Phyllis said nodding at the phone.

I looked at the handset and saw buttons across the bottom numbered from one to six. Two was lit up. I pressed it.

"Shawna Edwards?" I asked.

"Yes, Deputy Doyle. How may I help you?"

I asked her what I had asked Edwards. Shawna thought for a few moments. "Yes, I remember some men in a Ford extended cab truck with a broken headlight. I even mentioned it to them. They had been drinking, though I didn't think they were drunk when they stopped. They smelled like beer."

"Do you have their names?" I asked.

There was another long pause. "Well, I didn't actually check them in. I started to and Tim Bobbins, one of the other checkers there, said he'd take them. Tim is kind of protective and sometimes if he doesn't like the way the men look at me, he'll take over. It isn't necessary but Tim was my senior on the job there," she paused, "This is late Saturday, right?"

I hadn't thought to discuss the day we were talking about with Shawna. Greg and Cassie Carew had failed to come back Saturday night. Whoever had moved the car probably would have checked in late.

"Late Saturday works," I said.

"Well, normally we look at the tag and if it looks okay we ask where the deer or elk was taken and take a back tooth for aging. We don't record license numbers or anything like that, unless there was a problem."

"Was there a problem?" I asked hopefully.

"As I said, I did not check them. But there may have been. I was checking the next hunter and heard one of the men raising his voice. But Tim calmed him down. So it's best you talk to Tim," Shawna said.

"Thank you," I said after getting her contact info. She said "anytime" and the line went dead.

Phyllis looked at me and shook her head. I can't get Tim on the phone. He must be out. I don't think he often carries his cell phone on his day off. But I can leave him a message and have him call you."

"The sheriff's office is good for that call too, if he can't get me," I said.

"I hope you catch the men you're after," Phyllis said.

"Thank you."

I left the FWP office feeling dejected. Unless Tim Bobbins remembered something more about the men in the truck, I had no idea at the moment what to do next.

# The Accident

## October 21: Midday

The impact threw wiry, twenty-seven-year-old Bobby Wesley, who was driving, forward against his seat belt. The beer can in his right hand flew against the windshield and bounced off, splashing both his slim, twenty-one-year-old brother, Billy Wesley, and his burly, thirty-four-year-old dark-bearded friend, Nate Hanassey, with beer.

"What the shit?" Hanassey cried, "You drunk Fuck! You just not only hit somebody but you spilled beer all over my truck."

"Man," Billy, who had not been drinking at all, said, "I told you, you should let me drive!"

Bobby, drunk, looked at his little brother and then followed his brother's gaze to the vehicle they had just hit. It had veered off the road, and now sat with its back bumper less than a dozen feet from where they sat.

All of them sat there for a full minute or so before Nate opened his door and slid out of the truck leaving the door open behind him. Nate stood near the door just staring at the vehicle across from them. An icy breath of snowy air blew in.

Billy hesitated for only a second and then slid out after Nate.

Nate began to move toward the other vehicle. He had gotten just past the rear bumper on the driver's side when Billy grabbed his arm. But Nate had already stopped and was just staring.

"Let me check," Billy insisted.

Inside the Ford Bobby watched Nate nod.

Billy walked out of sight around the back of the other vehicle on its driver's side. Bobby could not see what Billy was doing, from his position in the truck. Bobby felt his stomach clench as he heard the door of that vehicle open.

Seconds passed. It seemed like Billy was taking forever. Bobby rolled his own window down and took a deep breath of the freezing air. Through his drunken haze he suddenly was frightened. If the people in the truck reported him as being drunk, if he got a DUI for this, he was going back to prison. He tried to think.

"Nate. Nate!" he cried.

Nate walked back to the passenger door and stuck his head in, shaking it as he did so. "Shit, man, we're fucked."

"Walk away before anyone sees you," Bobby said.

Nate, having consumed almost as many beers as Bobby, looked at Bobby puzzled for a moment.

"Associating with an ex-con? And we both have firearms," Bobby tried to explain. "Get lost!"

Nate nodded after a moment, finally understanding. He backed away from the door but then stopped, and shook his head as if clearing it. "That won't work, you dumb fuck! This is my damn truck," he said.

Bobby heard the door of the other vehicle slam shut. A moment later his brother came around the side of the vehicle and joined Nate. Billy looked pale.

"Both dead," Billy said.

"Shit," Nate said.

"We gotta think fast," Billy said. "I have an idea," he said and walked off toward the Chevy.

Bobby had to check. He drunkenly hoped his brother was wrong. Both dead? He got out and made his way to the driver's side of the Silverado.

Billy was taking a sleeping bag out of the back of the Chevy when he saw Bobby rounding the truck. "Don't touch the door," Billy yelled, running back toward Bobby. Bobby looked down; the door handle was smeared with blood.

Bobby shook his head. He had been about to open the door, but Billy was right. Instead he looked in the window. His eyes went from the branch entering the front windshield to the chest of the man it impaled. Part of the branch was riding atop the Chevy's steering wheel as if for balance. He glanced beyond the man for a moment and saw a bloody figure huddled in the corner by the passenger door also covered in blood.

Billy was watching him. "If you're going to get sick, get sick in Nate's truck. We don't want to leave no DNA."

A moment later Bobby was running back to Nate's truck. Almost instinctively, since he'd been driving, he stuck his head through the driver's window and puked.

Nate easily picked the deer up off the hood of the Silverado and carried it by himself to the open bed of the Ford and threw it in. Then he reached in and cut the string holding the tag onto the deer's left antler with his hunting knife. He threw that tag into the snow on the opposite side of the road from where the Chevy went off. Taking out his own tag, he retagged the deer.

Less than 5 minutes later the branch that had broken through the Chevy's windshield and impaled the driver had been cut on both the outside and inside by Billy with the chain-saw Nate always carried for firewood when he went hunting.

Nate got into his truck on the driver's seat, now covered with one of the sleeping bags from the Chevy, and waited for the Chevy to be backed out. Billy, sitting on the other sleeping bag they found in the Chevy, backed the Chevy out. There was no way to turn the Chevy there so Billy backed up until he came to a spot where the road was wide enough to turn around.

Moments later Nate began following the now turned Chevy. Next to him Bobby opened a new beer.

"You had to puke on my gad-damn driver's seat," Nate grumbled to Bobby.

In the passenger seat Bobby just shook his head and took another sip of the beer.

"That was good thinking on your brother's part," Nate said. He took a sniff of the air, shook his head, "but shit. You puke again you do it out the window."

Not quite a half hour after that Nate saw Billy pull to the side of the snow-covered road they were on and pulled up behind him.

Billy got out, stretched, and then walked over. Nate opened his window. Billy leaned in. "No reason for you guys to go any further. You don't want to be seen anywhere near the Chevy. We've been lucky so far; let's not push it. You guys can park here. Go hunting. I should be able to hide the truck and be back with you in a few hours."

"I want to help," Bobby said from the passenger seat. He had been sobering fast.

Billy shook his head.

"But I was driving," Bobby said.

"You took the rap for me once. That's enough. I get stopped I'll just say I was going for help. Either of you get stopped, you're screwed."

Nate turned to Bobby, "He's right, man."

Bobby just nodded. He watched Billy walk back to the Silverado and drive away.

"We might as well go hunting," Nate said, opening the driver's side door.

# Darkness

## October 22: Time unknown

Cassie Carew opened her eyes to darkness. She took in a breath that turned into a sob as pain wracked her body. Her head ached. Her chest and ribs hurt. She was on her back looking upward. Why couldn't she see anything? She blinked. Still only darkness hovered in front of her eyes. Her heart began pumping faster. Had she gone blind? She lifted her hands to her eyes. They felt cold. She could not see her hands at all. She closed her eyes and felt around the lids. There was some crusty material all over her face. She explored her eye sockets with her fingertips. Whatever it was, it was not covering her eyes. Realizing her hands were bare she remembered she had taken her gloves off in their truck and left them on the seat.

How had she gotten here? She had been with her Dad, hunting.

She listened for a moment. The silence around her seemed almost oppressive.

"Dad!" She cried out loudly.

Her voice seemed to echo back instantly as if she were in a small shower room.

Fear sent her heart racing. She was closed in somewhere with no light. Off to the side of her she heard a thump. Then another. Something was in the room with her. She had never been this scared before.

Whatever she was lying on was rock hard. She moved her right hand back to her side and felt the surface she was lying on. It was stone cold and hard. It felt jagged against her fingers, rough, uneven, and gritty. Was she lying on a stone floor? She moved her right foot across the floor. She had expected to hear her boot heel scraping the floor. But instead she felt the rough floor rub her heel. What had happen to her boot and sock? Moving her other foot, she realized both her boots and socks were gone. Who had brought her here? Who had taken her boots? Suddenly fearful she reached down to her side. Her fingers touched her leather scabbard. Her hunting knife was gone.

She sniffed the air; there was a scent she couldn't place, feral, musky. She realized the air itself was cold. She felt it on her face and hands. It was not a freezing cold. It was more of a chilly cold. She felt her jacket. She still had her hunting jacket on.

It took a moment for the significance of this to dawn on her. She had her hunting jacket on! She sat up. The movement made her dizzy. He body ached everywhere. She waited until the dizziness had passed, then fought the pain to rise to her knees.

Almost frantically she began patting her coat pockets. In her right inside pocket she felt something hard--that was where she put it, right?

For a moment her hopes rose. She quickly opened her jacket, the cold air intensifying the chill she felt, but she paid this chill no mind. She heard but did not actually heed a scratching sound now audible in the darkness off to the right. All she wanted at this point was the tool her father had given her for emergencies. Finally, she grasped the 5-inch leather strap she was searching for and pulled it from her pocket. The strap went through a hole in the top of a small piece of antler from which a bar extended. Also attached to the strap was a thin, flat piece of steel resembling a broken piece of hacksaw blade.

Cassie swallowed hard. This was the test. In a moment she would know if she could see. She felt the mostly rounded metal bar that extended three inches from its antler base. Two thirds of the bar's circumference was smooth metal: magnesium. The other third was a 3-inch long sliver of flint embedded into the magnesium rod.

She didn't need the magnesium now. Taking the flat piece of steel in her right hand she held it up over the bar extending from the antler, which she held in her left hand. She rotated the antler and its metal bar until she could feel the flint side facing upward. She hesitated just before striking the steel across the flint.

Almost afraid to, she sniffed the air. The only scent was that feral musty odor. No gas. It was safe to make a spark.

As hard as she could she struck the blade down across the flint. Her heart leapt as a brilliant flash of light streaked off the flint and for a glorious micro second lit her surroundings.

"I can see," she cried out softly. Almost in answer there was more thumping behind her, somewhere off to the right in the darkness.

She turned around and facing the sound she began to strike off spark after spark. Her heart beat wildly, her eyes strained to see into the strobe lit shadows what was making the sound.

She couldn't see what it was, but what she did see gave her a hopeless feeling: rocks; rocks spilling out on the floor, rocks piled up to the ceiling which seemed to be nothing more than a slab of rock.

The thumping sounds stopped, and what she felt as she stopped striking the steel to the flint was claustrophobia. Was she in a cave? How did she end up in a cave?

Her heart seemed to be thumping in her chest. "Think!" She told herself.

After a moment, feeling the dark edge in on her again, she reached into the right front pocket of her jeans and pulled out the hankie her mother had embroidered her name on. She needed to tear it. She pulled so it hard it hurt her hands, but the hankie wouldn't rip. Reaching down to her side, she touched her empty knife sheath. She had forgotten. The knife had been missing when she woke. She felt around her waist. Her belt was gone. Someone had taken that, too.

She reached into the right front pocket of her coat and felt around. To her joy her fingers touched a hard object. She grabbed it and pulled out the small multi-tool she carried there. 'Always carry a penknife,' her Dad had told her. Instead of a penknife she had opted for a tool that had a selection of screwdrivers and a serrated sawing blade as well as a regular knife blade. Now she was glad she did. He had also told her to always carry a candle. She had gotten out a candle at home to bring before they left on their trip. But she had forgotten to put that candle in her pocket. In her mind's eye she cursed herself, seeing it sitting on her night table.

With her multi-tool she managed to cut through the edge of the handkerchief. Grabbing the two sides of the cut, she ripped the handkerchief into rough halves.

"Sorry Mom," she whispered, thinking of her mother embroidering it by the window in her sewing room.

Defying the darkness she put one half of the torn cloth into her coat pocket and the other she carefully positioned on the floor near her knees. Then she took the fire-starting tool and turning the magnesium side of the rod up, she began scraping slivers of magnesium onto the piece of handker-chief.

The thumping began again in the same corner of the darkness. Cassie tried to ignore the angry-seeming sound as she worked on her pile of magne-sium slivers. Finally, she felt she had enough. Turn-ing the rod over so the flint side was up, she struck the flint with the steel.

Even though her Dad had had her try the starter, she never imagined the effect in the dark chamber where she found herself. The first spark ignited the pile of magnesium shavings she had built up. Mag-nesium burns at 2300 degrees Fahrenheit her Dad had explained, it could easily get even damp wood burning. What she did not realize, having tested it outdoors in daylight, was the incredible amount of blinding light that a 2300 degree Fahrenheit flame produced.

Almost instinctively Cassie closed her eyes and moved back from the flame, rising to her feet as she did so. Inside her eyelids a giant white spot hovered. She waited until it began to fade and then opened her eyes making sure she was not looking directly at the handkerchief.

In the light she could see the rocks opposite much more clearly. She also saw a thick nest of small sticks and twigs piled into an opening in the rock.

"A packrat," she said to herself, laughing just as the creature began thumping again.

The light was beginning to die down; she risked a glance at it. Now only the handkerchief was burning and she saw what was left would only last seconds. She went to the nest and picked up a few twigs and sticks, then moved back sticking the end of the driest seeming stick into the end of the dying flame. The tip of the stick caught. She held a small twig over its flame. Placing the burning sticks crosswise on embers of the handkerchief she added twigs so that the little fire grew.

Turning around in a circle, she saw she was in a stone chamber. Six wooded posts dark as charcoal rose from the floor to the stone roof. This was no cave--it was a mine.

When she had a small fire that she thought would burn at least for a short time she went back to the pile of sticks examining it as best she could in the fire's flickering light. Looking at it she realized this was a very large nest that had been built inside a large crevasse between the rocks. She reached for a stick that protruded from the edge of the stick bundle. As if to confirm that it was something's nest a quick and forceful thumping began as soon as she started to pull the stick out.

"Sorry, Mr. Packrat, but I need this more than you."

Now the smell, which she realized was musky packrat urine, was overwhelming.

"But, boy, you sure do stink."

The fire, she saw now, was dying out. Grabbing as many sticks and twigs as she could carry at one time; she went over and added some of the precious wood she had gathered to the dwindling flames.

However, she saved out the longest piece and thrust the end into the flames until it's flame blazed and added its light to the chamber.

She turned, and the movement made her small torch flicker and go out. The tip glowed red and smoked, but there was no flame to see by. She went back to the fire and thrust the tip back in. This time she held the stick in her left hand and shielded its flame with the bare fingers of her right hand as she turned.

Moving with the shielded flame she walked stiffly to the other end of the chamber. Here, on her far right was an opening that led into a lightless black passage. Bravely, she moved forward. This passage ended shortly in a T.

An ice-cold breeze coming from her right side caused her small torch to flicker. Moving her free hand over the flame to save it, she burned her fingers.

"Ouch!"

Luckily, the flame did not go out.

She froze, listened. There was no sound in the passage to the right, just darkness and an icy breeze.

To her left she thought she saw a flicker of light.

She walked into the left-hand passage. Just a dozen feet ahead, a wall of rock blocked her passage in that direction. The glimmer of light came from a tiny crack in that wall. Looking at it closely she saw that the crack went through four feet of solid stone before reaching the light. Her heart sank. This was a dead end. She'd have to go back. Then she realized she really had to go. Squatting, she made her toilet, and soon regretted leaving the roll of toilet paper she'd had in her jacket pocket in the back of her Dad's truck.

Back at the T the passage continued then curved around a corner to her right, from which the icy breeze blew. Carefully, shielding her light, she moved in that direction. The floor beneath her feet began to climb. The passageway seemed to curve as it rose. The stone beneath her feet grew colder, sending its chill through her bare feet. She pressed on. Then ahead of her, at a turn in the passage, she saw a much brighter glimmer of light coming around the corner. No longer needing her torch, she walked forward toward the light. She turned the corner. The light grew much brighter. She froze. The entrance to the mine hung above her like a skylight on a flat roof. Over this entrance rested a heavy, metal grate, through which snowflakes were blowing in through openings a half-foot square between railroad-track thick bars. The stone floor she stood on sloped more sharply upward here. From where she stood the grate was out of reach above her, but walking forward put the grate just inches above her head. Snow on the floor sent icy pain through her bare feet. Stunned, knowing somehow that trying to move the grate would be futile, she looked around for a place to put her torch. A tiny section of the mine wall where the cut rock formed a small ledge was within easy reach. Once the torch was safely balanced on the ledge, both her hands went to the metal of the grate. The cold burned into her bare fingers and the palms of both her hands. Her hands hurt like they never had before. Trying to ignore the pain, she pushed with all her strength. The grate did not move. She tried again, this time putting her legs and back into the effort. Nothing.

She looked up through the grate at the sky. Snow fell into her eyes.

As she looked over at her torch to retrieve it, a gust of wind blew in through the grate. The flame winked out. The tip of the stick glowed red and sent up a thin ghostly tendril of smoke.

From the light coming in she knew it was very late in the day. Her entire body hurt. She felt exhausted. Despair filled her. What was she going to do now?

After she stepped away from the part of the floor covered by snow that had fallen through the grate, she realized how thirsty she was. She began scooping up the snow and put each precious bit of moisture into her mouth.

# A Suggestion

## October 25: Afternoon

When I checked in with the sheriff later in the day, he informed me that Tim Bobbins had tried to contact me, and failing that had called the sheriff's office as I had instructed Phyllis at the FWP office.

The sheriff, based on the report I had sent him, had asked both Bobbins and Shawna Edwards to come in to see if they might be able to come up with something if they worked with a sketch artist.

I suggested that we include a hypnotherapist, and asked if he knew of one who might help the two FWP employees remember something about the vehicle with the broken lights.

Goldstone was skeptical at first until I explained that to locate a lost hunter I had found a few years ago, the family had brought in a hypnotherapist who had hypnotized their son. The boy had staggered out of the woods alone but couldn't remember where his injured father was.

With the hypnotist's help, the boy was able to describe his path through the woods well enough for me to backtrack his movements. I found the dad who had suffered a broken leg.

"In that case, it might not be a bad idea, Winslow," the sheriff had said. "I'll see what I can do." I knew he usually called everyone on his staff by their last name. His using my first name probably indicated he really liked my idea. "Let me look into it, and I will get back to you as soon as possible."

"One more thing," Goldstone said. "We found Cassie and Greg's rifles in the back of the truck. But the vehicle's jack was missing. Maybe we'll get lucky and someone will pawn it."

I was lying on the bed later, thinking, playing with Blu, and I guess I fell asleep.

Lomahongva appeared to me. She had a very serious expression on her face. "You have to sneak me into town," she said.

I was driving the Jeep toward the FWP checkpoint. There was a deer on the roof of the Jeep. "You can't let them see me," Lo said, anxiously, from the passenger side.

"How can I do that?" I asked. "There is no where to hide you in this Jeep."

I awoke and the dream gave me a helpless feeling. I did not know what more I could do to find

88

Cassie Carew. And yet, I felt I needed to do more. We had no idea where the girl could be. We were pretty sure she had been kidnapped. But, if the kidnappers had taken her into town, which Paul thought most likely, the case would be outside my area of expertise. It hit me again that thinking her kidnapped might just be wishful thinking. That her frozen body was hidden out there was also possible.

Later in the evening I emailed the Sheriff with a list of notes for the hypnotherapist. Although I lived far from any landline, I did have satellite Internet. I heard back from him quickly. The meeting was set up for 10:45 a.m.

I went outside for a breath of fresh air. Large flakes of snow cascaded around me.

# A Visitor in The Night

## October 23: Early Morning

Billy Wesley had stopped to put chains on his Ford Explorer in Beartown, by the large parking lot the BLM maintained for people who wanted to snow-mobile up to Garnet Ghost Town in the winter. It was after midnight and he hated putting chains on at all much less at night. But there could be more snow higher up, and he did not want to get stuck.

With his chains on he headed up Deep Creek, a road so named for the small creek that ran its length. Somehow in the distant past a very deep V had been carved between the mountains on either side of what was now a small stream.

Just before two am he pulled up into the dead-end lane that led up to the old mine he had discovered while his brother was in prison. Several inches of snow covered everything around the car. He shut the lights off and then the engine. The engine ticked as if adjusting to the cold. Darkness seemed to pour in around him and then freeze in a grey blur as his eyes adjusted. The snow outside now glowed faintly in the moonlight.

He had turned off the door light, so no light came on as he opened the door. The first thing he did was grab the heavy-duty, adjustable-beam headlight from the passenger seat. He turned the headlight on to its lowest setting and set the beam as narrow as possible, even though it was very unlikely that anyone would be close enough to see it.

He got out, then reached across the driver's seat again and grabbed the backpack he had packed. Lifting the backpack out, he shut the car door.

He went to the back of the vehicle and took out the plastic toboggan he had bought, put the backpack in it, and then loaded the rest of the things he had bought for the girl.

Pulling the sled to the front of his car, he examined the ground. Only his previous set of tracks could be seen under the snow. He felt relieved. He did not expect anyone else to be exploring the mine at this time of year, but you could never tell.

He wasn't worried about hunters. Most of the hunters he knew were road hunters. They drove around until they saw an animal to shoot. His brother and Hanassey were just road hunters, drunken road hunters, queer drunken road hunters. But this time that had worked out well for him.

At the top of his steep 50-yard climb he sucked in the ice-cold air as he caught his breath. After a brief rest he peered around the last giant, canine-tooth-like boulder toward the grate that covered the mine entrance.

The water bottles he had brought were heavy, and he was glad he'd thought of the sled. When he had brought the girl here, he had lucked out in finding a ratcheting farm jack in the Chevy. But he had to first walk up to the mine with the heavy, old-water-pump-shaped jack; break the rusting lock on the grate, and then prop open the grate with the jack. Once he had the mine open, he'd had to walk back down to the Chevy and drag the girl up to the mine. Even with the snow on the trail, that had not been easy.

Putting the girl in the mine and getting rid of the truck had wiped him out in a way he'd never imagined. He had started drinking beer on the way back to Missoula with Bobby and Nate. Normally he didn't drink much. But on the way back he drank can after can. Because of the beer he'd made a fool of himself with a woman at the game checkout. That had been bad enough that another guy had taken over checking out the deer Nate stole from the Chevy. At least Bobby and Nate had not asked questions.

There were a number of possibilities he now had to consider: the girl could be awake beneath the grate; the girl could be asleep by the grate; or the girl could still be in the room where he left her asleep or awake. Then it occurred to him that she could also be dead. He cringed at that thought. She had been alive when he dropped her off, but he had no idea of the extent of her injuries.

The cold seemed to bite into his bare cheeks. Then he realized it was very unlikely she was by the grate. It was too cold. He had taken her boots and socks and her gloves had been left in the truck.

Still, he shut his headlight off and crept as quietly as he could to the grate. He listened for almost five minutes, until he began to shiver. Hearing nothing, he turned the headlight back on high and pointed the light down through the grate. The floor of the mine beneath the grate sloped away from him. But the floor at the closest edge was just over five feet below him. He played the light from corner to corner. She was not there.

Fetching the jack he raised the grate as high as the jack could lift it. Taking an improvised sling from the backpack, he lowered; first the heavy water bottles then the rest of the supplies into the mine. Then he eased himself down, and as carefully and quietly as he could he proceeded into the mine.

He turned his light off as he neared the corner to the main chamber and listened again. In a moment he heard snoring. She was alive and asleep! His nose caught the scent of excrement. Of course she had to crap and pee. Toilet paper hadn't even occurred to him. Feeling around in his jacket pockets, he found the roll he always brought with him when he went hunting. There had to be at least half a roll left. He'd leave it.

He listened to the snoring a bit longer, then, encouraged, he turned the corner. To his shock a tiny red light seemed to glow in the chamber. He paused and soon realized he could smell smoke. Somehow she had made a fire. There was another deep snore, and, reassured, he turned the headlight back on, and leaving it on low, moved cautiously into the chamber.

The red glow came from a pile of ashes near the girl, where she lay sleeping on her side.

Pointing the headlight at the floor near her head so that the beam did not directly point at her face, Billy looked down at her.

He had barely looked at her when he had hauled her up and in here. Dragging her up the hill and lowering her into the mine, even though she barely weighed 100 pounds, had been tiring. Especially, after what he had to do to get the mine open. Plus, she had been covered in blood and that had made it difficult for him to look at her. He imagined she might be badly injured, and at the time he did not want to deal with that.

Billy had actually thought the girl was dead, when he'd told his brother and Nate that, after he looked into the Chevy that first time. But later, as he was driving the Chevy, the girl moaned, and he'd almost driven off the road. She was alive. He knew then that if he told Bobby and Nate, Nate Hanassey would want to kill her. If they found out she was alive and he didn't tell them they would be very angry. To give himself time to think, he tired to think of a place she would not be able to escape from, where he could keep her while he figured out what to do. This mine, he'd discovered explored the year before, while Bobby was still in prison, came to mind right away.

But now as he looked at the sleeping girl, he could see that she was really pretty. She was the kind of girl he drooled over in high school who never paid any attention to him.

He knew he could take her now. Wake her up. Strip her. Take her by force.

He thought about it for a long time. He would have to kill her afterwards. Wouldn't he have to kill her eventually?

He shook his head. He didn't even want to think about that right now.

He started ferrying the supplies he had brought her in from where he left them by the grate. Each item was as quietly as possible laid down next to her. When he was done he moved the light toward her face again. She turned slightly and he jumped. But another snore reassured him she had not awakened.

She is actually beautiful, he thought.

As quietly as he could, he began to move away.

When he reached the grate, his headlight was still on low. Shadows loomed and for a moment it looked like the heavy grate had somehow closed. A sense of panic filled him—a feeling of being trapped. And then as he swung his light toward the grate, he saw the Chevy's jack in place and the gap he had climbed in through wide open.

As he climbed out of the mine, the idea hit him. What if he was trapped with her?

It would take some preparation, but he might be able to pull it off.

# Checking His History

## October 26th: 9 am

"This is Colonel Waterson, Sheriff Goldstone, what can I do for you."

"I understand that Winslow Doyle was assigned to you in the Gulf War."

"Yes, he was. Is he in some kind of trouble?"

"No. As a matter of fact, right now, he is a temporary deputy in my department, and I cannot say that I am in any way displeased with his work. In fact, I'm thinking of offering him a permanent position. Before that happens I thought it might be a good idea to check him out."

"Understood. Do you have specific questions or would you like a general rundown."

There was a pause on the Sheriff's end of the line. "So you knew him personally?"

"Yes, as his Captain. He was one of the military policemen under my command."

"How was he as an MP?"

"I would not be exaggerating to say he showed exceptional promise. He had a real instinct for unraveling complicated situations."

There was silence as the Sheriff thought for a moment. "But something happened?"

"Sheriff, nothing happened in the sense that Doyle did anything wrong. He had talent and because of that he was taken away from his activities as an investigator."

The Colonel paused, and then spoke again.

"There was a sniper incident. An Iraqi sniper started firing on our MP headquarters one morning and was doing heavy damage. Doyle obtained a Barrett M107 and took the Iraqi sniper out with one shot. The sniper was dug in one thousand yards from our position. Doyle did not have a spotter.

"At the time, the powers that be considered a sniper to be a better asset than a newly (he had less than nine months in as an MP) assigned military policemen, and he was, against my protests transferred."

"How did he do as a sniper?"

97

"I didn't any get any direct reports, but I heard though friends that he was highly effective."

"Would you recommend him as a law enforcement officer?"

"Highly."

"Thank you, Colonel, for your time."

"You are welcome, Sheriff. Say hi to Winslow for me."

# Hypnosis

## October 26: 10:45 am

The sheriff's office was a small building that had once been a library. Jail cells had been added to the basement. The main office space was converted from the library reading room. As I came in through the door, a man in a deputy's uniform was going out. He stopped and looked me over. "Doyle?"

"Yes, Winslow."

The man was just short of six feet and had a high forehead and close-cropped brown hair and a handlebar mustache. He looked fit, and his blue eyes were piercing.

"Tom Bedder," he said, offering his hand.

I took it and we shook.

"We can talk some other time. They're waiting for you," he said, gesturing toward the reception desk.

A petite woman in her mid-forties, with very straight blonde hair, dark glasses, and a serious look on her face sat staring into a computer screen and typing behind the main counter. She wore an unbuttoned charcoal cardigan over a pretty turquoise and black batiked blouse.

"Nadine?"

"Yes?" her questioning tone was almost suspicious.

"Hi, I'm Winslow Doyle. It's nice to finally meet you." I offered my hand.

She gave me a forced smile but did not lift her fingers from the keyboard in front of her. "Everyone else is in the conference room," Nadine said, nodding toward a glass walled room where the sheriff sat with five others.

"Just go right in?" I asked.

"Just go right in," Nadine said.


"Mr. Doyle," the sheriff said, standing as I entered the conference room. "Now we can start. Winslow, let me introduce you." He turned to a taller blonde woman with her hair tied back in a ponytail. She wore steel-framed glasses and had pretty facial features but wore a serious expression. She looked to be in her fifties. But not a wrinkle showed on her pretty face, so I assumed Botox or surgery. "This is Doctor René Walters," he said. "She's a psychologist at the University of Montana in Missoula."

The woman took my extended hand. She had long fingers and her hand felt dry to the touch. She wore a light blue blouse and a skirt that went with her eyes. A very pleasant lilac scent wafted over me.

"Nice to meet you," I said. "Sorry if I kept you."

"Nice to meet you, Mr. Doyle. And that was not a problem. It gave me a chance to speak privately with Mr. Bobbins and make some notes about what he remembers about the day. It will help me with his hypnosis."

I nodded, and Dr. Walters smiled.

"And next," Goldstone said, "is Shawna Edwards."

Shawna was young, tall, perhaps just under six feet, and very pretty. She was wearing an FWP game warden uniform. She had brown hair that fell down to her shoulders, and brilliant emerald green eyes. Her skin glowed despite the fact that she didn't seem to be wearing any makeup. She had an outdoors ruggedness to her and a strength that reminded me of a marathon runner. When Shawna looked at me she smiled.

I was standing too far away to offer her my hand. "Ms. Edwards," I said.

She laughed. "Call me Shawna, please." Again she flashed that smile and this time she held my gaze for a moment as if taking my measure.

The young man next to her stood. He walked over to me and offered his hand. He was thin, maybe in his late twenties, and had unruly black hair that poked out from his head. He wore dark plastic framed glasses and had brown eyes. "Tim Bobbins. I want to shake your hand, Mr. Doyle. I have heard of you." He said it so gushingly that I felt a little embarrassed.

"I'm mostly just a dog finder," I said.

"But you also found that boy a few years back," he added.

I nodded. "It was actually the father I found," I said, correcting him. That was back before I lost Lomahongva. It seemed like an eternity ago.

"May I ask you both a question before we begin?" I asked.

"Fire away," Tim said. Shawna nodded.

"How well do you check vehicles? I mean do you look to make sure they haven't hidden an extra animal, or even a person somewhere?"

Tim laughed. "We actually do. But we've never found a person. We do look for hidden compartments, in fact, we check every possible game hiding area in every vehicle that comes in. Shawna nodded, agreeing.

"So normally nothing can be slipped by you guys?"

Both shook their heads, no.

The other person at the table was dressed in a deputy's uniform. She had short brown hair, covered by a "Sheriff" cap, and a sharp angular nose and jaw. She had dark brown eyes that bore into mine. She looked so tough I imagined some people mistook her for a man.

"Lois Renault," she said. She did not offer her hand, so I just nodded at her.

The woman next to her stood. She was a smaller woman with reddish brown hair, pinned back in a bun, ruby-framed glasses, and a blue sweater. I guessed, by the large drawing pad in front of her, she was the artist.

"Abby Bedoe," she said. She pointed to the pad and pencils by her as if that explained everything. She had a friendly expression, and I liked her immediately.

"Hello," I said, and I turned back to the sheriff. "How will this work?"

The sheriff pointed to Dr. Walters indicating she should take over.

Dr. Walters smiled. "After I conducted Mr. Bobbin's preliminary interview, Ms. Edwards let me know that she has an appointment in two hours, so Mr. Bobbins has agreed to allow her to go first.

"Deputy Renault, if you'll take Mr. Bobbins out, and," she turned to Bobbins, "we'll call you in when we need you."

"You can't do us together?" Bobbins asked.

"No, actually, we can't. If you listen to what Ms. Edwards says, it might influence what you remember. That is one trouble with hypnosis, images can be planted as well as unearthed, so we need to separate you for this to work. That's why we went to that private interview room even though I was just asking preliminary questions."

"Okay, I understand," Tim said.

When Deputy Renault and Tim had left, Dr. Walters addressed the sheriff, Abby and I as she moved to a chair next to Shawna.

"First, I have some simple preliminary questions for Ms. Edwards."

Shawna nodded. "But…"

"But what?" Dr. Walters asked.

"I'm a little nervous about this hypnosis, and I have a few questions."

"Feel free to ask, anything," Dr. Walters said, encouragingly.

"Well, can this harm me in any way? I mean in my head, of course, but also legally."

Dr. Walters thought for a moment about how to answer that question.

I glanced out the conference room window as a gust of wind blew snow off the snow-frosted trees around the parking lot.

"Let me see if I can answer your question to your satisfaction," Dr. Walters said. "First, you are not a witness to a crime. There is a potential complication that has occurred in using hypnosis for memory enhancement for trial in that ideas, images and memories, may be placed that are not really what the hypnotized subject experienced. That has led to some legal battles. But no one will be charged based on what you say here. You are simply here to perhaps help identify someone who may, and I emphasize may according to what the Sheriff has told me, be a person of interest.

"So legally you are good. Psychologically, there are at times dangers for some people with pre-existing disorders."

Shawna seemed to tense up.

Dr. Walters noticed this immediately and said, in a kidding way, "I have not done a psychological analysis of you, Ms. Edwards, but you look to me to be pretty normal."

Shawna laughed. "I hope," she said, noticeably relaxing. She looked to me as if gaging my reaction to her comment. I smiled. She returned my smile and seemed to hold my gaze for a moment.

Chuckles filled the room.

"Shawna," Goldstone said, speaking up. "You are under no obligation to do this."

"I'm fine with it," Shawna said, after a moment. She nodded to Dr. Walters to continue.

There are a few other possibilities," Dr. Walters went on. If you have ever had a very bad experience, for example," her expression grew serious and she looked at Shawna intently. I'd seen that look. She wanted to read any reaction to what Shawna would say next. "Such as being raped. If the hypnosis recalled such an experience, or the person who caused that experience, there could be repercussions."

Shawna shook her head. "No, nothing like that has ever happened to me."

"Good," Dr. Walters said. "Other possibilities include things such as something that you did not think was bad at the time but later learned was something you should not have done. Things like that can cause you anxiety and interfere with hypnosis."

Shawna shook her head again. "I can't think of anything like that."

"Good. Then are you ready to begin?"

Shawna nodded.

"Now Sheriff, Mr. Doyle, Ms. Bedoe, you need to be completely silent during this entire proceeding. If you need to communicate anything you must do it with hand signals and written notes. Is that clear?"

We all nodded, even Shawna. Then Ms. Bedoe raised her hand.

"Yes," Dr. Walters said. "Oh, yes. When I'm done and Ms. Edwards has given a preliminary description, if you have questions, raise your hand and I will turn Shawna's attention to you and instruct her to answer your questions."

"Understood," Ms. Bedoe said..

"Well, let's get started, with the preliminaries then.

"Shawna, close your eyes, and think back to whatever you remember about this Saturday past.

Let's start with when you woke up in the morning. You open your eyes. Do you have any feelings about the day?"

"I wondered what time it was. My alarm wasn't ringing. I turned and looked at my clock, and I was awake seven minutes early."

"What time do you usually get up?"

"6:30 a.m."

"Were you tired?"

"No. I felt good, and I was looking forward to the first day of big game season and the check. I especially enjoy checking in successful first time hunters. I find their joy uplifting."

"So you arrive at the check station. What is it like there?"

"I parked behind the trailer, we have a trailer to take breaks in and sit, or for shelter when it gets really bad out. I got out of my Subaru but didn't bother to lock it; we'd be there all day. It was cold, but not too cold, and the sun was out. A light breeze was coming off the river. It looked like it was shaping up to be a beautiful day. Tim came out of the trailer holding a cup of coffee for me. We do that for each other. I took it and sipped. He knows I use two sugars and cream and it was just right. Jim Bridges came out of the trailer, then, nodding to me and then toward the road. An old beat-up truck was turning in with an 8-point elk in the back. And Jim said, 'You're up, Shawna.'"

"Good," Dr. Walters said, "that's enough for me to start. Just one last thing; what is your favorite color?"

Shawna looked as puzzled as I was. "I guess, green," she said.

I knew there were many different things a person could use as a prop for hypnosis, including no prop at all. The hypnotist who helped the boy find his father used a pendant. To my surprise Dr. Walters took out one of the large-sized iPads. She turned the display on and in a few moments she had a green page on which a series of green circles where shrinking as they descended into the center of the iPad and vanishing as other circles rushed to do the same.

"Shawna, I want you to look down into my iPad and watch the circles as they descend and vanish. Try to concentrate only on the circles as I speak to you."

Shawna didn't reply but instead leaned over and putting her elbows on the table, and resting her head in her hands, began to look into the iPad.

"As you watch begin to feel your body relaxing," Dr. Walters continued. "You can feel your feet relaxing and this relaxed feeling is making its way up your body. It moves up to your calves, then your thighs, then to your upper body slowly making its way to your chest, and then, finally, up to your head. Now your entire body is feeling more and more relaxed as you follow the circles."

I had been paying too close attention and started feeling relaxed myself. I caught myself and snapped out of it.

"Now, Shawna, your relaxed body is becoming lighter and lighter. And as you feel lighter and lighter your eyes want to close. Your eyelids are feeling heavier and heavier. You want to close your eyelids. They are so heavy. Let your eyelids close Shawna, let them close."

I watched as Shawna's eyelids, flickered as if she was blinking, and then they closed.

"Now, Shawna, you are in a deep-deep sleep," Dr. Walters said, as she reached out, took the iPad and turned it off. "And in this deep-deep sleep you will only hear the sound of my voice. Do you understand, Shawna? Please answer yes or no."

There was something about the way Shawna said "yes." I had this impression of the word somehow rising from some intimate and private place deep within her.

"Okay, now Shawna, first I want you to sit up straight with your arms at your sides."

Shawna slowly sat up. Her eyes stayed closed. Her arms fell to her sides.

"I want you to remember back to the first day of hunting season this year. You wake up. You wonder why the alarm isn't ringing. You turn and look at your clock. What time does it say?"

Shawna moved. She turned as if looking at something. "Six twenty-three," she said languidly.

Dr. Walters looked at the rest of us and gave a thumbs up. I knew what this meant. She had Shawna there on Saturday morning. Now she would try to move Shawna up to the point in the afternoon where she met the hunters we were interested in.

"Okay, lets move on to your arrival at the game check station. You pull in behind the trailer, park, and then walk around to the front. It's a beautiful day. What do you see?"

"Tim, he comes out of the trailer with a coffee for me."

"You taste the coffee. Is it good?"

"Yes. I was afraid he'd put too much sugar in or not enough. Tim gets it wrong sometimes, but this is perfect."

"And now Jim Bridges is coming out and he nods toward a truck that is pulling up, with an elk in it," Dr. Walters continues.

"Yes, a nice elk, in this old beater," Shawna says, smiling with her eyes closed.

"What does Jim say?" Dr. Walters asks.

"You're up, Shawna," Shawna says.

"I want to move slowly ahead now to later parts of the day," Dr. Walters continues. "We are looking for a time when another truck comes, not a new truck but probably a newer one than that first truck. Move through your day slowly until you see a truck that may have more than one animal in it, but it has at least one deer, and the front right headlight is broken.

"Move slowly through your day. What kind of vehicles are you seeing?"

"Mostly trucks," Shawna said. GMC's, Fords, Chevys. Some cars…"

Shawna seemed to pause.

"What are you seeing now?" Dr. Walters asked.

"It's a Ford truck, a big one with an extended cab. I see it has a broken headlight on the right side. There is a deer head poking off the side of the truck bed. An antler is caught on the rim."

"The truck has Montana plates?"

"Yes, the plain ones. Just numbers and letters."

"Can you see the plate numbers?"

"A 91, that's all. I didn't really look at the plate."

"How many men are in the vehicle?"

"Three."

"Tell me what you can about the men," Dr. Walters says.

"One of the men gets out on the passenger side. He's young. Maybe ten years younger than me. He comes up to me and smiles. His breath smells like beer.

'Do you know you have a broken headlight?'

He looked at the headlight then nodded. Then said,

'So, hottie, you want to check me out?'

"I turn away from him. He was obviously a bit drunk. And then Tim stepped up behind us and told him he was going to check them out. The guy turned to Tim and said, 'like I really want to talk to you.' Another vehicle came in, and I just walked

110

over to it. I never looked back, so I didn't see what happened after that."

"Had you ever seen this man before?"

"No, I don't think so."

"You say he was around ten years younger than you. Can you describe him further? Picture him in your mind. Hold his face in focus and tell us what you see."

"He's just a young guy. He looks a bit like that guy who used to be in the old black and white television show, 'The Rebel.'"

Both Dr. Walters and I looked to Abby who was poised with her pencil over her large drawing pad. She shook her head; the reference meant nothing to her.

"Okay," Dr. Walters continued, "what is the shape of his head: round, oval, square?"

"His head is more egg-like, pointed end down, than completely round. He has fuzzy, dirty-blonde hair cut short like a crew cut that has grown out some. But the short hair makes his ears look like they're sticking out."

"What are his eyes like?" Walters asked.

"His eyes are hazel, I think. The pupils look a bit small. The eyes are set back and neither high nor wide. His eyebrows are thin and curved, and dirty blonde like his hair. "

"What about his mouth? Can you describe his lips, the way his mouth looks?"

"As he smiles at me, leers, actually, I think I see a hint of a broken tooth on the front right. His top lip is very thin, compared to the bottom lip which is slightly thicker."

"And his nose, is it pointed, long, wide, short?"

"Straight. Not too wide."

"If you drew a box with the top edges at the top of his ears, and the bottom edge at his earlobes would his nose fit in that box?"

"Yes."

"Does he have a beard or mustache?"

"No, but there is stubble on his face, as if he hasn't shaved in a day or so."

"How tall is he?"

"He is almost my height but not quite."

"And how tall are you?"

"Five eleven."

"What about his body type? Fat? Thin? Muscular?"

"He is lean, but fit looking, like a long distance runner."

"Any scars, moles, marks like that?"

Shawna shook her head. "No, nothing like that."

Dr. Walters looked to Abby Bedoe, questioningly.

Abby had been drawing quickly as Shawna spoke. She nodded back, flashed an 'OK' sign with her fingers indicating she had no questions, finished a line or two on the pad, and then turned it to face Walters and Shawna.

"Okay, now, Shawna. I am going to have you open your eyes and look down at the table. There is a drawing on a pad on the table. When you open your eyes I want you to concentrate on the drawing on the pad and nothing else. Alright?"

"Alright," Shawna said.

"Okay, now open your eyes and look at the drawing on the table."

As we watched, Shawna's eyes flickered open, and she looked at the pad and the drawing Abby had made.

"Does the man in the drawing look like the man you saw that day?"

"Somewhat."

"How is the drawing different?"

"His chin was more rounded."

"I am going to have Abby change that."

Abby, taking her cue, took the pad, used an eraser on the chin she had drawn and made the chin rounder. Then Abby turned the pad back."

"Does this look better?" Dr. Walters asked.

"Yes," Shawna said.

"What else is different?"

"His ears. His ears stuck out a bit more."

Again Abby took the pad and changed the drawing. Then she turned the drawing around.

"Does this look closer?"

"They stuck out a bit more."

In a few more minutes we had a drawing that Shawna said resembled the man she had seen that day.

"Okay, Shawna," Dr. Walters said. "I want you to close your eyes again."

Shawna closed her eyes.

"I am going to count to ten. As I say each number you will be moving back toward being more and more fully awake. When I reach ten you will open your eyes, be fully awake and feel refreshed. You will remember everything we've just said and talked about. Understood?"

"Yes."

"One, two, three, four, five, six, seven, eight, nine, ten."

We watched as Shawna opened her eyes and looked around at us.

"How did it go?" she asked.

"Great," Goldstone said.

"Does this look like the man you saw?" I asked, pointing to the drawing. I wanted to see if her conscious memory matched her memory under hypnosis.

Shawna looked down at the drawing. She looked at it for a few moments then nodded. "I think so."

# Morning Discoveries

## October 23: 1:20 pm

Cassie Carew woke for the second time in darkness. Her head seemed to be aching just as badly as it had the day before. She wanted desperately to hold on to the dream she had been having. Her Dad was with her in the mine. For some reason he couldn't help her to get out. "Try to stay strong," he said.

The air smelled of smoke. She was on her side, her face resting on her right arm facing the pack-rat's nest. She reached for her watch on her left hand and pressed the light button. It was 1:20 pm. Then it dawned on her what she'd just done. Shaking her head, she realized, checking her watch would have been an easy way to check if she could see. But she had not been thinking straight when she first woke up.

In the light from the watch she could see the ashes of her fire in front of her. She took her finger off the watch button. In the dark she gently blew into those ashes. A few tiny embers glowed but then winked out.

The night before, before her small fire died to coals and the mine was plunged into almost complete darkness, in her left jean's pocket she found a Kleenex tissue that she had placed there some time before and forgotten about. Now, she took this and tore small pieces of it off and combined them into a small teepee with nest sticks that she had piled next to her, collected the night before. Her fire starter ignited the paper and she blew gently. In a matter of moments she had a small fire casting light in her prison.

She stood and stretched. This made her head throb. Her body did not ache as much as it had, but a wave of dizziness hit her. No wonder she had slept so late. She wondered if she might have a slight concussion.

She began to turn around, and she froze. Right behind where she was sleeping there was a pile of things on the floor. The first thing that caught her eye was a package of 30 plastic water bottles. Her decision was quick. If someone wanted to kill her, they could do so easily without resorting to poisoning her. If the water was drugged she still had no choice. Despite the snow she had swallowed the day before she felt thirstier than she had ever felt. With her multi-tool she cut open the plastic wrapping, grabbed one of the plastic bottles, opened it and poured water down her throat. She finished half the bottle before lowering it.

A feeling of dizziness hit her. It passed after a minute.

Now, she hunkered down and looked at the rest of the things that had been brought in. She grabbed a cylindrical, cloth-covered bag, reached inside and pulled out a sleeping bag. It was musky smelling with an odd chemical hint. A $5.99 Needly Thrift price tag hung from the zipper. Why hadn't they given her, her sleeping bag, or her fathers? She let the sleeping bag fall. She lifted one of the two plastic bags and looked inside. There were two bags of beef jerky and a partly used roll of toilet paper. She felt like crying. Whoever had her in here was not planning on letting her out soon.

Finally, she reached for the last plastic bag. Inside was a headlight kit, containing a waterproof headlight and a plastic pouch containing eight AA batteries.

She cut the headlight out of the container. It felt light. She pressed the button on the bottom but nothing happened. After removing the back she could see that it didn't have batteries in it. The plastic pouch was hard to open, so she was glad she had her multi-tool knife to cut the plastic. She inserted two batteries into the slots for them and reattached the back of the headlight.

Holding the headlight in her hand she held her breath as she pushed the button. A beam of light blazed out of the front of the thing. At least now she had a flashlight. As she stood holding the headlight, the cold seemed to rise from the stone floor and steal what warmth was left in her feet. The headlight had two elastic straps: one circular one to go around her head and another that went from the light itself to the back of the loop. She tried putting it on her head. It was a little tight but it fit.

Grabbing the toilet paper, she hurried off to the dead end corridor she'd discovered the day before.

When she got back she folded up the sleeping bag, sat down on it, and stretched her feet toward the fire. Splaying the beam from the headlight across the walls of the mine she warmed her feet. Finally, her feet began to feel too hot. She pulled her feet back, and then mildly chastised herself. She had felt better with the headlight on but that had to be a brief luxury, one she'd try not to repeat. She shouldn't waste the batteries when she had the light from the fire to see.

She started feeling dizzy again. Adding a few more sticks to the fire she got into the sleeping bag. Soon after, she was asleep.

# A Second Hypnosis

## October 26: 1 pm

Everyone but Shawna was back in the conference room at 1 pm. After Shawna left Goldstone had suggested, he, Dr. Walters, Abby, and I have lunch at a nearby restaurant. Abby had a lunchtime errand, so couldn't join us. Bobbins and Deputy Renault were already seated at a table for two in the restaurant so Goldstone had us sit at another table. I got the chance to ask Dr. Walters what she thought of Shawna's replies. Dr. Walters seemed a little uncomfortable with the question. She hesitated before answering. "I think it went well. But, although Shawna agreed to having you all there at the session, what I may have learned about her personally as a patient, I feel I need to keep confidential."

Dr. Walters already had Tim's background material. So the session progressed pretty similarly to Shawna's, up until Dr. Walters began questioning Tim about the meeting with the hunters of interest.

Tim sat with his arms at his sides and had the same expression as the young woman who had been hypnotized before him.

"Now, Tim, you see the younger man in the truck get out and approach Shawna. He has obviously been drinking. You hear him say to Shawna, 'So , hottie, you want to check me out?' What do you do?"

"I like Shawna and guys like that upset her," Tim said. "I say, 'Sorry, guy, but it's my turn. State law. No out of order checking in allowed. So what do you got?'"

Dr. Walters asked about the license plate. Tim only remembered one number; a seven.

Tim's description of the young man was very similar to that of Shawna's. He did mention that the guy had a very prominent Adams apple and a small scar behind his left ear. But, otherwise, it was as if the two were describing an actor on the same television show they had watched.

"Okay," Dr. Walters said. "Now let's move on to the others in the vehicle. They have a deer?"

"Yes, a four-point. One of the other men tagged it, the big guy."

"Whom do you speak to next?"

I thought of a question, wrote it down quickly, raised my hand, and passed Dr. Walters the note.

Tim was already answering her last question.

"The big guy is walking up to me after I asked the younger man where he'd been hunting," Tim said. "The big guy says, 'We've all been hunting the same area.' So I quickly fill that information in. And I say let's check your deer. And we walked together to the back of the truck."

Dr. Walters now read my note, nodded to me and looked back at Tim.

"Where was Shawna at this time?"

"I look over at her as I'm checking the four-point they'd brought in. She's looking at an elk in the back of the truck that came in after this one. I look at her from time to time but she never looks in our direction."

"Is there anything wrong with the deer you are examining? Or the tag?"

"No. I take a tooth and everything looks okay."

"Have you ever seen this hunter before?" Dr. Walters asked.

Bobbins paused as if remembering. "I don't think…" The man seemed to freeze in place. His entire body went rigid. For what seemed like a full minute, it did not look like he was breathing. Then, suddenly, he shook his head and putting his forearms on the table for balance, leaned forward onto them. He looked at each of us around him like he didn't know where he was. I didn't think he was still hypnotized. He confirmed this a moment later.

"Did it work?" Bobbins asked. "Did you get what you need?"

"No," the Sheriff said.

Bobbins looked at him and then at Dr. Walters.

"Look at me," Dr. Walters said. "Look into my eyes."

Bobbins did so.

"What do you remember?"

"Looking at your iPad."

"Should we try again?" Goldstone asked.

"I don't think that would be a good idea," Dr. Walters said. She turned back to Tim and looked at him sympathetically. "We were doing well, and you confirmed Shawna's description of the younger man, but for some reason you snapped out of the trance before you could describe the man who'd tagged the deer. Do you remember any of what you said while in the trance?"

"No," Tim said, shaking his head.

Dr. Walters leaned back and thought for a moment. Then she looked at the Sheriff. "I don't think trying again would be good for Tim here. For some reason he jumped out of the session, and I don't want to be responsible for what might happen if we try again. There could be consequences."

"Tim," Goldstone asked. Do you think you could describe the guy without hypnosis?"

Tim shook his head. "He's just a blur."

# Checking the Entryway

## October 24: 9:13 am

When Cassie woke, cocooned in the sleeping bag, she looked at her watch, without taking her head out of the bag, and noted the time, then turned on the headlight she had taken into the sleeping bag with her. She had six more AA batteries. At least her head did not hurt as much. She needed to know how long the headlight would work on a new set of batteries. She had no idea if her captor would bring her more batteries and supplies, or if he or she would ever come back. The thought sent a shiver through her.

She was about to stick her head out of the sleeping bag and get up, when she saw something green against the red lining of the bag. Reaching down, she grabbed the green cloth and pulled it free from the folds of the sleeping bag.

To her joy she had in her hands two long green woolen gloves. She examined them quickly, realizing

123

that someone must have left the gloves in the bag and the Needly Thrift people had never checked the bag well enough to find them.

She put the right on first and then, when she took up the other she saw this was also a right hand glove. It didn't matter. They were soft wool. She turned it inside out and put it on her left hand. Now she had gloves.

But as she walked to the packrat nest for more fuel for her fire, a new idea came to her. The cold from the floor instantly made her feet ache. She'd been putting up with this, but now she stripped the gloves from her hands and, while sitting on her sleeping bag, slipped one glove on each foot. She stood. It wasn't perfect but her new 'socks' worked.

Wearing the headlight, she headed toward the T, did her toilet, and then went to the grate. Sunlight streamed through the grate. She flicked the headlight off for the moment and looked down at her watch. She added the time she had just used the headlight to the previous time she had noted in her head.

Although she had looked at the grate before, somewhat well, she decided she should now examine it carefully. She went around from corner to corner and pushed on the rusted metal where she could. But she could not budge it. Had the person who came in the night before last come in this way? He must have!

The sun coming through the grate was warm, and the light was heartening. She checked her watch, turned the headlight back on, and went back to the chamber. There she built a fire adding enough sticks to keep it going for a little while. Taking the half empty bottle of water she had opened the night before and one of the bags of jerky, she went back to the grate doorway. There she turned off the headlight and noted the time. She found a spot off to the side of the entry that had not gotten wet with snow and sat down. At least here she had lots of light.

Opening the bag of jerky she found a big piece and took a bite. Her senses seemed to churn at the taste of food. She hadn't realized just how hungry she was.

After eating three big pieces of jerky, her hunger abated. She thought for a moment about what she should do, and then began to take everything out of her pockets. She needed an inventory of what she had.

From her jacket pockets she pulled her multitool, the fire starter, and a bag of chocolate her mother had snuck in as a treat for her to find. The thought brought tears to her eyes. Where was her Dad? Something had to have happened to him. He would not have let anyone carry her away to bring her here. She had no idea how much time had gone by. Her mother must know by now she was missing. Were they looking for her?

The only other thing she found in her jacket was a Mylar heat shield--a large piece of thin reflective material designed to be used in emergencies to hold heat in, or to use as a shelter in the snow. She had forgotten about it, but it would be good to drape it over herself as she sat by her small fire to reflect heat back in.

# Ruminating

## October 26: 1:53 pm

I left the sheriff's office in the early afternoon after Tim Bobbins had dejectedly gone back to work. Dr. Walters had tried to reassure him that snapping out of hypnosis was not all that uncommon. But he left a very unhappy man. He gave me a long, lingering look before he left that left me puzzled.

Gladstone, the other deputies, and I talked briefly about the possibilities. Gladstone suspected that the girl, since she could not have been in the Ford at the game check station, had been dropped off somewhere, either in the mountains or along Highway 200. Goldstone thought along Highway

200 was more likely and decided that is where the focus would now be.

While we had been working with Bobbin's, Tom Bedder, the closest thing the department had to an Internet guru, had begun a facial recognition search for the young man, starting with the state's criminal database. That search went fairly quickly and came up empty. Bedder then entered the subject's image into two larger search engines. One was for a facial search on Facebook. The other was for the National Criminal Data Base. Both would take time, and there was no point in waiting around.

I got back to my cabin long before dark. The dogs jumped up and down by the Jeep's door, whining because they missed me. They both disappeared into the cabin via the dog door as I took off the padlock. I opened the door expecting it to have cooled down inside and that I'd have to start a fire. To my surprise, there was a fire bathing the room via the glass door of the stove with warm orange light.

That Adahy had started a fire was made clear by a drawing on the kitchen table. The only two people the dogs would have let in besides me were Adahy and his mother. Adahy had no trouble entering and exiting through the dog door. The boy had drawn himself, Blu and me. He and I stood outside the cabin door. Blu was just coming out of the big dog door that I'd put in when Lomahongva and I had had her wolfhound that she'd raised from a pup. The thought of that dog depressed me.

At the bottom of the drawing Adahy had written: 'How many Blu kittens does it take to screw in a light bulb? Answer on the other side.'

I turned the paper over. On the back it said: 'An infinite number of Blu kittens could not screw in a light bulb. But it is certain that long before infinity is reached, the bulb will be broken.'

I shook my head. Adahy was a very strange 9-year-old boy.

To the side of the front door, I kept a large steel ring. It was about thirty inches in diameter and had legs, which held it upright. When filled with firewood it held enough for a winter's night. It was half full when I left. In addition to making the fire, the boy had filled the wood ring for me, probably bringing a piece or two at a time from the woodshed and sticking them in through the dog door. I shook my head. It was clear the boy loved me and looked up to me. He worked hard at trying to please me. His father, Yona's husband, Bobby Redwolf, had died in an oilrig accident when the boy was one. I cared about the boy enough to try and hide the fact that every once in a while just being around him brought back memories of my Lo that I did not want to deal with.

Before going to bed I checked my email for messages. There was one. They had not yet found a match to the one face we had. But the sheriff had decided to release to the press the details of finding Greg Carew's body, and had requested that anyone, having any information about Greg or having seen his vehicle, please contact the sheriff's department.

The sheriff had opted to not put the picture of the young man of interest on the news. He did not want to give the man the information that we were, in fact, looking for him.

# Morning Ritual

## October 27: 7:30 am

I awoke from a dream in which I thought Loma-hongva would be upset with me. In the dream Shawna Edwards had smiled at me, and I realized I found Shawna attractive. Though there wasn't much to the dream, I found it disturbing.

I hadn't been on a date in what seemed a lifetime. I'd been a widower for six years and had thought more recently about dating, but I'd never gotten around to it. And I didn't think a woman as pretty as Shawna would be interested in me.

I tried to put the dream, and Shawna out of my mind and get along with my morning ritual.

My mornings had started out pretty much the same on most days. I was used to just waking up at daylight. But now, with Blu, I had a morning wake-up call where the kitten would walk on my head and face, purring as he did so. If I wasn't already awake this usually did the job. I'd pet him a bit which increased the volume of his purring, and then Irene would begin jumping up on the right side of the queen-sized bed Lomahongva and I had shared, while Mariah whined on the other. Today, Blu woke me from the dream.

I took the dogs for a half-mile walk every morning. But first, if it had snowed during the night, something I can tell with a glance at the kitchen skylight, I would go out and clear the snow off the solar panels. Near the southern corner of the cabin, stands a large tailings pile that rises to the level of the lower part of the cabin's roof. This pile has a climbable slope, which allows me to walk across a 2 x 10 plank stretching from the top of the tailings pile to the roof to reach the panels. This morning I could tell there was just a dusting of snow on the skylight. Leaving Blu inside, I went outside with the dogs following me and grabbed a broom. Although the dogs were free to go out the dog door and roam at will, they preferred going on walks with me. Luckily, Blu had yet to figure out the dog door. The dogs stayed close to home during hunting season, as they did not like the sound of gunshots.

130

This morning they ran around the cabin while I swept the snow off the solar panels.

I enjoy our morning walks. It's a good way to wake up and think about what I need to do during the day. The walks also made the dogs more obedient. Dogs are pack animals, and, by leading the walk each morning I established myself as the Alpha. We always went the same way. We'd set a well-worn path through the forest along an old logging trail to a spot where a big old tree stood. I called it the grandfather tree. Before Blu, I had another tuxedo cat named Wiley. He would sometimes follow us and then, suddenly, run ahead. On these occasions we'd find him sitting by the grandfather tree when the dogs and I arrived.

Each day when we returned from our walk, I would give the dogs treats and begin my daily yoga exercises while I cooked breakfast on the wood stove.

Today, after breakfast, I hesitated about what to do next. I was reluctant to check the Internet. I doubted they'd found anything, and that would be upsetting.

And my dream nagged me. Lomahongva kept saying, "You don't want to think of me."

But she had not meant thinking of her in general. Rather, she was referring to thinking about when I was notified that she had died. They were not pleasant memories. So, since I seemed to be able to speak to her in this dream, I said yes, I don't want to remember those things. But she said, "You are not thinking with me." Which was something she said somewhat often when we argued.

The last thing she said before Blu woke me was, "You did not know it would be a bad memory when you opened the door, before they told you of the bear."

I went online and checked for messages. There were none in my box. No progress had been made with locating the young man in the drawing.

I tried to think about what I could do next.

# On The News

## October 26: Noon

Nate Hanassey sat on a corner stool in the Oshkosh Bar & Grill and sliced open the sirloin steak that Bull Ryan, the bartender, had set before him. The place was well vented and smelled only faintly of beer. The scent of the steak filled Nate's nostrils. There were mushrooms to the side but no greens.

Nate didn't like greens. He smiled seeing that it was pink inside and that its juices flowed freely. He smiled at Bull, a tall, stick-thin man with a mop of dirty light brown hair, and Bull nodded back. The Oshkosh was one of Nate's regular delivery stops on his beer route. He and Bull had an arrangement. The brewery's beer was very popular in Missoula. So every so often Nate slipped Bull an extra case in exchange for a steak. Nate made up the case by shorting one of his company's other customers where Nate was blackmailing the closet-homosexual who did the inventories. Nate wasn't too worried about having this catch up to him. Bull would never rat him out, and Nate didn't plan on keeping the delivery job forever.

Almost directly above and in front of Nate hung a wide-screen television set up to be visible to all the patrons at the bar. The news had just started; and, though Nate paid little attention to the news in general, and never even looked at a newspaper, the young blonde woman on the screen with a model's body caught Nate's attention when she said, "And in breaking news, the body of a hunter, recently reported missing, has been found. According to the sheriff's department, the hunter, Greg Carew, 38, died under suspicious circumstances. More after the break."

Nate somehow knew that this was going to be about the truck he and his friends had dumped. As he waited for the commercial to end, a very uneasy feeling made him lose his appetite.

The reporter lady had said 'hunter.' She had not said 'hunters.' There was always the possibility that this had nothing to do with the truck they had hit and caused to run off the road. But Nate didn't believe that was the case.

The reporter came back on, and a moment later a shot of the truck they had run off the road appeared on the screen. A line of text beneath it read: 'Sheriff's Department Photo.'

"The body of Greg Carew, a hunter, missing with his daughter, Cassie, was found by the Garnet County Sheriff's Department yesterday. Carew's body was found in his truck in Lower Murkey Gulch in the Garnet Range. His 15-year-old-daughter, Cassie, also reported missing at the same time, has not been found. The sheriff's department is treating this as a suspicious death, and possible kidnapping. Anyone with any information about this is asked to contact the sheriff's department."

"Something wrong with it?" Bull Ryan asked as he came down the counter and saw that Nate had stopped eating.

Nate looked at him, confused for a moment, and then realized Bull was talking about the steak.

"No, it's great. But can you wrap it up for me. I gotta go."

"Sure, no problem."

"And can I use the phone in the office?"

Bull gave him a puzzled look.

"Local call. You know the boss don't let us take our cells with us on deliveries ever since that one guy hit that family while texting."

"Be my guest," Bull said.

Nate walked back into the office. Luckily there was a phone book by the desk phone. He almost tore the pages looking for the number. He always called Bobby's cell from his cell, speed dial 3. He had never called Bobby at work and did not know the number. When he found it, his hands shook as he dialed on the old-fashioned rotary phone.

Nate couldn't even sit down. He felt like his blood was pounding in his veins. His eyes focused on a small snow globe on Bull's desk. Nate figured it was probably a gift from Bull's daughter who was 8. Nate transferred the phone to his left hand and picked the globe up in his right. As the phone rang Nate squeezed the glass ball in his right hand so hard his hand hurt.

Finally, the phone was answered. "Beasley's Supply."

Nate did not recognize the voice.

"May I speak to Bobby Wesley, please?"

There was a long pause on the other end of the line. "Just one second," the voice that answered said sternly.

Bobby worked at a large plumbing supply company. He did maintenance and the trivial work needed. Finally, Nate heard the phone being picked up.

"Bobby Wesley, here. Can I help you?"

"It's me," Nate said, barely controlling himself.

When Bobby spoke it was a whisper. "What are you calling me here, for? You talked to the boss, and he did not look happy about me getting calls. You know I'm on probation with this job…"

Just then, one of the bartenders came into the office and began looking in a filing cabinet for something. Nate had been ready to shout but forced himself, now, to control his voice.

"Just checking," Nate said, "Hey," he added as if he had just thought of something interesting to say. "It was just on the news. They found that missing 'hunter.'" Nate put full emphasis on the singular word, 'hunter.' "And they're saying his daughter was with him, that they didn't find her."

Nate watched the bartender leave the room.

At the other end of the line Bobby was quiet for a long time. Finally, he said. "Oh, my God. I'll tell them I have an emergency there, and see if I can get right over. Should I meet you at the hospital?"

"Someone's listening, I get it" Nate said. "Make it the bus stop by your house."

"Okay. I'll see you at the hospital in about 20," Bobby said, playing along. Nate could hear the panic in Bobby's voice.

The phone went dead. Nate slammed the receiver in his left hand down. For a moment he tried to control his temper. Finally, he looked down at the snow globe in his hand and in a rage threw it against the wall furthest from the phone. It shattered in a burst of glass, water, and fake snow.

136

# A New Morning in Darkness

## October 25: 8:07 am

On the fourth morning of her imprisonment, Cassie awoke feeling warm in the old sleeping bag that had been left for her. But her right side, the side she always slept on was sore from lying on the stone floor of the mine for so many days. As far as the injuries she had received during the accident were concerned, she knew, now, that they were not severe. Her headache was gone. And she hurt more from sleeping on the stone floor than she did from the bruises she'd received when she, she assumed, hit the dashboard after taking her seat belt off.

In the dark she could make out the tiniest of embers in her fire, which was just about out. She lifted herself to a sitting position with the sleeping bag still around her. She listened. Aside from the sound of a packrat moving around, there was no other sound. She was still alone.

It occurred to her that whoever had brought her here might have found her after she wandered off from the accident. That would explain the strange, smelly sleeping bag. And if she had wandered off, it was possible that her father was all right. She didn't want to think too hard on whether that was realistic. As far as she knew her, Dad was alive. She noted the time, turned the headlight on, and got up.

The pain that she had seemed to feel all over was almost gone now, and she found she was able to move faster. She quickly gathered some wood and built her fire up. Then, she switched off her precious headlight and made a mental note of the time. The mitten-socks were good. She once saw a show on television about two guys who, after being dropped off in the wilderness, had to make it back to civilization on their own. One of the guys always wore just socks on his feet without shoes or boots. If he could do that, even in the winter in snow, she could.

As the light from her fire grew, she examined the chamber. She had 21-1/2 bottles of water left. She could add to that by gathering snow that had fallen or blown through the metal grate and melting it in one of the empty water bottles.

There were no new supplies. Whoever had dropped off that first group of stuff had not come back. She preferred he not come back. But then, what would happen to her when she ran out of jerky?

What if whoever it was never came back? Or, on the other hand, he intended to make 'use' of her... and at some point kill her?

She had no way to be certain her abductor was a 'he,' but she felt that it most likely had to be a guy. Whoever had carried he in had to be pretty strong.

# At Billy's Trailer

## October 26: Afternoon

Bobby Wesley sat silently in the passenger seat as Nate drove them both out of Missoula toward the nearby town of Clinton.

Bobby's brother Billy lived in a small trailer in a wooded area on the opposite side of highway 90 from the Clinton Market. Nate took the exit ramp, not slowing down from the 80 mile-an-hour speed limit until they were almost to the stop sign. But he did not stop. Instead he swung through the right turn onto the bridge road so fast Bobby felt like he was on a roller coaster. Bobby knew Nate was angrier than Bobby had ever seen him. They were just lucky no other vehicles had been coming in either direction when they made that turn.

There were two cars making the turn onto the bridge road from the frontage road and Nate had to slow down. He turned left onto the frontage road and spoke for the first time since he had picked up Bobby at the bus stop. Then he had simply said, "Get the fuck in."

"If that brother of yours has that girl in his trailer I'm going to kill the both of him."

Bobby Wesley's heart was already pounding. He said nothing. He knew if Nate tried to kill his brother, he would have to try and do something about it. But Nate had five inches on him and outweighed him by 60 pounds. Even though Bobby exercised regularly and was no longer the skinny weakling he had been when he was first sent to prison, he knew he was no match for Nate in any kind of fight. For now he said nothing. He just clenched his teeth and looked into the tree's lining the service road on the passenger side.

The houses and trailers seen through the trees grew further apart. Nate seemed to be driving at a normal speed, and they passed a two-story log cabin that was just barely visible behind the evergreens and drove the last 200 yards to the turnoff to the driveway that looped through the woods to Billy's trailer.

As Nate turned Bobby took a deep breath. To himself he thought, 'Don't be there, little brother. Please don't be there.'

Billy's trailer was a singlewide 50-footer with beige siding that was going to rust. There was a rusted wheelbarrow with a broken left handle and a flat tire covered with five inches of snow not far from the door. Gravel at the bottom of parallel tire tracks marked the empty parking area.

"His car is gone," Bobby pointed out.

Nate turned to him, a scowl on his face. "I can fuck'n see that myself," he said, as he pulled to a stop on the grass in front of the front door.

Bobby said nothing as Nate got out of the truck. His hand shaking, Bobby opened the passenger side door and got out himself.

The snow in front of the house was almost untouched but for a path that led from the door to the gravel drive. Nate walked up to the door and pounded on it four times. "Open up, you damn pussy!" he roared.

There was no sound but for the low distant hum of traffic on the highway.

"He's not here," Bobby offered.

Nate turned and looked at him for a moment. "He'd better not be." He turned back to the door as he fished in his right hand jacket pocket. "You better hope he isn't."

It took Nate, who had been convicted of burglary twice, seconds to pick the flimsy door lock on the trailer. Nate grabbed the knob and turned it.

The door opened. He pushed the door in and let go of the knob. The door swung in on its own. The smell of beer, cooked bacon, and dirty laundry drifted out.

"Last chance, Asshole. If you are in here, you'd better damn well come on out."

There was a cry of a bird that blended in with the traffic sounds from I-90. But there was no reply from the trailer.

Nate turned and looked at Bobby for a moment. Then from his left pocket he pulled a snub nose revolver. Bobby knew it. It was a .38 police special.

"Come on," Bobby said, pleading.

Nate just glared at him and pushed into the trailer. Bobby hung back. If Nate found his brother and the girl inside, he would kill them. Bobby was sure he would. He felt like a coward, and he tried to summon his courage, but he could just not force himself to go inside.

Bobby had been holding his breath, dreading a gunshot, or more likely two, when Nate stuck his head out the door.

"They're not here," Nate said. "Get inside and help me look for clues as to where he might be."

"I'm sure he'll be back," Bobby said, thinking he had better get Nate away from here anyway he could. Nate would kill his brother if he showed up now.

"I said, get in here!"

Bobby reluctantly climbed in. His brother Billy was not a great housekeeper. Nate was looking around the kitchen, so Bobby headed the opposite way, toward the bedroom.

Bobby tried to give everything in the bedroom a look but found himself barely examining things. He was about to move on when Nate said from the kitchen, "Found something."

Bobby hurried to him. Nate was kneeling over a garbage can he had pulled out from under the kitchen sink. He held up two receipts.

Bobby took them. One was from Needly Thrift: a thrift store in town, a charity, which took clothing and other donations that were sold to support the homeless around the state. The date on the tag was the day after the accident. The single item listed on it was a sleeping bag. The other receipt was from Hunters & Fishermen. This receipt was for some jerky and a waterproof headlight and battery set.

"Your brother already has a sleeping bag?" Nate asked.

"Yeah," Bobby managed.

"So why is he buying some cheap-ass $5.99 sleeping bag?"

"I don't know," Bobby said.

Nate grabbed Bobby by the arm and swung him around.

"He bought this for that girl. The one that obviously was not dead. That has to be what all this stuff is for."

Bobby said nothing. Finally, he slowly nodded.

"Where would he take her?"

Bobby shook his head.

"Don't shake your damn head at me!" Nate cried angrily, grabbing Bobby again and shaking him.

"You know most of the places he knows. Where would he go?"

Bobby shook his head. "He had three years while I was inside to find new places. I can't think of any place he'd take her that I know of."

Bobby looked at Nate, who, now, had a far-away look in his eyes.

"We have to find him and the girl. I don't want to go back to prison."

"Neither do I," Bobby said.

Bobby looked at Nate for a long moment. When Nate got this way in prison, there was only one way to calm him down. Now Nate was on a hair trigger. If Billy showed up before Bobby could get him out of here, Nate would kill him. Bobby moved close to Nate and brought his lips up to Nate's bearded face. As he kissed Nate on the lips, he reached his right hand down and rubbed his palm over Nate's crotch through his tight jeans. For a fearful moment, Nate tensed and Bobby steeled himself least Nate hit him instead of giving in to the invitation of sex. To Bobby's relief Nate gave into the kiss, extending his tongue into Bobby's mouth. Relieved, Bobby moved his hand up to Nate's belt buckle and began undoing it.

# A Pleasant Invitation

## Friday October 27: 8:45 am

When a knock came at my door before nine in the morning, I assumed for some reason it was a desperate Callie Carew looking for an update on the search for Cassie. The dogs were both out again, and I figured they were nearby and would have barked if there was danger. I had been cleaning my frying pan after a breakfast of bacon and eggs and with the pan still in hand, opened the door.

My visitor, who to my surprise turned out to be Shawna Edwards, was out there petting the dogs. Shawna was on one knee in the snow with Mariah's head hung over her knee scratching Mariah's ear with her right hand while she tried to pet a wiggly Irene with her left. I caught just a bit of the woman's smile when a dark streak zipped past me.

"Blu!" I cried. A

The dogs jumped at my cry, and Shawna stood up, and looked at me quizzically.

"I didn't want him to get out," I said in explanation. "There're two many things around here that could hurt him."

"Gotcha," Shawna said, turning and spotting the kitten just a few feet away by a building where Lomahongva kept chickens while she was alive. "Will he come when you call him?"

"Not usually," I said. Then I turned to the kitten. "Blu," I called. He ignored me and looked from me to Shawna and then darted back toward the cabin between us. He moved so fast he was like a dark streak. Shawna tried to grab him but slipped and fell in the snow for her efforts.

"Are you...?"

Shawna waved away my concern as she stood and brushed snow off.

The kitten ran up the board from the tailings pile onto the roof.

Shawna looked at me, and lifted her palms in a what-now gesture.

"He doesn't come when you call him, but he can be tricked," I said.

I walked to the side of the cabin. Standing on the lower slope of the tailing pile, my head was just level with the roof. The heat from my wood stove had melted the snow on the actual roof. But a build-up of unmelted snow ran around the eaves and this shielded me from view. Shawna came up behind me. Pointing with my fingers I guided her to stand on the other side of the board going to the roof.

"He likes to watch birds from the roof," I whispered. "But this is how to trick him."

With that I executed a short imitation bird whistle. I had gotten pretty good at imitating a blue jay. When nothing happened I whistled again. I listened. Wherever he was he wasn't moving. Shawna looked at me questioningly.

I whistled again, and this time I was rewarded with the sound of small feet running across the roof. I pointed, warning Shawna to be ready. A moment later Blu nearly flew onto the board, Shawna grabbed and lifted him.

"Thank you," I said.

"So your name is Blu?" Shawna asked him. He looked right at her and meowed.

"Let's get him inside," I said.

Once safely in the cabin, Blu ran to his food dish. I turned to Shawna. "Well," I started laughing and so did she. "What can I do for you? Unfortunately, there's no new progress on the case."

"Before I get to why I came, who is that old miner on the road up here?"

"You met Two Guns?" I said. "His name is Denny O'London, but everyone calls him 'Two Guns' because he always wears two guns. How did you meet him?"

"I'm working in this area today, don't have your phone number, so I stopped to ask where you lived."

I nodded and laughed. "And it's lucky you got away. He's lonely, and he'll talk your head off. It's hard to walk away without being rude. But he's a great guy and knows more about this area than anyone. Next to him I'm a greenhorn.

Shawna nodded in understanding. "I must have said I had to go ten times before he seemed to understand." Shawna paused, and then looked me right in the eye. "Actually, I should get to it. I came to ask you out."

I must have looked surprised and my mouth may have fallen open. Shawna looked away.

"This is a little embarrassing," she said. "There's a dance tonight in Missoula put together by the Friends of the Wilderness. And I bought tickets. I wasn't going to go, but then I thought I'd ask you."

I looked into her emerald green eyes and felt like a deer caught in headlights. Stunned, I said nothing for a moment.

"I know it's rather last minute, and I understand…"

"I would love to go," I said, interrupting her.

"Really?" She asked.

"Really." I was a little in shock. It had been years since my Lomahongva died. Until recently, I had never even given a thought to dating. Now this woman had asked me out, and I'd just surprised myself by accepting.

"If you don't mind my asking, and don't get me wrong, because I am flattered by your invitation, but why not just ask someone like Tim Bobbins?"

Shawna shook her head. "I'm not Tim's type, and I find you interesting. Since I asked you do you want me to pick you up?"

I had to think about what to say for a moment. I had never been picked up for a date.

"Logistically that.... Why don't we just meet?" I asked.

Two hours later I was, along with Lois Renault and Tom Bedder, doing door-to-door interviews along Highway 200 to find out if anyone remembered seeing a red Ford extended cab truck on the afternoon of October 21. Meanwhile, Sheriff Goldstone, either by phone or in person, personally interviewed Greg and Callie Carew's small circle of friends and acquaintances, Cassie's school principal, and her closest school friends. The Sheriff found no red flags. None had been expected. But Goldstone, by conducting his interviews, eliminated any possibility other than the one where Cassie had been the victim of a stranger abduction.

The dance was held in the ballroom of one of the newer hotels in Missoula. After parking my Jeep, I walked in through two open doors with a Friend of the Wilderness Ball banner. No one was checking entrants. Inside, tables covered with white tablecloths surrounded a dance floor like a circle of covered wagons stopped for the night.

After checking my jacket, I stood to the side of the door and looked for Shawna. It had been a very long time since I was on a date. Lomahongva had died in 2011. I had married her in 2003 while in the army. I hadn't even done much dating before that. After five minutes of searching the crowd for her, I wondered if I had been stood up, or if something had delayed her. I was about to try and find someone to ask if they'd seen her when I felt a tug on my sleeves. I turned and there she was, looking at me with those green eyes.

'Wow," she said, "We're color coordinated."

When I looked confused she touched the lime green shirt I had bought that afternoon and then her own blouse. They were almost identical in color.

"I thought we were supposed to be," I said with a smile.

The laugh I got back was beautiful. She'd told me the dance was informal and that she'd be wearing jeans and a blouse. I had bought the shirt and new black jeans that afternoon. The fact that the shirts matched was just a coincidence, but a nice one.

"Let me introduce you to Jim Bridges," Shawna said. She led me to a tall man with a long face in his mid-thirties who reminded me a bit of actor John Wayne. "Jim," Shawna said, 'This is Winslow Doyle, who you spoke to on the phone."

Bridges held out his hand, and his grip was firm. He didn't try to squeeze mine too hard, and I liked that. "Good to put a face to the name," Bridges said. "You are a deputy in the sheriff's department?"

"Just for now. Mostly I look for lost dogs."

Bridges nodded as if he understood. It was awkward.

"Come on," I want to dance," Shawna said and led me away.

Luckily for me neither Shawna nor I were experienced dancers, so we were able to enjoy just moving around on the dance floor doing whatever felt right.

Over the course of the evening, she introduced me to a number of people, none of whom I knew or had heard of.

After dancing for a while, Shawna, asked if I'd like to get some air.

We walked out and crossed the hotel parking lot to the park that bordered the river. Light gleamed in the windows of buildings at the university. The river was a dark ribbon between the snow-covered banks. It gave a low roar that filled the cold night air.

"You know, when I was in my teens we got a channel that showed reruns of a show from the sixties called Stoney Burke. Jack Lord starred in it playing a rodeo cowboy. I loved that show because Stoney, no matter what happened to him, would not let go of his dream to be the champion bronco rider. You look a bit like him in that role."

"I try to avoid horses whenever possible" I said.

"I had a crush on Jack Lord back then," Shawna said, with a teasing smile.

"How did you come to work for the FWP?" I asked to change the subject.

"My father worked for them for 27 years," Shawna said. "I followed in his footsteps so to speak."

"Is he still a game warden?"

"No, he died just before I joined up."

"I'm sorry," I said, embarrassed.

"I was sorry to hear your wife died. For me, with my Dad, it's been awhile and it doesn't hurt as much now." She shook her head. "Sorry, I didn't want to bring up stuff like that."

"That's okay."

I usually hated it when people brought up my Lomahongva. They had good intentions, most of them. But it made me feel like I was begging for sympathy. But with Shawna it seemed like we were sharing a sense of loss.

I tried to change the subject again. "Isn't Tim here?" I asked.

Shawna gave me a wry smile. "He has never been very comfortable at an event like this."

At the end of the evening, since we had driven separately after all, I walked her to her vehicle. It was an early 2000s Subaru Forester that looked like it had just been washed. Dents on the lower portions of the vehicle indicated to me it had been driven a lot in Montana's wilder areas.

"I had a really nice time," Shawna said.

"I did too," I said, and it was the truth.

Suddenly, she leaned forward and kissed me on the lips. She was almost as tall as me so didn't have to stand on tiptoe to do it. I kissed back with my arms at my side. Shawna's arms came up and went around my neck. I put my arms around her back and pulled her in. The kiss lasted for a beautifully long time and then she pushed away.

"Good night," she said. "Call me."

All I could do was nod. Still feeling her lips on mine, I watched her drive away.

# A Plan

## October 25: Mid-Afternoon

Since he had dropped off the supplies and looked at her sleeping on the floor of the mine, 'The Girl' was the only thing on Billy Wesley's mind.

Now, as he pulled into the parking lot of the Hardware Super Center he was formulating a plan.

Before he dragged her there, he used the jack from the Chevy truck to prop up the grate. The grate was so heavy, he couldn't even budge it himself, so he figured he didn't need any kind of a lock. But he had worried, that she somehow might be able to get the grate up and escape. Prior to lowering her into the mine, he'd laid her down in the snow and taken her boots and socks off. Her gloves had been on the seat of the truck, and he'd left them there. Without anything to keep her feet or hands warm, she wouldn't, he thought, try to get away in the cold and snow. He'd taken her wallet to make her harder to identify, but he hadn't looked in it. He didn't even know her name.

He'd left the jack, her boots, everything hidden in the rocks near the grate. He'd used the jack again when he brought the sleeping bag and other supplies. But for his ultimate plan to work, he knew he needed something different to open the grate, since he was going to be going down into the mine with her.

In the store, he found what he needed: a 12-volt, portable, battery-operated winch, some sections of steel cable, the hardware needed to connect the cable to the winch, and a heavy-duty marine battery. He also bought an 8' x 10' white poly-tarp.

His next stop was Walmart. Sooner or later someone was going to find the Chevy, so he'd been listening to the news on the radio in addition to watching it on television. So far the truck and the body had apparently not been found. Still, he kept an eye out for Nate or Bobby. He'd avoided them since they got back and didn't want to speak to them. He knew they should be at work, but you never knew. He found the most important thing on his list first: a box of plastic bags that came with snap ties like the ones that cops used instead of handcuffs when there were more detainees than available cuffs. After that, he quickly gathered up the rest of the things on his list ranging from energy bars to water, checked out, and drove downtown.

Warren Jenkins dealt drugs. Billy didn't like the idea of going to him, but "War," as he was called, was the only drug dealer that Billy knew that had never had anything to do with his brother or Nate Hanassey. For a while, as a teenager, Billy'd been a regular pot customer of War's.

Driving into downtown Missoula made Billy a little nervous, as there was always the possibility that he could run into Nate who made deliveries to the downtown bars.

War had a basement apartment in an old two-story building near the tracks, and Billy got there without seeing any sign of Nate's delivery truck.

At War's an old concrete stairway led down to a solid steel door. Billy gave the door three hard knocks with his fist and waited, standing in front of the peephole.

He was thinking of leaving after five minutes. He could not knock again. War didn't like people knocking on his door over and over. But then the door swung open, and he found himself staring into the muzzle of a Glock .380 auto. Behind the gun War stood, naked from the waist up and smiling.

155

Billy swallow. "What the hell is with the gun?" he asked, trying to act braver than he felt. "You could see it was me through the peephole."

"Just making sure you don't have a backup of narcs around," War said. Billy always thought War's face with his dark hair and hooked nose made him look like an Indian brave--or maybe a skinny Italian gangster. But War's head had the only skin showing that wasn't 70% ink. The rest of his almost athletic upper body was covered in tattoos of all kinds. They weren't jailhouse tattoos. War had never spent a day in jail, much less prison. Artists with talent did these. The face of Albert Einstein on War's left shoulder always caught Billy's eye.

War poked his head out the door and glanced around in all directions. Satisfied that there were no narcs lurking, he gestured with the gun for Billy to come in.

"Haven't seen your ass in a while, Wesley. What are you looking for?"

War kept his condo dark with heavy curtains covering the windows. A stick of jasmine incense burned in a stone Buddha.

"Something to really knock somebody out," Billy said nervously.

A wide smile broke across War's face.

"Nothing too dangerous. Something mild. To help her sleep."

"I heard about your brother taking the rap for that girl."

Billy said nothing.

156

"You didn't talk so we're good." War nodded. "I can fix you up."

A little later Billy handed War three $20 bills for three white pills in a small paper bag. Afterwards he headed home, feeling sick. The purchase brought back memories of the incident with Amy.

# Revelations

## February 15: 2013

The girl War had been referring to was Amy Wizzick. Billy had been introduced to Amy by War at a rave. A lifeguard at the time, working at the municipal pool for the summer, Billy'd gone to the rave to purchase pot from War. Amy, an attractive, slightly overweight redhead, had been swaying to the music near War as Billy made his purchase and seemed to take an instant liking to Billy and his lifeguard tan. She asked Billy to dance, and just as he started to follow her out, onto the dance floor, War pulled Billy back. When Amy was out of earshot War'd shouted into Billy's ear that he'd just slipped Amy some 'E' with a time-release surprise. Patting Billy on the back, War then gave him a gentle push out onto the floor.

Billy had never had sex with anyone, but he'd heard girls who took ecstasy always wanted to have sex. As Amy began bouncing about the floor, Billy pulled her close and shouted in her ear that he had some very good weed and would she like to go to his place to smoke some. Amy had agreed.

Billy was living with Bobby at the time in an apartment rented by Bobby. Both their parents had died in a car accident when Billy was 15. Bobby, 22 at the time, had taken Billy in. Bobby slept in its one bedroom, and Billy slept on a pullout couch in the living room. Billy and Amy had shared a joint in his car on the five-minute ride to Bobby's apartment. In the apartment there was a note to Billy on a table by the door saying Bobby was out and didn't know if he'd be back that might or not.

Assuming it was Billy's, Amy pulled Billy into Bobby's bedroom, and began kissing him. To his surprise she put her tongue in his mouth.

After a few minutes where Billy'd been exploring her mouth with his tongue, Amy broke off the kiss and pushed his face away.

Billy looked at her confused.

"Listen," Amy said seriously, "I don't want to fuck. Will you promise you're not going to try and force me?"

158

"Yeah," Billy said.

"And I can't spend the night. My parents will kill me if I'm not in bed in the morning."

"Okay, I promise I'll get you home."

"Good," she said, and touched his lips with the forefinger of her right hand.

"Then, if I let you suck on my nipples, you'll promise no actual sex?"

Billy's eyes went wide. "Yes," he said, and he meant it. He had kissed a few girls after dates, and he'd necked just a bit with Mary Walsh once but nothing like this. He was actually beginning to like this girl.

"You promise?" Amy asked. "You won't try to go farther?"

"I promise," Billy had said. "Until we get married, or you say it's okay."

"Married?" she said, somewhat alarmed.

"I promise," Billy said, embarrassed. "No actual sex."

She'd started undoing the buttons on her blouse, and he'd tried to help. Awkwardly they'd gotten her blouse off, tearing the last button off in the process and then, with her help, he'd managed to unhook her bra, which snapped in front and bared the front of her chest. Billy had no sooner brought his lips to her flesh near her left nipple, when Amy seemed to collapse.

"Hey, hey," he had said, shaking her. But she didn't move.

Billy shook her. He slapped her face lightly. Her chest rose and fell, so she was breathing, but she was not awake.

He realized, then, that the surprise War said he slipped her was probably some kind of delayed action roofie. Less than an hour had passed since he'd met the girl. Billy was harder than he'd ever been. Amy lay there with her breasts bare before him. She would have jerked him off at least, wouldn't she?

He began unbuckling his belt. But before he could pull his pants down, something inside him stopped him. No actual sex he'd promised. He didn't know if that meant a hand job, but he couldn't ask her.

He left Amy in his brother's bedroom and gone out to the couch where he'd relieved himself before going to sleep.

Unfortunately, Bobby came home after all sometime later completely drunk. He'd gone into his bedroom, shut and locked the door as he normally did, stripped, and fell asleep next to Amy on the bed without even realizing she was there.

When Amy awoke in the morning, sunlight streaming in through the window, she found herself partially undressed with a naked older man lying on top of her left arm in a strange bed. Terrified that trying to move would awaken him, she had taken her cell-phone out of the pocket of the shorts she found she still had on, and dialed 911. She had no memory of meeting the man next to her the night before. When asked what her emergency was, she'd simply whispered a desperate, "Help!"

When the police knocked loudly on Bobby's apartment door, Amy had screamed and struggled to free her pinned arm in an effort to escape. Bobby woke, and confused by the screaming girl, grabbed her. The police found, when they broke in the front door and then the door to Bobby's bedroom, a naked man holding a partially-clad, screaming girl.

The police also found a framed coin collection in the apartment that had been recently taken in a burglary. Bobby told them he'd found it in an alley and had been looking in the paper for a posting by the person who lost it.

The police at the scene wanted to arrest Billy, too. After finding him naked, hiding in a closet, covered in dried semen, they instantly assumed he'd been part of what they were to call a sex kidnapping.

The police didn't have any evidence that linked either Billy or Bobby to the burglary where the coin collection was taken. Amy went to the hospital and was examined for rape, and no evidence was found that she had been sexually assaulted. But Amy was 15. Bobby could be charged with statutory rape.

When they threatened to charge Billy and Bobby with kidnapping, Bobby told the cops that Billy had had nothing to do with the girl in the room. Then Bobby confessed he'd blacked out and did not remember bringing the underage girl there for sex.

They let Billy go. Later, when Billy pleaded with Bobby to let him tell the police the real story, Bobby refused. They wanted him for the burglary they couldn't prove. Billy had had nothing to do with that. Pressured, too, by threats to prosecute his brother, Bobby sacrificed himself to keep his baby brother out of prison.

# A Stop At Home

## October 25: 2:16 pm

In the bathroom of his rented trailer, with the kitchen radio tuned in to the news station, Billy looked in the mirror and decided that an initial un-shaven appearance fit in best with the story he'd planned to tell 'the girl.'

Now a memory returned to him. Before their truck had hit the girl's, she'd looked right at them. He could remember seeing her eyes and her shock at the realization of what was about to happen. The memory of that scared look on her face touched him. But this feeling of empathy for her was one he could not afford and he shook it away. He was going to have to choose between her and his brother...unless he could figure something else out.

As he put his shaving things away, he thought about what else he'd have to do before leaving. He'd already put the pills he'd purchased from War in his shirt pocket. Three plastic garbage bag fasteners he'd removed from the box of garbage bags were in his left front jacket pocket. He'd checked to make sure that the winch worked with the marine battery he bought. To his surprise the winch had been much quieter than he expected. Now all of that equipment was back in his Ford Explorer.

He reached into this pocket and took his wallet out. Should he leave it here? No, that wouldn't work. He'd have to have his wallet when he met the hunter who would supposedly put him in the mine. But he should get rid of the receipts for his recent purchases. He took them out and threw them in the wastebasket. Taking a few pulls on the toilet paper roll, he tore off enough toilet paper to bury the receipts out of sight.

"Here goes," he said to himself in the mirror.

Before going outside he took two wire hangers from his clothes closet, then rummaged around in his dresser until he found the infrared game locator he'd purchased a year before. He hadn't used it much and didn't even know if they were still legal. The device detected heat and could be used to locate wounded game. He put new batteries in it before putting it and the wire cutting pliers he grabbed from his tool drawer in his right front jacket pocket.

On the way to his car, he had to wonder if he'd ever see his trailer again.

# Preparations

## October 25: 4:13 pm

Billy Wesley pulled into the dead end near the mine. Before he killed the engine of his Ford Explorer, he glanced at the digital clock on his dashboard. The clock read 4:13 pm.

Although he wouldn't try to go into the mine until early in the morning, he wanted to approach the mine in daylight to get his game hoist set up and ready for his early morning descent. He used the sled to pull the winch, battery, cables, and hardware he'd bought up to the mine. He left the supplies for later.

The mine entrance was in the center of a rocky outcropping that resembled a jagged crown. Behind the grate boulders rose up as high as 20 feet. In a gap between two boulders, Billy had hidden the girl's boots and socks, his backpack with the sling, and the ratcheting jack he'd found in the Chevy.

As he neared the grate he took the game detector out and turned it on. The device showed no heat was coming from the area below the grate. To confirm that, he snuck close and peeked down through the grate. The girl was not there.

He didn't think that she would hear anything from outside the mine, but he still tried to move quietly just in case.

He climbed up to the boulders above the grate and with the cable he bought secured the winch to a boulder. He connected the marine battery to the winch and extended the winch's cable enough to attach its hook to the front of the grate. The winch's control unit was a two-button rubber-protected box with wires connecting it to the winch. The control's wires were long enough to let the control rest by the side of the grate. He twisted the hook end of one of the hangers around the base of the control and stretched the hanger so it formed a long loop narrow enough to fit thought the six-inch openings in the grate. He cut the other hanger where the ends twisted together, then straightened the wire out giving himself a long-handled hook to grab the loop on the control with. He planned to hide this wire hook in a crevice in the mine. Lastly, to keep them dry, he covered the winch and battery with the tarp, weighing the edges down with a mix of snow and loose rocks.

Now he wondered if he dare risk seeing if it worked? As there was no sign of the girl, he decided to try. He could always move away from the grate if he heard her coming. As long as she didn't see him, his plan could still work. With a push of the 'up' button, the winch began to hum. The cable pulled taut. The grate began to rise. It worked! He lowered the grate slowly back to the ground.

With the hook he'd be able to access the control and exit the mine when he needed to.

# Into The Darkness

## October 26: 2:30 am

In his Ford Explorer, now parked almost a mile from the mine, the little wind-up alarm clock Billy had in the car woke him from a sound sleep. He turned the overhead light on and could see a covering of new snow on the vehicle's windows. The front seat hadn't been wide enough for him to lie down and he woke stiff and sore. He shook off his discomfort and wiggled out of his sleeping bag.

As he pushed the sleeping bag off he brushed against a stone he had glued to his dashboard that he thought looked like an Indian arrowhead. The arrowhead gave him an idea, and he pulled the piece of flint from the dashboard.

Snow fell on him as he loaded all his supplies that he didn't want leave outside to freeze into the sled. The snow was good. It would hide all signs that someone had pulled a sled to the mine. He grabbed his rifle and started off.

When he reached the spot where he had originally parked, he reluctantly threw his rifle into the woods. He needed every detail to fit the story he was going to tell.

Before cresting the top of the hill near the grate he turned his headlight off. In the dark he walked a few feet closer to the grate then turned the game finder on and listened. There was no heat signature and no sound. He could smell the faint scent of wood smoke from inside the tunnel, but nowhere could he see a spark of light. He risked turning his headlight back on. The entrance was empty but for a few inches of snow that had fallen through the grate.

With the winch he opened the grate and then listened carefully again for any sounds from inside the mine, holding his breath as he did so. He heard nothing.

He used the sling to lower two cases of bottled water, 10 more bags of jerky, 30 tins of sardines, saltine crackers, and a big box of energy bars. Lastly, he dropped in the metal clothes hanger that had been converted into a long hook.

He prepared himself for the last steps. Walking over to the crevice where he'd hidden everything else, he took his gloves off and tossed them in. One fell into one of the girl's boots. Taking two of the three plastic garbage bag fasteners out of his pocket, he secured one somewhat tightly to his right wrist and then secured the other to his left wrist. Next he took his own boots and socks off and added them to the crevice. The cold snow made his feet instantly ache, and, though he was tempted to kick snow over the opening of the crevice to hide it, he realized that would just be more painful and decided not to bother. Lastly he turned his powerful headlight off and added it to the crevice. He'd decided against bringing in his headlight. His being too well supplied might make the girl suspicious. He'd make do with the tiny penlight he always carried. He took the penlight out and turned it on.

The snowfall seemed heavier now. After lowering the winch's control through one of the holes on the side of the grate, he removed the flint arrowhead from his pocket and quickly whipped it across the left side of his forehead with his left hand. He could feel the hot blood from the head wound pouring down his face. Keeping both hands, as best he could, away from the blood, with a snap of his wrist, he sent the arrowhead sailing away into the night.

Taking a deep breath, he climbed down into the mine, picked up his wire hook, and laid himself in the snow under the grate. Placing his hands under him he slid himself forward toward the tunnel entrance until he was past the patch of snow beneath the grate. Only then did he stand. He pulled the winch control to him with his wire hook.

Using the winch control he slowly lowered the grate until the entrance was closed. Then he used the hook to ease the control back through the grate, and lay it next to the grate out of sight. A crack in the stone wall to the side of the grate opening provided the perfect place to hide his wire hook.

He'd thought about taking the supplies into where the girl was as he'd done the last time but thought better of it. There was no point in having his plan ruined because he happened to drop something and wake her.

His bare feet, now on the cold stone floor, still wet from walking through the snow, ached like they never had before. The cut he had given himself began to burn and his blood was still running down his face. So as not to leave bloody footprints he had decided to crawl into the mine.

As he crawled toward the dark opening of the mine he turned his penlight off and put it in his inside jacket pocket. In the tunnel entrance he put his left hand against the wall to feel his way.

He stopped every so often and listened. For most of the journey he heard nothing. But as he made his way to the last bend of the tunnel before the chamber, he heard the deep breathing of sleep. He smiled to himself.

Slowly he turned the corner, trying to move quietly. He saw a faint glow of coals from a fire. He would have to ask her how she managed that. Letting his eyes adjust to the dim glow of light, he made his way into the chamber, near the sleeping girl.

He turned onto his back and removed the three pills he had gotten from War from his shirt pocket. He was only going to take two because at one point, he'd thought about somehow slipping one to the girl in a water bottle, but now he decided to not even try doing that. The girl might find that last pill if she searched him before he woke up. He swallowed all three.

Needing to get it done before the pills rendered him senseless, he took the last plastic garbage bag fastener out of his left front pocket and laid down on his stomach. Working it as best he could, he put his hands behind his back and slipped this fastener, first through the fastener on his right wrist, then through the one on his left wrist. With the plastic garbage bag fasteners arranged so they'd make it look like someone had bound his hands behind his back, he pulled this final one taut securing all three together.

He could still feel his warm blood running down his left cheek. The wound really stung now. He put his bloody cheek to the floor and waited for the pills to knock him out. All he could do was hope the girl would believe that the same person who had put her there, had brought him in also: helpless, handcuffed and unconscious.

# A Dream and its Aftermath

## October 28: Morning

Lomahongva ran ahead of me on the forest path. The track, an old forest road, ran by the log cabin we had built together and continued on deeper into the woods where now abandoned mines had once rung with the sound of gold mining.

"Lo!" I cried.

But she did not hear me or chose to ignore me. I began running. "Lo, wait."

This time she paused and looked back at me. She looked right at me as I ran to her. But, then, without acknowledging me, she turned and ran on.

"Lo," I cried. I could hear the desperation in my own voice. I felt desperate. I could not lose her again.

Snow filled all of the old road but for a narrow track. As the winter snow grew deeper, the dogs and I packed it down by walking on it. The track, eventually, became the only place I could walk without snowshoes and the dogs could run.

I lost sight of Lo around a bend where snow covered pine branches hung like giant tongues. I increased my pace until it felt my heart would burst. In my rush I knocked snow from branches, which, freed of their burden, sprang at me like snapped mousetraps.

And I came to the cliff where the trail ended Lo was nowhere in sight.

"Lo?" I cried weakly. The snowy landscape swallowed my voice.

I got down on my knees and buried my face in my hands. "Lo," I whispered to myself. Suddenly I heard her voice behind me.

"Winny," she said softly. Lo was the only one I had ever allowed to call me Winny. I did not move or open my eyes, knowing somehow if I moved or tried to look she would be gone.

"Yes?"

"Your new woman knows why the young man woke up. All you need do is ask her."

"I don't have a new woman," I protested. "I love you. I will always love you."

"I know that," Lo whispered gently. "But I had to scare you. You have to understand that 'you are afraid' is far less important than the question 'what are you afraid of?'

"I will always be in your heart. A new woman will never keep me away," she whispered as I woke up from the dream.

As I sat up I saw daylight streaming in through the window by the desk.

I thought of the dream and tried to rerun it through my head. I knew the feeling of guilt that overwhelmed me had to do with the feelings I might be beginning to have for Shawna. But what did that have to do with a young man waking up? Or the question, 'what are you afraid of?'

After taking the dogs on their morning walk, I called Nadine to see if there had been any news of the guy that Shawna had described.

"Hello, Deputy Doyle," Nadine said very formally. "The sheriff would like to talk to you. Please hold."

"Winslow," Goldstone said, coming on the line. "I hate to say this, but I don't know how much longer we can keep you on full-time. We've got nothing on this case for now."

I understood. It was only because Callie Carew had come to me, that I was working on the case. But a normal deputy had duties that involved more than one case. And those duties were not of interest to me as a career.

I must have been silent too long as Goldstone filled in the void. "I've asked René, Doctor Walters, if we could try hypnotizing that kid Tim again. But she said that given the way he woke up she didn't feel comfortable trying again. She said she knew the urgency of finding Cassie, but as the connection to the men in that vehicle to the death of Greg Carew and the missing daughter was tenuous at best, she

174

did not feel that any damage to the young man was warranted."

"Understood," I said. "Do you want my badge back?" But as I asked that, something began to take shape in the back of my mind.

Goldstone was silent for a few moments. "Why don't you hang onto it? If anything that comes up that leads out your way, you'll have it."

We hung up, and I sat there and tried to construct the idea trying to gel in my mind. And then I had it. What Lo, or my subconscious, was trying to tell me in my dreams.

I had taken down Tim Bobbin's phone number when I met him. I tried calling. I got his answering machine.



"Oh! Hi," Shawna said, with enthusiasm when I called. "I was hoping you'd call but didn't expect you too, so soon."

Suddenly, the phone call felt awkward. I had really enjoyed my date with Shawna. And though I liked her and was considering calling her again for personal reasons I felt at least some guilt about seeing someone new. I had called to ask her about Tim Bobbins. Now, given her response, I hesitated to bring the actual reason for the call up.

"Would you like to go to dinner with me tonight?" I asked. I instantly felt almost fearful that she might turn me down, and realized because of that, that I really wanted to see her again.

There was a silence on the other end of the line that left me more and more anxious as the seconds ticked by. "I realize this is short notice, and if," I began.

"No, I would love to see you tonight," she said. "But I have a lot of work to do, paperwork that I usually do here on my home computer, and...." she paused. "How about we meet somewhere?"

"Okay," I said, feeling elated. "Where would you like to go?"

"How about the Oriental Buffet?" she said. "Unless you need drinks?"

"No, and I love that place," I said.

"I have to run right now. She you around 7?"

"Okay," I said.

When I had hung up the phone, I wondered if she'd think, once I asked her the question I had called for, that that was the only reason I called. It mattered to me what she would think and this, too, gave me pause.

I called Phyllis at the FWP office and found out that Bobbins had the day off. She gave me the young man's address. I tried Tim Bobbin's phone number two more times. The call went to his machine both times. I drove to his apartment in a Victorian style house on Front Street in Missoula, but there was no reply to my knock.

I met Shawna at the Oriental Buffet, a buffet style restaurant that served American, Chinese and Japanese food. I had been eating there for a number of years. It sat nestled in the center of the Central

176

Village Shopping Center. Many of the stores in the center, but for a very popular fabric store Lo used to shop at, had changed hands over the years, but the OB stood the test of time. I walked to the glass windowed front in the crook of the L shaped shopping center. Shawna wasn't waiting outside.

A guy with a motorcycle helmet held the door for me, and I walked in. Shawna was standing by the fountain across from the checkout counter. She had on a leather aviator's jacket and matching purse. She wore dark slacks and running shoes. I couldn't help but admire how pretty she was. She smiled when she saw me, and she got a whole lot prettier.

"Hi," we both said at the same time and both laughed.

An older but somewhat ageless Asian woman came up to us. "Two?" she asked. Shawna and I both nodded. The woman led us down to a booth on the far right hand side, and asked, "What would you like to drink?"

I looked at Shawna.

"Hot tea," Shawna said.

"Two hot teas," I added.

As the woman left Shawna took her winter jacket off and put it down on the seat. For the moment I kept my on. We proceeded to the rows of plastic hooded food tables that lined the back of the restaurant, grabbed plates, and we went our separate ways. I did watch her for a moment. She was a beautiful woman. I noticed at least two men checking her out.

I always started my meals at the OB with sushi. So I headed to the sushi table and helped myself to rice rolled fish or shrimp and then took 4 small plastic containers provided for taking the condiments back to your table. I added to three containers small portions of wasabi, pickled ginger slices, and French dressing, and filled the fourth with Sriracha sauce at a different counter where I helped myself to sliced lemons.

Shawna was already at the table when I got back. She had poured both of us tea from the small silver teapot on the table into the small handleless cups provided,

"I hope you don't mind," she said, pointing to the tea.

"Thank you," I said. I squeezed lemon over my sushi pieces and dropped the rinds into my water glass.

"That's a good idea," she said, pointing to my water glass.

I looked at her plate. You could tell some things about people by what they ate. On her plate Shawna had a few pieces of fried chicken wings, some mussel shells covered in an almost white cheese, and spinach covered in the same cheese.

"Those used to be much better," I said, pointing to the cheesy mussels, "when they used real cheese years ago."

"Yeah. I know. That's what got me coming here in the first place."

I took one of my sushi pieces, wrapped a ginger slice around it, dipped it in wasabi, Sriracha, and the French dressing and popped it into my mouth.

"How did you come to be living in the wilderness?" Shawna asked. It was a question I was expecting.

"When I was young my parents family owned a punch-bowl like section of land near Roscoe, NY. They had an isolated 125 acres, a six acre lake and house built by the guy who built the Merrimack, not the civil war ironclad but the frigate whose hull the confederates built their ironclad upon. I loved it there. I always wanted to live there, but the family decided to sell it when I was about 18 and it left me with a desire to live in the wilderness.

"I was wounded in Iraq and met my wife Lo who was my nurse. She was from Montana, I'd gone to college here. We discovered both of us loved the wilderness, and eventually decided to buy the place where I live now."

Shawna nodded. "Hoping that she would leave it at that and not ask about Lo, I asked, "How did you end up in Fish, Wildlife, and Parks?"

"I grew up on a small ranch near Roundup, and I loved it. Rode horses, explored. When my brother, he's two years older than me, was 18, he was in a car accident. Messed his right leg up pretty bad. He didn't have insurance, and my parents went through everything they had to cover the bills. They lost the

179

ranch. I studied Forestry at UM and ended up taking the job at FWP. I love it."

"I'm sorry about your brother and your parents," I said.

"It's just life," Shawna said and picked up a chicken wing. "I am starved."

We ate, and I watched her eat. I liked her. But I wondered if she was still going to like me when I asked her what I needed to.

I cleaned my third plate of sushi and waited for Shawna to scoop the last of the cheesy muscles on her plate from its shell. As she put the food in her mouth, she caught me looking at her and knew something was up. She didn't say anything just turned her head and gave me a 'what's up' look.

"I enjoyed the dance the other night and was going to call, but when I called this morning it was to ask you something other than to ask you out."

"So you bit the bullet and went out with me?" There was a good-natured smile in her question.

"I jumped on the opportunity to see you again," I said, sincerely.

"Good. So what's the problem?"

"I need to know about Tim Bobbins. I wouldn't ask, but the girl is still missing and the longer it takes to find her the worse her chances are."

"Why would Tim have anything to do with that? Is he somehow a suspect? Because…"

"No, he's not a suspect. But you weren't there when he was hypnotized. Has he spoken to you about that?"

180

"No, but I haven't seen much of him since then. We're scheduled to be on game check duty together this weekend.

"What's going on?"

I looked at her for a long moment before speaking. "Tell me about Tim."

"Tell you what? He's a friend."

"And he has secrets?" I asked.

Now she frowned. She thought for a moment, obviously thinking about her answer.

"Everyone has secrets. I have secrets and so does Tim. How are his secrets any of your business?" Now she sounded angry.

This obviously wasn't working, and I had to change things. "He went into hypnosis and as soon as Dr. Walters began questioning him, he snapped out of it."

"Why would that have to do with any secrets he might have?"

I looked Shawna in the eye. I hoped my expression was pleading.

"He woke up just as Dr. Walters took him to the day the girl and her father went missing. Right after he said that he had taken over for you and began checking out the deer in the back of the truck."

"I don't understand."

"The question she asked was 'had you ever seen this hunter before?' And Tim snapped right out of the hypnosis. I'm asking if you know any reason why trying to recall a hunter he was checking would scare him, or bring back unpleasant memories?"

181

Now Shawna looked away. Her left hand went to her mouth and she sat there thinking.

"You told me at the dance that the dance was not Tim's thing."

Shawna turned back to me. "Where did you get the idea that whatever woke Tim out of his hypnosis session is somehow important?"

"The truck may be important. Who they are may be important."

"I understand the girl is still missing, but how are you connecting all this?"

She obviously considered this conversation as a threat. I had to level with her.

"My late wife came to me in a dream and told me that you know why the young man woke up. There was a lot more to the dream than that. Part of it had to do with some guilt I'm feeling about liking you. I didn't get it at first and then I spoke to Sheriff Goldstone today, and he used the term woke up referring to Tim, and he added that Dr. Walters refused to try and hypnotize him again.

"I know dreams can often be meaningless…"

"No," Shawna said, interrupting. "I know you can solve problems in dreams. I've done that myself." She paused and then smiled, "And you dreamed about me?"

I nodded. And then realized what her problem was. "I have a idea about Tim, and I am guessing that you've known him a lot longer than you've known me, and you're concerned about betraying a friend?"

Shawna nodded. "Some men are quite the opposite of sympathetic to Tim's secret."

"What if I don't ask you to tell me the secret? But just tell me where I can find him?"

"He lives on Front Street. I don't have the address written down…"

"I've been to his apartment and I've called. I stopped by his apartment just before coming here. He isn't home."

"Maybe he doesn't want to talk to you," Shawna said. She took her phone out and pushed two buttons. Obviously, she had Tim on speed dial. She listened for a moment and then said, "It's me, Shawna. Call me when you get this." She hung up and put the phone back in her purse.

"Do you have any idea where he might be now?" I asked.

Shawna looked at me for long time. She seemed to be making up her mind. Finally, she nodded as if to herself.

"You promise not to be judgmental?"

I smiled despite myself. Lo used to say to me, "Don't be so quick to jump to conclusions."

Shawna glared at me taking it the wrong way.

"I was just remembering something my wife used to say to me. She pretty much cured me of being judgmental."

Shawna went quiet, thinking. "Okay, I'll take you to a place he hangs out." She turned and looked at me with a very serious expression. "I hope I'm not making a mistake."

# A Place of Secrets

## October 28: Evening

Shawna had walked to the Oriental Buffet from her home. So when we left we rode together in my Jeep to downtown Missoula. Shawna did not speak after telling me to find parking somewhere near N. Higgins and Broadway. She seemed deep in thought. And I hoped she would not regret her decision to help me. I lucked out as a car pulled out of a spot on N. Higgins close to Front, and we parked there.

We actually had a long walk. Shawna led me to a little, nondescript back alley lit by a single streetlight. Kitty corner to the light pole a sunken stairway led to an orange door with a blue light above it. The door sat almost hidden under a wooden stairway. She stopped near it and looked up at me. "You are going to be nice?" she asked.

"I don't have any reason not to be," I said. I understood where she was coming from. I'm a big man and pretty tough. I know some men my size like to throw their weight around. I'm not one of them. "I'm not a bully. Never have been. Though I've bashed a few bullies in my day."

184

Shawna smiled, "I'll bet you could."

I started for the door, and she grabbed my arm, stopping me.

"How about I go in first, see if he's there, and ask if it's okay for you to talk to him?"

This gave me pause. My first thought, going back to my training as an MP was, 'is there a back door? And will he hi-tail it out?' But Shawna's eyes were pleading with me. This was about her sense of not being someone who would betray a friend.

"If you promise to remind him that a girl's life may be at stake?"

"I will," she said. She lifted herself up on her running-shoed toes and kissed me on the lips. "Be right back."

She went to the door and opened it. All I could see was a dark corridor with small purple lights on the wall and part of a bar with colored lights a ways in. The door shut, and I was alone in the alley.

Snow hung to the sides of the buildings, but the alley was just a wet looking black in the light from the pole. I heard footsteps and looked down the alley. Two young men, both in their early twenties and wearing matching sweaters came down toward me holding hands. One had spiked blonde hair and the other had brown hair cut in an almost feminine style. They had turned in the direction of the orange door when they finally noticed me. They both froze. Their hands fell apart.

"Beautiful night," I said, as friendly as I could.

"Yeah," the blonde said. He sounded nervous.

I turned away from them and looked in the other direction. I heard their footsteps and then the door opening.

I looked up at the sky between the buildings in the alley and could just make out three bright stars in the partly cloudy sky when a hand touched my arm.

I jumped, startled, and flipped around.

Shawna looked at me in surprise. "I didn't mean to scare you."

I could feel myself blushing. I just tried to smile. She must have come out just as the two men went in.

"Tim's waiting for you, at the far end of the bar."

"Great."

Shawna looked at me very intently. "I appreciate your letting me go in and talk to him first. I realize that's something cops ordinarily don't do."

"I'm only a part-time deputy."

"And I enjoyed dinner and I would be willing to see you again, if you would like to see me again."

I could have said something but acted instead. I took her gently by the shoulders, pulled her just a bit closer, leaned down and kissed her gently on the lips. She brought her arms up, put them around my neck and kissed me back hard for a moment but then let go and pulled away.

A mischievous smile crossed her face. "Well, just watch yourself in there," she said in a teasing tone. Whatever had been said between Tim and she had helped her mood considerably. "I wouldn't want you to change sides," she said, punching my arm.

And with that she turned and walked away.

I opened the orange door and stepped inside. When the door closed behind me I saw that the streetlight had actually brightened the place. The purple lights along the wall were identical to the bare bulbs that accounted for the ceiling lights. The only other real light came from behind the bottles on a wall behind the bar, which illuminated the different colors of the liquid poisons in the bottles. This bar illumination accounted for more than half the visible light in the room.

Rather than the typical stale beer scent that permeated most bars I was familiar with, this one had a rich exotic scent, like musk mixed with fine liquor.

The walkway I was on was not a real corridor but rather a walkway with a waist high partition on the left as you came in that separated the entryway from a open area, presumably a dance floor. I could see booths along the far wall. The couple, that had passed me on their way in not long before, sat in one. The blonde young man glanced at me, watched me for a moment then turned back to his companion.

The partition ended after about 10 feet and then the room opened up. The bar was just a few feet ahead where a thin man, with short red hair, and a large pearl in his left ear, wearing a red T-shirt, leaned with both palms on the bar and looked toward me expectantly.

As I made my way toward the bartender a slightly heavyset young man with slicked down brown hair and earrings in both ears stepped up to me. As I turned toward him I saw that he had heavy make-up on his face and wore eyeliner to give him a very feminine appearance.

"Hi," he said in a falsetto voice, "They call me Pumpkin. As you are new here, may I buy you a drink?"

He was careful not to touch me though both his hands were positioned, palms up, just inches from my arm. The nail polish on his fingers looked black in the dim light.

"No, but thank you," I said politely and stepped away so that he was no longer in my personal space. I took a step toward the bar and the bartender behind it when I caught a wave from the far end of the bar. I looked and even though the person was seated far enough past the lighted liquors for the spot to be almost in darkness I recognized Tim Bobbins.

I nodded to the bartender and made my way toward Tim. I could feel Pumpkin's eyes on my back the entire way.

"Deputy," Tim said in greeting as I sat down on the stool besides him. He was dressed in a white shirt and blue jeans. He had a glass of what looked like scotch, neat, in front of him.

"Winslow, please," I said. "I appreciate you being willing to talk to me. And I apologize for putting Shawna on the spot to do so."

"No problem," Tim said. "She told me I could slip out the back way if I wanted and she'd tell you I wasn't here. But she'd already outed me just by bringing you here."

"I hope this doesn't cause problems between the two of you." I said.

"There is a girl still missing. And if I can help I will. And as far as Shawna goes, she did what she thought was right." He laughed. "So how can I help you?"

"Your being here answers part of my question," I said. "Or I should say suspicion. I'll be frank and let you get on with your evening. My gut tells me we really need to identify the people in that truck. Apparently you broke out of the hypnotic trance you were in when Dr. Walters asked you a very specific question. Had you met the person who claimed the deer you were checking before?"

Tim shook his head, more as if to clear it than to say no. "You know I've thought about it. And I've tried to conjure up that guy's face. And I just can't. The faces of other people I checked pop up and I can see them clearly, but not that guy."

"I am assuming that as you are here in this bar, that you are gay. So, I need to ask you. Have you ever had a sexual experience with a man that was painful? This would be something that you would rather forget, or an encounter that you only partly remember."

Tim was quiet for a long time. His face showed concern and then discomfort. It seemed as if he was

189

struggling to decide whether or not he should tell me something.

"I don't know if this will help you. I dated girls as a teen and discovered I didn't much care for them. I found I'd rather fantasize about other guys I'd seen in the men's locker room. But the guys at school seemed to notice this and I decided my guy watching wasn't something I should do at school. So I went to the city pool and did my man watching there.

"Most of my memory of what happened is pretty much blurred. It happened one day when there was just one guy and I left when the pool closed. The only impression I have of him is that he was big and had a lot of body hair. He was about to take his suit off and get dressed. His back was to me and I was just secretly watching him. I had just taken my suit off and being a teenager…well, I had an erection. I was about to cover myself with my towel when he turned and saw me.

"He forced me to give him oral sex. And that messed me up for a few years as far as approaching other men." Tim looked at me, then. "Do you think it could have been the same guy?"

"It could have been him, or the hunter in the truck looked like the guy who raped you. You don't remember anything at all about him other than that he was big and had a lot of body hair."

Tim hesitated. "I don't know if this will help you, but the only image I get is the words he had tattooed just above his crotch. "Suck Here." The letters were about a half-inch high.

Something clicked inside me. "Was it a professional tattoo, artistic, or something done with a pen?"

"Not artistic. Just something that looked like it had been inked in with a blue pen."

I nodded my head. "That sounds like a prison tat. And that could be very helpful. Thank you."

"Glad to help."

I started to get up."

"Deputy, I mean Winslow," Tim said.

"You know Pumpkin is very particular. She's a bit of a slut but she only goes for very attractive guys."

I felt myself blushing. I didn't have anything to say to that, though I guess I was flattered.

"And for that matter" Tim added, "I also find you very attractive."

I shook my head stood, and began turning away. Then a question hit me. I turned back.

Tim gave me a surprised and open smile, misinterpreting my actions.

"Have you ever, since then, been with a man with a similar body type?

"Yes," Tim said. "That's not my ideal type, but I find myself attracted to the type."

"So you've been with men of that type, since then, more than once?"

"Dozens," Tim said, with an embarrassed smile. "I...."

I didn't wait for him to finish. "Thanks," I said and left.

# A Slim, Almost Non-Existent Thread

## October 28: 10:53 pm

I was not at all concerned with Tim's sexual preferences as I was with the actual possibility that the person who had forced him to have sex was indeed the guy in the truck with the broken lights.

Because Tim had admitted liaisons with men similar to the one who had raped him the possibility that Tim had problems with the type in general was less likely. Still, that the man who had attacked him was the same man he saw at the deer check in station was a long shot. But it was worth checking out.

That the tattoo above the man's genitals was a prison tattoo was clear from Tim's description. And descriptions of felon's tats were easy to trace.

It was going on 11 but I called Goldstone. I explained my thoughts and he scoffed at the idea that our guy from the damaged truck could be the same guy who attacked Tim. The fact that he had been in bed and almost asleep did not help his disposition.

"I will check this out," he said reluctantly. "If there is anything I will call you back," Goldstone said. He did not sound happy or enthused but I was sure he would check it right away.

I was halfway home when my cellphone rang. I pulled the Jeep over and took the phone out of my pocket. It was the sheriff.

"You may be onto something with the tattoo," he said. There is a guy living in the Indian Springs trailer park in Missoula, Nate Hanassey, who happens to own a Red 1997 Ford Pickup. All the numbers the FWP people remembered are in his plate. He's been in Deer Lodge twice. Where are you now?"

"On my way up 200 toward home. Not quite to the Paws Up Ranch."

"I've called Frank Davis. He's one of my newer deputies who you didn't get to meet, because he's taking a special two-week course at the university in Missoula. Since he's staying in Missoula for the course, I asked him to check out the truck. Do you want me to tell him to wait for you?"

"I don't think if this Hanassey guy has the girl he'd bring her to his trailer park."

"I don't either."

"But yes, have the deputy meet me just outside the trailer park. And then we can walk in together. That way maybe this guy won't see us, and we won't spook him."

"Sounds good," Goldstone said.

"Just give me the address," I said as I pulled and turned the Jeep around.

The trailer park Nate Hanassey lived in was off W. Broadway in Missoula closer to the airport than the heart of town. So I got off the 90 on Airport Road and was just turning left on Highway 10 to backtrack toward it when my phone rang. I pulled over to the side of the road and answered.

"Doyle, this is Frank Davis. Did you talk to the chief?"

"Yes, I'm on my way to meet you."

"Understood. I wanted you to know I just checked. The truck is in front of the guy's trailer."

"You drove by his house?" I asked, unable to keep the concern out of my voice. "You didn't alert the guy in any way?"

"That's a negative on alerting the guy. He's at the very end of a dead end street, and I only drove by on the cross street. The Missoula Sheriff's department drives by this area regularly, so it shouldn't have alerted him. I used field glasses to establish the truck was there."

"What is your ETA?"

194

"I'll be there in a jiff. I'll blink my lights twice when I pull up so you know its me."

I hung up the phone and soon pulled into the entry road behind the deputy's patrol car, blinked my headlights twice and stopped.

Davis got out as I got out of my Jeep. He walked up to me with his hand out.

"Frank Davis," he said.

"Winslow Doyle," taking his hand. He had a firm grip and didn't try to impress me by squeezing the hell out of mine. So far I liked him.

"Good idea to blink your lights," he said. "Anybody could have pulled up behind me. How do you want to do this?"

"Is it too far to walk from here?"

"It's doable. And if we move closer someone might notice my cruiser. Here," he indicated the entrance where we were parked, "we can pretend I'm ticketing you. Missoula knows I'm here, so we are good."

He put the bubble gum lights on top of his cruiser on, fetched a flashlight and locked the vehicle. I went back, got my flashlight, locked my Jeep, and we started down the road into the trailer park.

Since Davis knew where we were headed, I followed him. There was a layer of thin ice on the roadway that crunched beneath out feet. We walked about a city block before Davis turned left. About halfway down this street there was an alleyway. It was snow-covered and had two tire ruts running down unto the shadows between trailers.

I had already noticed there were halogen lights on poles about every hundred feet along the roadways. These were put in by the trailer park and not the city so they had minimal illumination. But still there was enough light for anyone looking out their window to see us. The alley did not have any lights.

"Davis?" I said and we crossed the alleyway.

Frank turned to me.

I pointed to the lamps along the paved road we were walking. "Are there lights like this on Hanassey's street?"

He nodded.

I gestured with my flashlight toward the alley.

"Does this run by his trailer?"

"It should."

"Can we get close to his truck?"

Davis just nodded.

He turned into the alley placing his feet in the far left rut. I followed in the right rut. About halfway down the alley he turned his flashlight off. I did the same and walked up so I was abreast of him. There was light coming from the trailer windows facing the alley. One trailer, not far away had a yellow back porch light on.

"He's at the very end," Davis said gesturing toward the shadowy area down the alley. "If we're lucky the truck will be in the trailer's shadow."

I gave him a thumbs up and we continued on into the deeper shadows. My heart began racing as we neared the last trailer. The trailer next to it had no lights on and its grass had obviously not been cut over the summer.

We both slowed our pace and then barely eased ahead at the corner of the trailer so we could peek around it.

The trailer did indeed block the light from the one halogen bulb near the middle of the dead end street. Light came from the trailer itself but only from the front window. It cast a yellow rectangle on the snow just past the tail end of the truck. It was so dark it was hard to tell the truck was red, except for the tail end where the window light gave it some illumination. It looked almost black. Luckily it had been parked forward in the space next to the trailer. So the front end was toward us. We were able to walk just a few paces across the snowy yard to reach the truck.

Davis bent down, and holding his flashlight close to the front end on the passenger side of the truck, turned it on. I could see that the headlight and turn light were intact. They glowed in the flashlight beam. I felt my heart sinking. This wasn't the truck? Just to make sure that the lab guys didn't have the wrong lights in the report I stepped close to the driver's side lights and put my flashlight on them. The lights were intact. For a moment my heart began to sink and then in a flash my spirits rose.

David came over by me. "Maybe he fixed the broken light?"

"You bet he did," I said.

"How can you tell?"

I put my light on the driver's side light bulb. "Notice a difference?" Davis looked for a long moment then nodded his head. Unlike the lights Davis had put his flashlight on, the driver's side light did not gleam. On this side the glass was dirty. I turned my flashlight off and David did the same

"Good call," Davis whispered. "So what now?"

I looked at the end of the trailer that faced us. There were no lights in the back rooms. The furthermost room, which I assumed was a bedroom, had storm windows with screens facing outward. There was lattice around the bottom of the trailer. I pointed my flashlight through it. There were piles of firewood and some trash under the trailer but nothing like the entrance to a secret cellar. If the girl was in the trailer she had to be above ground.

"We need to know if the girl is in the trailer. How do you feel about breaking the rules a little bit?"

"Depends on how little a bit."

I leaned in close and whispered in his ear.

Davis nodded, "That works for me."

I took my folding knife out of my back pocket and, going to the closest window screen on the suspect's trailer, cut along the right side and then the bottom.

"Should I just go to the door?" Davis asked.

I shook my head. I motioned from him to stay put. I walked swiftly toward a fenced area I had seen on the other side of the alley about 100 feet away. As I got to the fence I rattled it. The air sud-

198

denly filled with the sound of dogs barking. I turned and gave Davis a thumbs up and ran to a spot by the next trailer down. Far enough to be out of sight but close enough to back-up Davis if he need me.

"Hey, someone fucking around out there?" a gruff voice called from inside the trailer of interest.

Davis moved out of sight around the trailer. I heard him knock on the door. I could hear the door open but couldn't' make out what was said. I moved ahead to the rear of the trailer so I'd be even nearer if needed. The light in the back room came on. A curtain parted. I saw Davis looking out the window and pointing to the cut screen.

About five minutes later Davis came out. It had begun to snow. I knew it would be snowing much harder in the mountains. I wondered if Cassie Carew was indeed alive and had shelter, or if her body was now being buried even deeper in snow. We walked down the alley together before Davis spoke.

"He bought the burglar who cut the neighbor's screen story. And he let me in and I got a pretty good view of the entire place. There is no where he could have a girl hidden."

When we reached our cars I asked Davis to stick around for a few minutes while I called Goldstone. I reported to the sheriff what we had found. Goldstone didn't have any questions for Davis so I waved that he could go. Davis walked over to me.

"Can you hang on a second, Sir?" I asked Goldstone.

Davis put his hand out and we shook. "I don't know if we can get someone to watch this guy but at least we know the girl isn't here."

"Thanks."

As Davis drove off I got back on the line with Goldstone. "There is really no where to hide around here for a 24/7 surveillance. Any chance you can get a warrant for a GPS tracking device?"

Paul said he'd work on it. It was late. I was very tired and I had animals at home to feed. Still, I was very tempted to stick around and watch the guy. This was the truck that had hit and killed Greg Carew. I was sure of it now. But there really wasn't a safe place to watch Nate Hanassey from. I got in my Jeep and headed home.

# Grad Students

## October 29: 6 am

Rylee Blouin woke in the dark to what she thought at first was her alarm clock. A first year grad student in Communications Studies at the University of Montana, she was slim and petite, and wore her auburn hair so short she was sometimes mistaken for a boy. She did not have classes today. So why was her alarm going off? She sat up and shook her head to clear it.

Finally, she was able to focus. Her alarm clock sat silent as her smartphone gave off an urgent ring. She made another mental note to change the ringtone—something she'd intended but forgotten to do. The phone sat on the night table next to her bed in her private bedroom in the three-bedroom apartment she shared with two other girls. She picked up the phone and looked at the display, noticing as she did so, the time was 6:02 am.

The display said: YASH.

She lowered the phone to the bedspread and looked at the streetlight coming through the venetian blinds on the single window in her room. Why would he call so early? She thought about just not answering the phone, which continued to chime like a small bell.

She had dated Yash Havish three times. He was smart, funny, and gentlemanly. He was not the worst guy she had ever dated.

At 5' 4", with rather small breasts she considered herself pretty but not beautiful. Being French Canadian she thought of herself as the typical French girl next door even if her mother kept telling her she could be a model.

Here in Montana Yash had been the only one to ask her out. Being with Yash had just been fun until he had taken her to an expensive restaurant and said, "I think I am falling in love with you."

And that was that. She liked Yash but only as a friend. She could not encourage love in someone she could not feel a romantic attachment for.

As to the ringing phone, she finally made her decision. She lifted the phone to her ear and pushed talk.

They both spoke at the same time.

"Yash, I like you but…"

"Rylee, thank God I got you, I need your help."

"You need my help?" Rylee asked doubtfully. Her instant thought was that this was some sort of trick to get her to be with him again.

"Yes," Yash replied. He had an accent, which she assumed was from Bombay where he had come from, and sometimes she had found it hard to understand him when he spoke fast. He was speaking very fast.

"We just got a job, Ken and I, and we need a driver for the van right away." Ken was Ken Sweethorse, a Biology grad who minored in engineering. From her dates with Yash she knew all about their research project. The van was a large white Econoline. A small satellite dish sat on the top. It housed a large and very expensive quad copter drone and the computer equipment to control both the drone and the cameras and other equipment the drone carried. Across the sides of the van THE CONDOR had been stenciled with the image of the giant bird after the words, with a small University of Montana logo beneath it.

Yash was the computer guy and drone pilot and Ken the one who operated the camera and special equipment. In addition to being pilot and camera guy their job was to create new software and engineer new equipment for the drone. They had already come up with a directional microphone that could pick up sounds from three hundred yards away and transmit them to the van.

On their second date Yash had shown her footage they'd collected of two grizzly bears mating. That had made Yash seem like every other guy she had ever met, but he had acted embarrassed when she had said she'd seen enough. That night she'd dreamt of a bear who came up to her and hugged her.

"It pays $30 an hour," Yash said, filling in the void left while she thought things over.

"Really?" She said, surprised it paid that well. "Why do you need a driver? Don't you just go and park and then look for animals?"

"This is not about an animal! This is about that missing girl. They have a suspect. They don't have a warrant for a tracer bug so they want surveillance."

"Is it going to be dangerous?" Rylee asked. But she had already, mostly, made up her mind.

"No, we'll be far from them. But it will be a moving surveillance so we need a driver. Will you…"

"I'll be over in fifteen minutes," Rylee said, hanging up. Yash lived only a block and a half away and kept the van at the house where he rented a room. She actually got there in fourteen minutes.

Thirty-five minutes later she sat at the wheel of the parked van. They were backed into a driveway of a sort for a warehouse where a number of abandoned vehicles were parked. From the suspect's trailer, some distance away, their van would look much like the abandoned one they were parked alongside. They had pulled into the spot after driving to the back of the building where Yash and Ken had offloaded the fully charged Condor out of site from the trailer.

"Can I have the binoculars?" Rylee asked. The

Ken, who was sitting in front next to Rylee, was the same age as Yash, taller than both she and Yash at 5'11," and Native American. He was good-looking with an oval shaped head, shoulder length black hair and a smooth, beardless face.

Ken was silent for a long moment. "Nothing to see. The truck is just sitting there." His left arm appeared in front of Rylee holding out binoculars.

"Thanks," Rylee said.

She held the fifty-power set up to her eyes and focused across the open grassy area at the red truck parked alongside the trailer two hundred and thirty yards away.

"There's someone coming out of the trailer," she said. "A guy with a beard."

Ken grabbed the binoculars roughly away

"Hey!" Rylee cried.

"Sorry," Ken said, lifting the glasses to his eyes. He watched for a moment then spoke loudly so his voice carried to the back. "It's the guy. He is now going around the side of the truck."

Rylee didn't need the binoculars to see the man moving to the driver's side door of the truck. As she watched he got in and a moment later began to back out of his parking spot.

Rylee started the van's engine. "Are we going to follow?" she asked.

"Turn the truck off!" a voice Rylee didn't recognized commanded over a speaker in the console.

"Will do," Yash said in back where he sat by the computer, and then said to Rylee. "That was the sheriff. Turn the engine off."

Rylee did so and turned to look back at him. "I thought this was a surveillance?"

"You are not to get anywhere near the suspect," the voice on from the console said loudly. "Is that understood?"

"Understood," Ken said.

"The surveillance is going to be done by the Condor, not by us," Yash said softly. "We have to stay out of sight."

Ken moved to the back of the van and sat down next to Yash. "Condor's engines are a go," Ken said. "You want me to lift off?"

"No, I'll do it," Yash said. "You need to man the camera." He turned back toward Rylee. "As soon as he's out of sight, you can start the engine. I'll let you know which way he's going. And you will drive that way. But like I told you on the way over, we always want to stay far enough away, so we are completely out of sight."

"Understood," Rylee said, realizing her palms on the steering wheel were sweating. She watched the red truck disappear from sight down the trailer park road. Her heart was beating faster than it had in a long time.

# Wait and Listen

## October 29: 10 am

At 10 am I found myself parked in the open area on the Bearmouth Chalet side frontage road near the Bearmouth Exit off I-90. Goldstone had thought it was a good spot to wait. One advantage of going the Bearmouth way was that I didn't have to pass by Two Guns' cabin. Denny's loneliness made stopping to say hello time consuming. Not stopping would have been rude. So I usually had to allow extra time when I went his way.

The first words Goldstone spoke to me when I answered my phone were, "Bad news." He said it matter-of-factly in an unemotional tone. I figured it couldn't be too bad.

He had explained that the judge they had gone to had refused to give them a warrant to bug Nate Hanassey's truck. The judge said they didn't have evidence that Hanassey had ever replaced his head-light much less that he had been in an accident.

I had to wonder why he wasn't more upset at the news.

"But…" I began.

The Sheriff interrupted me. "But there is good news," And I could tell by his tone he was hopeful.

"Frank Davis recruited some students from the University of Montana doing a drone study..."

After he explained it and told me how to hook up my iPhone to the surveillance feed, I expressed my concerns about using civilian college students. Goldstone assured me the college kids would not be anywhere near the suspect. All they were doing was operating the 'whirly-gig.'

Their drone had followed Hanassey to the house of another ex-con Bobby Wesley, who had been waiting for him outside. In the image on my screen I looked down from just behind the passenger seat a little off from the side of the truck at Bobby Wesley tapping the fingers of his right hand, on his knee.

"Won't they notice the drone?" I asked.

The kid who manned the camera zoomed out then, I assumed for my benefit. The red truck became a red speck. The drone hung behind the truck at an incredible distance.

I learned that quite a few people where listening in when Tom Bedder came on and pointed out Wesley was on parole and could be pressured for association with a known felon. Goldstone said maybe later.

On the iPhone on my lap I could see the red truck cruising down I-90 getting near the Clinton exit. If it didn't get off at that exit there were only a few more exits between the truck and me. And if he was headed for the exit to the area where Greg Carew had met his death that would be Bearmouth where I was parked.

I was almost disappointed when the red truck's turn signal began blinking just before the Clinton exit.

"Sheriff, do you want me to drive up that way?" I asked.

"Let's see what he does," Goldstone said.

That seemed like very good advice as I watched Hanassey drive the short distance from the highway exit to the Clinton Market's parking lot. He pulled in right by the front door and both men went in.

"We are near the Clinton exit. What do you want us to do?" an Indian sounding voice said.

"Can you leave the drone hanging back and still drive into the Clinton Market's parking lot?" the sheriff asked.

"Yes."

"Get off at the exit. They are parked in front of the store. Park out of sight in the back behind the store."

"Will do."

The two men emerged from the market 15 minutes later, each carrying a case of Pabst Blue Ribbon and a grocery bag. They got back in the truck and took off. They headed toward the highway but instead of getting on I-90 and heading in my direction, they passed the highway entrance and made for the T on E. Mullen Road and headed South East.

I was wondering where the two were going when Nadine came on. "Wesley has a brother, Billy," he lives off E. Mullen."

"Maybe they're going there?" Goldstone said. "Any chance the brother looks like our guy in the composite Edward's helped us with?"

"Checking," Nadine said.

There was silence then Nadine spoke again. "Got a high school year book photo. Billy is a dead match for the guy in our drawing."

"Do you want us to move in," Tom Bedder asked. I didn't know where Bedder was but assumed he was somewhere near Clinton.

"Let's see what our whirly-gig gets us first," Goldstone said.

"Condor," the young man, who sounded like he had come from India, said. "The bird is called Condor."

"Okay, Condor," the sheriff said. As he said it the red truck turned off E. Mullen into a short driveway toward a trailer hidden among the trees.

210

"That's Billy's place," Nadine said.

"Are you still in the grocery store parking lot, Condor?" Sheriff Goldstone asked.

"Yes," a male voice I had not heard before said.

"And the suspects did not see your van?"

"No, sir. We're behind the store. We couldn't even see them leave."

"What's your name, son?"

"Ken."

"Okay, Ken. You guys stay there until I tell you to move," the sheriff said.

"Understood," Ken said.

On my iPad I watched as the two men exited the truck and began walking to the trailer.

"If the trailer is plastic I may be able to scan the inside with thermal imaging," the young man from India said.

"You are...?" the sheriff asked.

"Yash."

"Yes, do that, Yash." Goldstone said.

The image of the trailer on the screen went red and orange. The camera zoomed in. It seemed from the shadows of familiar things like a coffee maker and a small television that they could see inside.

"I am not reading any bodies in the trailer," Yash said.

"Thanks, Yash," the sheriff said.

"Do you want me to switch back to the normal image or keep it on thermal?"

"Let's keep it on thermal and see if they go inside."

The two men went right to the trailer. It seemed the heavier of the two, which I knew was Hanassey, did something with the door and a few minutes later, he opened it.

"Picking locks, what do you know," Bedder said.

I couldn't help but laugh.

Suddenly there was a squawking sound on my iPad. It grew loud and then changed into voices. Two distinct voices.

"I'm trying our new directional microphone," Ken said. "We haven't got all the bugs out yet, but I thought it might help."

"Why the heck didn't you put it on the truck while they were driving?" Goldstone asked, sounding annoyed.

"It doesn't work well enough to completely overcome moving car sounds, and the controls need a more delicate touch than I can manage while our vehicle is moving."

I could hear the sound of voices becoming clearer in the background.

"Can you clean that up a bit more?" Goldstone asked. "Can you record it?"

"10-4," Ken said.

I wondered if Ken got that from a movie.

The jumbled sounds slowly became clear voices as we all waited and listened.

"Where the fuck can that brother of yours be?" a loud gruff voice said.

"I don't know," a higher pitched male voice replied.

"Let's search the place," the gruff voice said.

"What do you think I've been doing?" the other voice pleaded.

It was hard to discern what was going on exactly as the two just moved around in the small space, but then the bigger of the two men, who was on the left hand side of the trailer, walked toward the opposite end, turned in the middle of the trailer and took a few steps forward. We watched him bend down. It looked as if he was searching for something in a waste-paper basket beneath what looked like a sink. The smaller man moved up behind him but not next to him. There was a wide box shape on their right that reached the ceiling, which most likely put them in the trailer's bathroom near the shower.

"What's this?" the gruff voice asked.

It looked on screen as if he were holding something up, showing it to the other man over his shoulder.

"Why would he buy one of those?" the higher voice said.

"How the fuck would I know! He's your damn brother. Maybe he wants to have her above him while he fucks her."

There was a silence.

"Damn, we should have searched the entire trailer before."

"You told me you thought he'd be back." The gruff voice sounded annoyed.

"Not if he's where I think he took her."

"Well, then lets go." The gruff voice said. It appeared he threw whatever they had been looking back in the wastebasket.

I watched the two men exit the trailer.

"Go back to regular imaging?" Ken asked. "Thermal uses more power."

"Go back," Goldstone said.

"Crap," Yash suddenly said. "The Condor is very low on power. I'm going to need to land it."

"Do you have to? Goldstone asked, "Can we see which way their truck is headed first."

"No can do. I've got to land this now."

# Condor Recovery

## October 29: After 10 am

Rylee Blouin stood behind the two cushioned chairs fixed to the floor in which Yash and Ken sat in front of the three-screen computer console. She had watched, and listened, mesmerized, as the heat images of the two men in the trailer showed them searching it. They were connected by phone to all the cops watching, and all of the technology seemed amazing to her. But, to Rylee, the situation had hardly seemed real until the men found something in the trash that one of them suggested could be used to suspend the girl while having sex with her. At that moment the reality of it sank in, and she felt a weird mixture of both fear and excitement.

At that moment she had looked at the interior of the van and then out through the front window at the mountains on the other side of the highway from the Clinton Market to assure herself that she was somewhere safe.

Her heart went out to the kidnapped girl who was not. When she looked back at the computers, she noticed a small red pulsing light, blinking on the far left computer screen.

Rylee hadn't been able to watch Ken and Yash as she drove, but when she had the van parked, hidden, behind the Market, she had gone to the back of the van to watch. While the vehicle they were following was moving, the two young men had kept checking or changing the flight controls and the camera. Once the red truck reached the trailer they were able to set the controls so the drone would hover safely in the air. The only changes made were when Ken turned on the thermal view and then adjusted the microphone.

Soon Ken and Yash had become completely focused on the center computer screen in the array of three and the situation playing out there. They were as mesmerized by it all as she had been. She didn't think they had even noticed the red blinking light. She hesitated but then decided to say something.

Yash had explained before they started that they'd all be on the conference call with the cops, which was going to be recorded, along with anything they picked up with the directional microphone they'd be focusing on the bad guys. It was best not to talk if they could help it. If one of the bad guys spoke at the same time one of them spoke, what the bad guys said might be lost. On the middle screen the bad guys exited the trailer. Ken asked if he should turn off the thermal imaging and was told to do so.

Yash's eyes were riveted to the screen where the camera now focused in on the two men. She tapped Yash on the shoulder. Presenting obviously annoyed body language, Yash turned and gave her a questioning look.

She didn't say anything, but, instead, she pointed at the blinking light. Suddenly, as she did so, a picture of a battery that had been in a lower section of the screen grew to fill the screen. Now the screen showed an image of an almost completely depleted battery with the word WARNING in red above it, and a beeping sound began.

"Crap," Yash said in alarm. "The Condor is very low on power. I'm going to need to land it."

"Do you have to?" the voice she'd come to know as the sheriff's asked. He was obviously in charge, "Can we see which way their truck is headed first?"

"No can do," Yash said, his voice almost panicked. "I've got to land it now." With that Yash leaned over the console and flicked off the communication switch. Now the sheriff and his men would not be able to hear what they said.

"Deploy the chute?" Ken asked.

"Don't touch that button." Yash shouted. "The last thing we need is for it to get hung up in a tree."

Yash hit a switch on the console and began playing with the flight controls. Rylee watched as the view on the screen changed as the drone turned and then moved over treetops. Rylee assumed the direction it was heading was away from the trailer. At the right edge of the computer screen the end of the tree line was visible as well as a peripheral view of the highway.

"Can't you head for the main road?" She asked.

"It could be seen," Yash cried, "Or worse run over!"

"You turned off the group chat?" Ken asked sounding surprised.

"Not now!" Yash cried, clearly freaking out now. The light on the far screen blinked faster.

A gap appeared in the pattern of trees ahead.

"Be a dirt road, be a dirt road," Yash cried.

As the drone moved over the gap in the trees they could all see it was a dirt road.

"Thank you, thank you, thank you," Yash cried as he began lowering the drone for a landing.

Suddenly the screen went dark. Yash stared at the screen in shock. The left hand screen read: UNIT POWER FAILURE, ATTEMPTING TO REBOOT.

"Crap!" Yash cried. "Do you have the coordinates?"

"That should be Sunshine Hill Road. I'll check it on Google Earth. Why did you turn the chat off?"

Yash looked from Ken to Rylee. "I have a confession to make. A deputy called me this morning and asked if we could use the Condor for surveillance necessary to find the missing girl. I told them I would check with Professor Kern. But I couldn't reach the professor."

"So we are not authorized?"

"No," Yash said, sounding as if making a great effort now to calm himself. "We need to get to the Condor now. Or I might be arrested for stealing it."

"5522 Sunrise Hill is what Google says.

Yash looked at Rylee. He didn't need to say anything. She went to the drivers seat, sat down and turned the engine on.

"Over the highway and then left," Ken said.

A moment later they were on their way.

Six minutes later Rylee drove slowly as she checked the right side of the road for the turn onto Sunrise. On their left open grass separated them from the highway. Yash was in his chair looking at their GPS position on the computer, but the road they were looking for didn't seem to be exactly where the software said. Ken stood holding the back of the driver's seat helping to look.

"Oh, no," Ken said.

"What?" Rylee asked.

In front of them the red truck was turning into the road.

"The red truck we've been following," Ken said. "Best if they see only you," he said as he slipped into the back of the van.

As Rylee watched the red truck which at first sped up as it came toward them, began to slow. The tall man in the driver's seat, sitting next to the big man with the beard, held up his hand through his open window. He wanted her to stop.

Rylee checked the rear-view mirror. No one was behind her. She pulled to a stop in the center of the road so that her window looked directly into the truck's window. Keeping the van in drive with her foot on the brake she rolled down her window.

"Lost?" the driver asked.

Rylee's heart was beating like it never had before. The voice wasn't the voice of the man who had talked about hanging the girl up for sex. That meant that the bearded man was. And the bearded man was looking at her in a way that terrified her. She tried to keep her voice calm as she replied.

"Yeah. Can't find Sunrise Hill road."

"You missed it," the man said, pointing down the road behind her. "About a block back. It's really hidden by the trees."

Rylee turned; looking back behind her instinctively, though the van had no back window.

"Thanks," she said.

"You're welcome," the man said, and drove off. A second later the horn of the red truck honked. Rylee looked in her side mirror. The red truck was stopped not half a block away. The man's arm was out the window. He was pointing. Rylee stuck her hand out and waved. As the red truck drove off, Rylee sat there unmoving until Yash shook her shoulder. "We have to get the Condor. Let's move!"

There was no sign of other traffic around in the rear view mirror. She began backing up. The road was where the man had pointed. Sunrise was a dirt road that didn't seem to get much traffic as the snow on it had only one set of tire tracks coming out. Pine trees hovered over it on either side. Rylee drove slowly as the road twisted like a snake. They passed an uncompleted A-frame with tarpaper on the roof which was the first sign of anyone living on the road at all. Finally, Rylee drove around a corner and there the Condor sat on its side at the edge of the road. The unit lay tilted in a deep rut. One of its propellers hung broken.

Before Rylee even came to a full stop the men jumped out the back. Yash ran up to the Condor as if it were his lost child. As the two lifted it to the road behind the van, Rylee called, "Don't you think you should turn the COM back on? You have some explaining to do to our cop friends."

"No," Yash cried. Not till we get it fixed." Which he was already beginning to do.

"Are you going to tell them that the guys in the red truck saw us and I talked to one of them?"

"No," both Yash and Ken cried almost simultaneously. "Don't do that. They need us," Yash said.

"And the missing girl needs us," Ken said.

"If you tell them, they might tell us to go home." Yash added.

The sheriff wasn't interested in too much explaining. Yash just told him that they'd recovered the Condor, they'd put a new battery in, got the Condor in the air, and they were searching for the red truck again as they spoke. The sheriff suggested they search the East bound side of the highway first. The Condor found the red truck in minutes.

Soon after that Rylee turned the van back onto the I-90 heading toward Butte, while the red truck was locked onto the screen in the back of the van.

# A Strange Sound

## October 26: 6:31 am

Cassie woke to a strange sound that at first she thought was the packrat. But as her head cleared a cold terror seized her. It sounded like snoring. Someone not more then a few feet from her was snoring loudly.

Her kidnapper, it had to be. She listened as carefully as she could, trying to determine how big the person was. The snoring was not at all like her dad's. In addition to having a different rhythm, it was not as loud as her dad's. Whoever he was he was asleep. If it was indeed a he? For all she knew her kidnapper could have kidnapped another girl. Then she realized if it was her kidnapper and he was in fact asleep, she had an advantage.

Slipping halfway out of her sleeping bag, she felt her coat pocket, found her multi-tool and opened the knife. Then, sliding the rest of the way out of her sleeping bag, she took her flashlight and holding it down just an inch from the stone floor, she turned it on. For a moment the glow was blinding. She turned away briefly while her eyes adjusted. Then, in the dim glow that flashlight cast, while it pointed to the floor, she looked in the direction of the snoring sound.

A figure lay there face down. Whoever it was wore dark jeans and a blaze orange hunting jacket. As the person on the floor continued to snore, she watched not knowing what to do.

In the shadows the sleeper's body type looked heavier. It looked like the person had short hair. But those two things proved nothing. Pale bare feet lay against the floor. Had someone taken this person's boots and socks as they had hers?

Avoiding shining the flashlight directly on the person's face, she examined this person's feet. They were big, at least a size 10-1/2. Encrusted between the persons toes, dirt had been allowed to accumulate. The nails were unpainted, dirty and didn't show signs of recent trimming. But why kidnap her and then a guy?

As she shifted the flashlight so that she could get a better view of the sleeper, her impression changed then from suspecting her new mine mate was her kidnapper to thinking that this was another victim. Whoever it was had their hands bound behind them.

Her need to know pushed her resolve. She moved the flashlights beam slowly up toward the sleeper's head, feeling reassured by the steady snoring which showed no sign of wakefulness.

When her light finally illuminated the person's head, a black-looking substance gleamed around it.

He had a stubbly growth of facial hair. Then she saw the gash on his forehead. He lay in a pool of his own blood. Cassie gasped. Her gasp seemed loud in the small chamber but still the sleeper snored on. Was he faking sleep? But the snoring seemed too steady and real.

She was now pretty sure that this was not the man who kidnapped her but rather a victim like herself. With the index finger of her right hand she gently poked him in the center of his back. The snoring paused for an instant then started up again. She poked him again, this time harder. The snoring stopped. The man groaned and seemed to try to lift his head. But instead his head just seemed to wiggle a bit. His own blood had stuck his face to the floor.

"Wait a minute," she said. She stood and went to the remaining water bottles in the package she had gotten, and took out a new bottle. She brought it back to the sleeper and opened it. He wasn't snoring but seemed to be breathing heavily through his open mouth.

She splashed some water about the edges of his face where it touched the floor and seemed stuck. Using her fingers she worked the skin free. Having nothing else to use she used her jacket sleeves to wipe up the wet blood and water around his face. All through this, he just kept breathing heavily and showed no sign of awakening.

Cassie wondered if this guy, who she was now thinking of as 'the sleeper,' had a concussion? The gash in his head, though now crusted, looked like a nasty blow had caused it.

She would have heard if he had been walked in and hit in the chamber. Pointing her flashlight at the floor she saw a trail of blood coming in.

She didn't want to put his face back down on the stone floor, so she picked up one of the plastic bags nearby. She had tried burning the bags but the fumes from the burning plastic smelled awful. She slid the bag under his face. As she lowered his head back down he began snoring again.

Cassie looked at him a moment. He had short dirty-blonde hair and from the side it looked like he had an innocent baby-like face. His ears stuck out a bit too far. He probably got teased about that, Cassie thought. The thought came to her that perhaps she should search him. Even though he was lying face down she was able to lean over and pat the outside pockets of his hunting jacket. She found a set of car keys in the right pocket and some Slim Jims in the other. Throughout her searching him he never stirred. She was convinced now he was either drugged or badly injured.

The man's hunting jacket was apparently zipped up and though she tried, she could not get the zipper to open while he was face down with his hands bound behind him. Figuring there was no way she could search inside without turning him over, she used the knife on her multi-tool to cut the tight binding on each of his wrists. They had been so tight she thought they might have cut off the circulation to his hands. She moved his arms to his sides and tried pulling on his shoulder. As she pulled on his shoulder he suddenly moaned. She stopped. She could no longer hear him snore or breathe. Was he hurt somewhere? She decided for now to leave him as he was. Unable to think of anything else to do for him, she decided to start up a small fire.

As she gathered twigs from the seemingly endless packrat's nest she looked toward the still figure and hoped he wouldn't die.

# Line of Sight

## October 29: Before Noon

Goldstone heard me start my engine and asked, "Where are you going?"

"No point in letting them see me if they get off here like we were thinking."

From the Bearmouth exit a vehicle could go south or north. The area where the body had been found could be reached by going north. If the suspects turned left off the end of the exit ramp, they'd come to a T at the base of a huge mountain. East on the T went past the Chalet and to the Bear Gulch Road where we suspected they were headed. Going west at the T gave you a drive down a long dead end that followed the Clark Fork River.

"I'll park back always on the dead end. That way they might not even notice me."

"Good thinking," Goldstone said.

When I had driven far enough down the dead end to still see back to the T, but far enough away to almost be unidentifiable, I parked without turning around. I was pretty sure a vehicle parked facing away from a suspect was far less suspicious.

I looked down at my iPhone and saw that I was just in time. The red truck was slowing for the Bearmouth exit with Bobby Wesley driving less recklessly than Nate Hanassey had.

I turned in my seat and watched the actual truck turn at the T. The driver and passenger, blaze orange clothing visible, seemed to be facing the front and took no notice of me.

Curious, I opened my driver's side window and listened. I could hear the highway traffic, but I heard nothing like the sound of a drone. I left the window open.

On my iPad I watched the red truck pass the Bearmouth Chalet. I knew the road curved around the mountain and I would now be out of site. I turned the Jeep around and drove back to where I had initially been parked by the T. Once there I opened the passenger side window.

On my iPad the drone seemed to have a close-up view of the red truck but I knew it could be quite a ways away. But I assume it would be coming past me somewhat soon and listened for it, curious as to whether I would be able to hear it, and on hearing it, be able to see it if I looked. My real concern was would it ever get close enough to Nate Hanassey for him to hear it? In my cabin I could hear helicopters and planes coming from miles away.

It seemed like five-minutes before I thought I detected a slight buzzing sound above the din of the traffic on I-90. The sound seemed to come from outside the passenger side of the Jeep. I couldn't see anything from the driver's seat, so I got out keeping my iPhone in hand.

It took me a few moments to find it. It was a hundred yards almost directly above me when I spotted it, and it quickly moved on toward the Chalet. I knew they tried not to fly directly over the highway for fear of being spotted by the suspect or other drivers who might be distracted and cause an accident. It didn't look very big from the ground, and I was only able to follow it for seconds before it got so far away that I could no longer make it out.

"We're getting off at the Bearmouth exit. Where should we deploy?" the voice I'd come to understand was Yash Havish's, the guy in charge of the van surveillance, asked.

"Winslow," Goldstone asked, "where are you now?"

"Back in the parking area by the T," I told him.

"You're in your red Jeep?"

"That's a roger."

"Yash, once you get to the red Jeep parked by the T, follow it. Winslow will lead you guys to a spot where you can park."

"You'll find them someplace safe?" Goldstone asked, and I assumed he was talking to me."

"I'll take care of them," I said.

A moment later a white van came out from under the highway overpass and was soon pulling up behind me.

I got out of my Jeep taking my iPhone with me and walked to the van window. I stopped and stood still, frozen, mesmerized as I caught a glimpse of the young woman with very short auburn hair who began rolling it down. Her face looked so very much like my Lomahongva's, they could have been twins.

"You don't look like a Yash," I managed to say.

"Rylee Blouin" she said offering me a hand.

"Pleased to meet you, Ms. Blouin," I said.

"Rylee, please," she said, "Deputy."

"Winslow, please," I'm only a part-time deputy."

"Winslow," she repeated the name as if it amused her.

There was a door between the front seats and a thin, dark-haired, dark-skinned head peeked out. "Hi, I'm Yash, gotta get back to the console."

A moment later another head peeked out. "Ken," a man with long hair and Native American features said. "Nice to meet you." Then he disappeared too.

"So I am going to follow you?" Rylee asked.

"That's the plan," I said. "Let me get your phone number, a direct line to me, and give me yours," I stopped. "You do have a cell phone?"

"Yep," she nodded and held up a pink one. "Why don't you just type your number into my phone and I'll do the same on yours."

She had to show me how to put my number into her phone, but knew how to put hers in mine. When we were done I felt just a bit embarrassed.

"Back to low tech," I said. "I will put my left hand out the window, point my hand in the air and wave it in a circle if I want you to stop. Is that clear?"

"I think I got it," Rylee said.

I looked down at my iPhone. The red truck was turning onto Bear Gulch Road.

"They're headed in the general direction I thought they would be." I said. "Let's hope you guys can help us pinpoint exactly where they're going."

Just then Goldstone spoke over my iPhone. "Is there room in their van for you, Winslow? I'd rather they have some protection just in case they run into our suspects."

I looked at the empty seat next to Rylee. She caught my eye and said, "Sure, you can ride up here with me."

"No problem," Yash called from the back.

I drove the Jeep back to the spot on the dead end road where I had previously parked to watch for the red truck and locked it. Rylee drove up and I got into the van on the passenger side. I was hoping the van would be able to handle the rough roads.

Before she turned the van around Rylee smiled at me. I guessed she was around 22. I always thought 22-year-olds would think of me at 35 as an old man. I studied her for a moment while she was concentrating on driving. Shorter, petite and a little skinny where Lo was voluptuous, Rylee's resemblance to my Lomahongva was still incredible.


Thirty-five minutes later the van was safely parked on some clear-cut private property just off four corners, which was posted as private, and an unlikely place for most hunters to enter. Yash and Ken had, after I told them there weren't many turnoffs on the road the suspects were traveling, actually landed their drone next to the van and swapped in a new battery. To me the thing sounded like a giant bee and looked like a grimy white flying saucer with a camera and microphone hanging down from its bottom. With a loud droning buzz the thing lifted into the air and was off.

Within minutes of it's taking off the boys found the red truck again. Rylee and I were sitting on a bench that folded down from the wall so that visitors could watch the computer monitors along with

231

the two at the controls. Yash had explained the bench was for faculty to monitor students running the unit.

The students focused on their work and spoke little. Aside from the console and the seat Rylee and I sat on the only other thing in the van was a bookcase-like tower of wire cages, holding supplies. Two rolls of duct-tape in the top cage made it seem the tower watched Rylee and me with giant eyes. I did learn on the drive here that Rylee was a graduate student majoring in Communication Studies at the University of Montana, and she had been recruited because she lived a few houses away from Yash.

The drone followed the truck around for hours, coming in twice during that time. While Yash landed it, I watched Ken take the battery out, replace it with one freshly charged, and step back. The drone seemed to leap back into the air.

It was getting late when, to my surprise, the suspects' vehicle headed down the long dead end road I had searched while looking for Carew's truck the other day. Where they could possibly be headed--I did not know. I watched them park in the same short turnoff that I had and get out.

"I'll turn the microphone on," Ken said.

The camera zoomed in on the two men. The technology amazed me. It seemed as if someone was standing with a camera just a few feet from the men.

An instant later the voice of Nate Hanassey rang clear. "What do you mean you're not sure this is the right place?"

"I haven't been around here in years. Billy and I found it before I went to prison."

"Shit," Hanassey cursed.

We listened to the crunch of their boots on the snow. The men didn't speak at all until they had rounded the curve and looked in every direction.

"I must have missed a turn," Bobby Wesley said.

"Fuck," Hanassey said, "It's almost dark. You gonna be able to find it in the dark?"

Bobby shook his head. "We'll have to come back tomorrow."

"Fuck," Hanassey said.

We watched them get into their vehicle. This time Hanassey got behind the wheel and began the drive back out the dead end.

I looked out the front window of the van. It was just after sunset. It would be completely dark in 20 to 30 minutes.

We followed the red truck's progress until it passed through four-corners not four hundred yards from us in the direction of the highway.

"We're low on power," Ken said.

Yash turned to me. "Can we bring it in?"

"I think so," I said. Then added loudly for the sheriff and the others in the group listening. "It looks like they're headed home. I think we can call it quits for today. I'll wait with the drone crew for a half hour to make sure Hanassey and Wesley are on the highway then get these guys home."

"Let's do that," Goldstone said. "We can pick up our surveillance tomorrow."

"Bringing the Condor in," Yash said. The van was not quite tall enough for me to stand fully and so, crouching, I headed for the front and the passenger door. I got out and stretched leaving the door open behind me because I thought Rylee was coming out, too. She seemed to have taken up studying me. I wanted to make sure I did nothing to lead her on. I found being of interest to this much younger woman who reminded me so much of my Lo, disconcerting.

As I stretched and looked to the sky for the incoming drone, the wind began picking up. I looked back to the van. Rylee did not come out, and I felt slightly disappointed. The wind increased in power. Snow devils swirled about me. At the top edge of the logged bowl where we were parked I could see tree limbs swaying. A moment later I heard a cry from the truck.

"Shit," Yash cried out so loudly I could hear him over the wind.

I swung back up into the van and asked, "What happened?"

It was as if they didn't hear me.

"I've deployed the chute," Ken said.

"No!" Yash wailed. "What were you thinking? It's too soon. Now the wind's got it," Yash cried.

234

The three were grouped around the monitors. Yash and Ken sitting on the edge of their seats and Rylee leaning over them. I caught a glimpse of the camera's view on the screen spiraling around and then tree limbs and then the view went black.

"Oh shit, oh shit, oh shit," Yash was crying.

"We have the coordinates," Ken said. We can get it.

"Is it by a road?" I asked.

Both Ken and Yash looked at me, now, disbelief over the situation on their faces.

"There are no roads there," Yash said, pointing to the screen.

I looked at the screen. Now there was a topo map on the screen with a red pin indicating the spot where the drone had landed. It was pretty far from where we had watched Hanassey and Bobby Wesley.

"No," I said recognizing the general area. It had been logged and so there were not many trees. But it was far from level, the topo map showed many close-together wavy lines delineating deep gullies. The drone, itself, was situated on the far slope of a very deep ravine. The location was not that far from us but getting in there in the dark would be treacherous. "We won't be able to get in there tonight," I said.

Yash looked at me in disbelief.

# A Change in Plan

## October 29: Early Evening

They were a few miles from the frontage road when Nate slowed his truck to a stop.

"Why you stopping?" Bobby asked.

"Why go back to town?"

"We could go to my brother's trailer?"

"And then drive all the way back here? We got beer. We got jerky. Sleep in the truck tonight and start out at daylight."

"I was hoping to sleep in a bed."

Nate gave him a look that said that wasn't happening. Bobby knew not to protest.

It wasn't until Nate started backing up that Bobby realized they were by a little side road that was almost invisible from the road due to the snow. Nate swung in in reverse and backed in about 20 yards or so. Pines on either side hid them from the road.

Nate had just finished his fifth beer and had stepped out of the truck to pee, when lights announced another vehicle coming down the road. He stepped back and watched out of sight behind a small fir as the vehicle approached. As the vehicle, a

236

van, passed, its headlights bouncing off the snow re-
flected back enough to give him a view of its side.

It was the van he had seen near Billy's trailer.
Nate did not like coincidences.

# Memories After a Long Day

## October 29: Evening

That evening I went to bed early expecting an early
morning start to lay in wait for the red truck. As far
as the sheriff was concerned the condor was unre-
coverable for now and no longer an option. But I
had trouble sleeping. To say the young man from
India, Yash, was upset about leaving the Condor behind was an understatement. He had been vehe-
ment, or perhaps I should say manic, about recover-
ing the drone immediately. My arguments about the
inadvisability of trying that in the dark on treacher-

ous terrain with the possibility of Nate Hanassey and Bobby Wesley coming back at any time going unheeded.

"But I have to get it back!" Yash repeated almost in tears.

When I tried to explain that if Nate and Bobby saw the van and they realized they were being watched, that would ruin any chance of us finding the girl. Yash had just looked at me funny. Then he tired to argue that the bad guys were home for the night, and I had to tell him over and over we had no way to know that. Finally, he tried to assure me that they would be very careful not to be seen.

I called Goldstone who ordered the young man to wait until the sheriff's department decided it was safe to go back or face charges for impeding a sheriff's investigation. (I suspected Goldstone was bluffing, but bluff or not, it worked.) I followed the van back to Missoula, and insisted Rylee take a very upset Yash and somewhat upset Ken home, then drive the van to her apartment where she would keep the keys until contacted.

But sleep evaded me, I kept hearing the young man, Yash, repeat over and over in his Indian accent, "But it is my responsibility to safeguard the Condor."

# New Snow

## October 26: Afternoon

Cassie had been listening to the young man breathe for what seemed like hours. His breathing had not changed. It held to a steady in and out rhythm that seemed strong. At least she told herself that.

She had tried pouring a little water on his face to see if that would wake him, but that only caused him to shake a bit. His eyes never opened.

She picked up the headlight and headed for the mine entrance. She wanted to be alone and get some fresh air.

As she came into the chamber beneath the grate, she saw that it had snowed and the light was now dimmer than it had been. To her surprise she found a new pile of supplies that been left. She assumed her capture had left it when he dropped off the young man. In addition to the water bottles, that she could see were beginning to freeze, there were some grocery bags. She realized she was starving. She moved eagerly toward the bags.

After she had eaten a few pieces of the jerky that had been left, she focused again on the grate above her. The openings in the grate seemed to glow a gray-blue with the snow completely covering them. Snow had actually pushed through at the edges so that it seemed the grate had grown into the chamber.

She looked at the grate for a moment then headed back to the chamber. She listened to the young man's breathing as she passed him. It seemed the same. She went to the packrat's nest and dug until she found a longer thin stick, then hurried back to the grate.

She chose a spot in the center of the grate and pushed the stick through the grate. The stick pierced the snow easily. She pulled the stick back out and snow from the small hole fell down on her. She stuck the stick back in and this time moved the stick as best she could in a circular motion, knocking snow out as she did so. This time when she pulled the stick out there was a small opening. Through the tiny inverted-funnel of the hole she'd made she could see the sky and falling flakes of snow. She thrust the stick back in and began scraping the sides of that one section of grate. As she worked, section by section, her view of the sky slowly grew.

An hour later Cassie sat down exhausted. A section of the grate about two feet square, sixteen sections, had been cleared of snow. It was like a small window in an igloo. Her arm was tired. But at least she could see the sky. She left the stick she used propped up against the wall by the entrance.

As she carried one of the cases of water into the chamber she was afraid she'd find the young man dead. But she heard his breathing before her headlight found him. He had not moved.

She put the partly frozen case down and began moving the rest of the supplies in from the entrance.

# Too Many Coincidences

## October 30: Around 4 am

Nate woke in the driver's seat. His head hurt. His mouth tasted like shit. It was still dark out but a vehicle was approaching. He almost dismissed it as a hunter starting off early or trying to get to a stand before first light and was about to close his eyes, when the vehicle, going fast passed. Damn if it didn't look like that same damn van again.

"What are you doing?" Bobby asked, awakened by the truck starting. "It's still dark out."

"Go back to sleep. I'm just curious about something."

Bobby closed his eyes as Nate began to drive.

Hours later, the sun just coming up, Nate urged Bobby on. The Native American kid, duct-taped in a kneeling position to a small tree, stared at Bobby defiantly. His hands were duct-taped behind his back, and the duct-tape around his neck barely let him move his head. The young man was helpless. He should have looked scared. But then he hadn't seen what Nate had done to his friend. Bobby's belt buckle was at the guy's eye level. He held Nate's 1911 .45 in his right hand.

"Come on," Nate said almost cheerfully. "You got to watch me do the other guy. I've been wanting to see somebody do this since I saw that guy in the dueling banjos movie get away without doing it."

Bobby began undoing his belt.

"Yeah," Bobby said, "Because the hillbilly trying to do it died."

Nate made a big show of looking around. "I don't see anyone around with a bow and arrow."

"What if he bites me?"

"That's why I gave you the gun," Nate said. He didn't mention that the gun, his, was unloaded. He didn't want Bobby to shoot the guy. He didn't want to have to look for casings and bullets.

242

# To Nightmare

## October 30: Before Sunrise

I dreamt that Lomahongva was sitting on a snow-covered stump among pine trees whose branches hung so heavy in snow they drooped. Tears flowed from her eyes. Her long black hair was covered in white flakes. I ran up to her and took her hands. "What's wrong?" I asked. "Aren't you cold?" she wore only a white deerskin dress.

"I am not cold," she said in that voice I missed so much. "I cry for the young men."

"If young men are lost, I will find them," I said, trying to reassure her. "You know I am good at finding."

"No, my wild wind. You cannot find them. They are here in this forest with me where you can find neither them nor me."

I woke then to the sound of buzzing, that I thought at first was an alarm clock. I had set my alarm for 8:30 am when I was to get in touch with Goldstone to see what the day's plan would be. Now

I realized it was my phone. I jumped up from bed and ran to get it, but it stopped ringing just as I picked it up.

My missed calls had a number showing I did not quite remember seeing before. I pushed the buttons and the phone rang once before it was picked up.

"Hello?" a very anxious and familiar voice asked.

"You called me?"

"Deputy Doyle, Winslow?"

"Yes. Rylee?" I asked recognizing the voice and the slight French accent.

"Yes. This is Rylee," she said. There was relief in her voice, but she still sounded very anxious.

"Why did you call?"

"The van's gone," she said. I was about to interrupt when she rushed on, "I jog every morning at 6:30. I found a note on my door this morning and the van gone. Yash apparently had an extra set of keys for the van. His note said he couldn't wait, that it was 3 am, and he and Ken were going to get the drone and be back at 7:10 to pick me up so I could drive again."

Goldstone had told them he wouldn't be using them again. They must have thought that if they showed up, he would let them help.

"It's twenty to eight and he's not here. I have a very bad feeling."

"Could he be home sleeping?"

"I can see his and Ken's apartment from here. They started rooming together once they started working together. I didn't see the van. So I called.

When they didn't answer I went and knocked on their door. There was no answer. I pounded on the door for a full minute."

"And they left at three in the morning?" I asked having a very bad feeling myself.

"That's what it says."

"Thank you, Rylee. If they do show up call me immediately. Otherwise I'm going to have to assume the worst, and so I'll be looking for them."

"Winslow?" Rylee said. Something about her tone made me think this wasn't going to be good.

"I have a confession to make."

"What? I don't understand," I said, having no idea what she'd have to confess.

"Yesterday, when we went to retrieve the Condor, the first time, when the battery ran out. We ran into the red truck. I mean the driver saw us and stopped and asked if we were lost. He didn't see Yash or Ken, but he saw me and he saw the van. I should have told you yesterday."

"Yes, you should have," I said sternly, knowing that if I had known that I might have acted differently.


When I explained what had happened to Goldstone on my way to the coordinates where the drone had gone down, he was understandably upset. When I tried to take the blame, saying I was concerned Yash might try something like this, he stopped me.

"We can't babysit every citizen that might do something stupid. I need you at your best and that means getting a good night's sleep. What's going to hit the fan here is me allowing civilians in on an investigation. If something has happened to those students, I'm the one screwed. Let's just hope they broke their legs, or something, hiking through the woods in the dark."

"Or they just got stuck in this new snow," Winslow said. "That van didn't have super high clearance."

We were both silent a moment thinking about that, when Goldstone spoke again. "Maybe we can get the GPS location of that van itself, since we don't know where they parked. I'll check and get back to you if I can. Let's hope you can get a signal there."


Even though it was a Monday there were some tracks in the new snow. The numbers of hunters around always tapered off during the week, but there were plenty of hunters who took the first week or two of hunting season off as their vacation. The thing I worried about was that Ken and Yash had driven in while the new snow was falling. That meant if they went off the beaten track their tracks might now be covered up making finding the van if it went off road while the snow was falling difficult to find.

The road closest to the location I had for the downed drone didn't even have a name, it was simply called road 1893. There appeared to be but one set of tire tracks in the new snow before I got there. They were too close together to be the van's. Either the van had been here and left, or the young men, not knowing the area at all, had not figured out that this was the best way in.

I had dressed in my hunter's blaze orange jacket and threw my Ruger No. 1, a one shot rifle chambered for the .300 Weatherby with a Nikon scope, over my shoulder by the strap to look the part of a hunter. I never needed more than one shot when I hunted. If I thought I'd need more than one, I didn't shoot. A producer once wanted me to be a guide on a hunting show on a cable channel. I refused. I hated the shows were the guide took a rich man out and gave him a shot at an elk or bear, and then had to tell the guy to shoot again, because he'd missed or just wounded the animal. In my book if you couldn't kill game with one shot you should not be hunting.

Another thing I didn't do that many hunters did all the time was use my rifle's scope as a telescope. I didn't point my rifle unless I intended to shoot it. I had a pair of 50x binoculars and used these to scan the area in front of me. All I saw was white snow, dark cylinders of tree trunks and some small trees. To me, the distance from where I was to where the drone had landed wasn't very far as it was under a mile in. To city people like Yash and Ken, traveling over rough ground, that could be a very long way.

Since I'm tall and hike quite a bit, three and half miles per hour is an easy gait for me on level roads in the winter. I can do two-and-a-half miles per hour with snowshoes on fairly level ground. But it took me almost Forty-five minutes to reach a spot near where the drone had landed. Climbing gullies and clinging to stumps to keep from stumbling down steep slopes on slick snow, made progress slow. Finally, I came to a spot at the top of a ravine where I could glass the area where the drone had landed on the far side. I scanned the area with my binoculars. There was no sign of the drone, but it looked as if the snow had been disturbed in the area.

When I got to the spot ten minutes later, I could make out the shape of indistinct tracks beneath the new snow. It looked as if two people had found the drone, picked it up, and carried it over the top of the ravine. I began following the tracks.

At the top of the ridge the wind had leveled the snow and covered the tracks. But by walking around in a wide semi-circle I was able to pick up the faint tracks again. The boys had obviously had a hard time getting across the sloppy ground. There were a number of indications where one had fallen and then dragged the other down with him.

I tracked them for almost a mile and a half, losing their tracks from time to time, but finding them by logic and in one case a big sweep of the area. An hour after finding the spot where the drone landed, I stood at the top of a ridge and looked down on the Condor team's van. It was parked in a little cul-de-sac hidden from the main road by a turn through some trees.

Using my binoculars I glassed the van and the road behind it. There was snow on the van's roof. Behind the van snow had filled in its tracks. It would have been very hard to locate if I'd been searching from the main road. But what bothered me was that there was no sign of movement in or about the van. Again I had that sinking feeling as I made my way toward it.

When I was ten feet away I called out as loudly as I could, hoping the two had just fallen asleep inside it. "Yash? Ken? You guys in there?"

A gust of wind blowing particles of new snow was my only reply.

I went to the driver's door and knocked hard. The metallic thump was swallowed by the wind and snow. I knocked hard three more times. I hoped I'd see a head peek through the opening behind the seats. But no head appeared. The silence from the van was total. When I had been in the van watching the screen with them, overhead lights had been on. There were no lights on now.

Had they left? Where would they go?

I walked to the back of the van. When I looked down at the snow behind the van to check the tracks, my heart sank. In the snow just where the double doors came together a thick red substance dripped into the snow creating a brownish-crimson stain on the white surface.

Careful not to step in what I was sure was blood, I tried the handle on the right hand door. It did not move.

I went back to the driver's door. It was also locked. I went to the passenger door and this opened. I stepped up into the van and looked back toward the console.

Yash Havish's upper body lay draped over the console. The computer screens that had been on it had been pushed off to the floor. His hands were duct-taped to the far edges of the table. His pants and underwear hung from one shoeless foot on the floor of the van. His legs were splayed wide, held by duct-tape wound around his ankles and the console's legs. Some blood hung on the inside of his right thigh running from the direction of his anus. The van wall behind the console had been sprayed with blood. I turned away feeling sick. The young man had had his throat cut while he was being raped. There was no sign of Ken in the truck.

I got out of the van as quickly as I could and sucked in air. I didn't want to be sick, but I knew sometimes your body decided that for you. Once I felt myself again I walked toward a copse of trees off to the far side of the cul-de-sac. I found Ken Sweethorse a minute later.

Most people remember three things from the movie Deliverance, the music, Ned Beatty playing the role of Bobby, being told to squeal like a pig as he was being raped, and Jon Voight as Ed bound to a tree with his belt around his neck and the tree. Whoever had bound Ken to this five-inch thick lodge pole had used duct-tape. His hands were taped behind his back and to the tree. The duct-tape went around the trunk and his neck.

Half the top of his head had been caved in. Blood ran down the side of his face to his shoulder. There was also blood around his mouth and blood dripping from it. I though I caught a glimpse of some thin rubber material in his teeth. I could guess what had happened.

# To Nightmare 2

## October 30 Late Morning

I held the crime scene until the forensic team arrived. Tom Bedder arrived shortly after and drove me back to my Jeep. The plan was for each of us to drive around in our separate vehicles hoping to find some sign of the red truck.

When I got to the entrance to the dead end we'd watched Nate and Bobby drive down the day before, new snow showed no one had driven down the road recently. I drove in anyway, because I remembered a hidden turnoff just before the dead end. When I reached the turnoff, it, too, was covered with snow.

I got out of my Jeep and walked in a ways. The road twisted and turned a bit but then dropped downhill through open ground. At the top of the hill I could see no one had been that way in some time.

Later, I called Bedder. He had not had any luck either. I called Sheriff Goldstone.

After reporting that neither Bedder nor I had seen any sign of the truck, Goldstone said, "Maybe that kid bit one of them bad enough they needed to go to a doctor or hospital."

"Can you check that?" I asked.

"I have been. But, unlike gunshot wounds, bites don't have to be reported."

"What about searching Billy's trailer? Those two found something in the bathroom wastebasket that gave them an idea where Billy was. It might still be there."

Goldstone was silent for a long time. Finally, he said, "We don't have a warrant. That would be an illegal search." I understood. On one hand an innocent girl's life might still be in danger. On the other two innocent students had been brutally murdered, and anything that might interfere with the conviction of the people involved could not be tolerated. By the way he said it I took him to mean that searching Billy's house was something he really wanted to do.

# An Illegal Search?

## October 30: Dusk

It was dusk when I pulled into the yard by Billy's trailer. There was barely enough light to see the yard. I had made up my mind. I would break in, search the wastebasket, and find out just what the two men had been talking about. Then, I'd slip out, hopefully, without leaving a trace. Unlike in the mountains there was barely any new snow here. But in the snow there were many new tracks. And what looked like dark stains in the dying light. Blood?

I looked up at the windows. No light was visible inside. Had Nate and Bobby come here? I still had rubber gloves in my coat pocket and put them on. I pulled my Casull and made my way carefully to the door, keeping an eye on the windows of the trailer as I did so.

Just as I reached for the doorknob I stopped. The knob and the side of the trailer next to the door were covered in something dark. The stain by the side of the door looked like a handprint. I reached into my pocket with my left hand and pulled out a small maglite. With a push of the button, the stain was revealed to be a bloody handprint.

We had probable cause. I turned the maglite off and put it back in my pocket. I holstered my revolver and got my flashlight from the Jeep. With my flashlight on the doorknob and stain I took three photos with my iPhone. Then, I clipped my phone to my chest and set it to record.

I put the flashlight under my left armpit, and drew my Casull. Then knocked on the door with my left hand. "Sheriff's Department," I called out loudly. "Open up!"

There was no reply. I repeated myself. The only thing I heard was a gust of wind and silence.

Carefully, so as not to disturb the bloodstain on the door, I tried turning the doorknob with the fingertips of my gloved left hand. It turned. Lifting my gun in my right hand, I pulled the door open with my left and stepped inside.

I sniffed the air. The trailer had a faint locker room-like smell. Keeping the flashlight away from my body, I swung it first to the right. I saw what appeared to be the kitchen area and no one appeared to be hiding there. Then I swung the light to the left and saw a corridor to the far end of the trailer. This quick look showed me no one was standing in the open in the trailer. I pointed the beam of the flashlight down on the floor. Droplets of blood gleamed in the light and seemed to be leaving a trail to the left. Moving to the left, careful not to step in the blood, proceeding sideways, I made my way down a narrow corridor toward the bedroom at that end of the trailer.

There was a door coming up on my right. I kept looking both left and behind me, as well as ahead, just in case someone popped out from hiding. I stopped next to the door, which I assumed was a closet. I pushed the door open with my flashlight with my gun ready.

Shirts, pants and jackets hung on plastic hangers. A pair of dress shoes sat on the floor, next to some old sneakers. The closet smelled musty. No one was hiding in this closet.

The next door down would be the bathroom, which I thought the most likely place for someone to hide. The bathroom door was closed and there was a bloody handprint on it. The trail of blood drops turned here and ended at the closed bathroom door.

I moved down to the bedroom after checking behind me again. I wanted to make sure no one could surprise me as I entered the bathroom.

The bedroom was a mess. Someone had tossed clothes from a chest of drawers on the floor. Whoever had been bitten was looking for clothes?

Satisfied the bedroom was empty, I moved in the other direction. I stopped just before I was abreast of the bathroom door. From the hallway I had a pretty good view of the open kitchen area. I had only given it a quick look before. Now I noticed one bloody glass on the counter next to an empty pint of Canadian Whiskey, and a wooden knife rack beyond it. The slot for the largest knife sat empty. Was the knife in the kitchen sink? Or did someone in the bathroom have it?

If the receipt the two men had been looking at was still there, it would be in the bathroom wastebasket. The door opened outward into the hallway. I held my breath and listened for thirty seconds. I heard nothing. I put my flashlight back under my left armpit, raised my gun, turned the knob with my left hand and swung the door open. No one stood in the open doorway. I transferred the flashlight again to my left hand and moved it about, keeping the gun in my right hand ready.

In the light from my flashlight, I first noticed there was much more blood on the floor than there had been in the rest of the trailer. The shower was to my right and the shower curtain closed. I kept my gun on the curtain and pointed the flashlight directly at it. The curtain seemed to be covered in blood, but from the inside. There was too much blood on the floor to enter without disturbing it. But the curtain was close enough that I could reach it with my flashlight. I leaned in, gun ready, and eased the curtain back with the tip of the flashlight. Bobby Wesley's naked body sat slumped in the bottom of the shower stall amid some bloody towels. Gaping flesh hung open at his neckline. With his right hand he held a bloody towel near his crotch.

I took my phone out and called Goldstone. As soon as he was on the line, I said, "I'm at Billy's trailer."

"I told you we needed a warrant to search that trailer!" Goldstone shouted over the phone, angrily. "Do you know what you just did?"

"I had probable cause," I said.

"What probable cause?" Goldstone demanded, unbelieving.

"I stopped on the chance the suspects were here. There was blood on the door handle and a bloody handprint on the wall next to the door. I took photos and video as I entered the trailer"

"Oh," Goldstone said.

He was silent for a long moment. "You should have waited for backup," Goldstone said, back to his normal tone.

"I betting you didn't find any doctors or a hospital that treated a man for a bite to the privates?"

"No," Goldstone said, his voice indicating he knew what I was going to say next.

"I found Bobby Wesley in the shower. He's dead."

"Damn," Goldstone cried. "Hanassey is not going to leave any witnesses." He was quiet a moment. "Were you able to get to the waste basket?"

I looked at the bathroom floor. "No. I don't think I can get to it without stepping in any blood."

"Then don't. Wait there for forensics."


"Did you touch anything?" Glenn the forensic team leader asked an hour later. He was a tiny man who had come from Laos. He was very good at what he did.

"No. Did you find a receipt in the wastebasket?" I asked.

Glenn nodded. He held up a plastic bag so I could read a receipt. "This is the only thing I found in the wastebasket other than tissues and toilet paper wrapping."

It was a receipt for a battery-powered hoist. Unless Nate and Bobby had taken the receipt they had been talking about with them, it had to be the one.

But what hint could an electric hoist large enough to lift a moose off the ground have given them?

# To Dream

## October 30: 9 pm

I did not want Rylee to learn about Yash and Ken from the newspaper or some other way. I had ridden in their van with them. I had sat next to her and felt part of the group for a short time. The bad news should come from me.

Still I felt a little funny about being the one who told her about her friends. I realized that part of me wanted to see the young woman again, see a young woman who might be as much as 14 years my junior, just because she looked like my Lo.

I unbuckled my gun belt, left the gun behind the driver's seat, and locked the Jeep. The temperature had gone up. The air felt almost balmy as I knocked at the white door of a blue house by the base of

Mount Sentinel. Streetlight gleamed off the frozen snow and puddles in the street. A small cat door had been set in the center of the door.

With a creak the white door opened. Rylee stood in the entryway wearing a yellow sweater and cut-offs. As the realization that it was I at the door registered, the broad smile she was wearing dimmed a bit. She stepped out of the door and looked down the street in the direction that we both knew Yash and Ken lived. When it registered that the van wasn't there, she looked up at me with a question.

"Was there an accident?" she asked. Her body seemed to be shaking. Her eyes were pleading with me to make the news not too bad.

I was tired and not thinking all that clearly. I wanted to get it over with. "I am afraid that they both have been murdered," I said.

She seemed to take this in and then began to fall. I grabbed her even before I was consciously aware that she had fainted. Lifting her in my arms, I carried her into the house closing the door behind me. I found myself in a dining room with a table large enough for six. This room was dark with open doors to darkness running off from it. The living room was lit up so I headed there. There did not seem to be anyone else home.

There was an old couch on the wall facing Mount Sentinel with an old coffee table in front of it. Some text books, a notebook and pen where open on the coffee table.

I lay Rylee down on the couch. I knelt down next to her. I didn't know what to do. In all my training I'd never had a lesson in what to do with a woman who fainted. I began stroking her forehead and her cheeks.

After a few minutes she began to stir. She opened her eyes and looked into mine. "I got them killed, didn't I? Because I didn't tell you that those men saw us?" she asked.

"No, you didn't," I said after a moment, trying to calm her.

She began sobbing.

I put my arms around her and held her close.

I don't know how long she cried. I just imagined for some of the time that it was my Lo I was holding. And held with all the tenderness I'd felt for my wife. I continued to hold her until she'd stopped sobbing.

# A Sleeper Awakens

## October 27: 9:22 am

Cassie woke to a voice shouting in the darkness a few feet away from her. She reached out and grabbed the flashlight from where she had left it next to her sleeping bag. But for the moment she did not turn it on.

"Hello? Is anyone there?"

The young man was finally awake.

"Help! Help!" he cried even louder. "Dad?"

Cassie remembered she had cried out for her father when she first woke.

"It's okay," she said. "But your Dad isn't here."

"Who are you?" the boy cried. Cassie liked to think of him as a boy though she knew he was actually a young man. His voice was slurred. He might be awake but whatever had been given to him had not completely worn off yet.

"Where are my boots, and gloves? Did you take them?"

"No, I did not take them. And I'm Cassie," Cassie said as she turned on her headlight.

At the light the boy threw his hand up covering his eyes. Cassie realized the light could be blinding in the small room, and she lowered it to the floor near her feet so he could see she was also shoeless.

"Whoever put us in here took my boots and gloves, too. My father and I were in an accident and I woke up here. I don't know what happened to my father. Have you heard anything about a truck being in an accident?

Billy shook his head, no. "I took the first week of hunting season off and was hunting. I haven't heard any news."

"You were hunting with your Dad?"

He looked at her for a moment. "No, my Dad died years ago."

Because he looked embarrassed she looked away before she said, "Anyway when I woke my gloves and boots were gone. But I wouldn't have anything for my feet at all if I hadn't found some mittens in this sleeping bag that was left a day after I was put down here."

The boy looked at her in wonder. "You're saying someone trapped us in here?

She nodded. She realized whatever he had been given was making it hard for him to make sense of things.

"What is this place?" He asked looking around.

"I think it's an old mine."

"How long have you been here?"

"Three or four days I think. It's hard to keep track of time."

"What have you been eating?"

"The person who imprisoned us has left food and water," Cassie said and pointed the light at the new supplies piled at the side of the chamber. The plastic bottles of water gleamed in the light. It looks like they left more when they dropped you off. It's a good thing since I was almost out of water and food."

The boy kept looking at the pile of food and water.

"I smell smoke. Did you have a fire?"

"Yes, I can make one if you want," Cassie said. "There's a packrat nest over there." She pointed to the crevice where sticks still protruded. "I've been taking the sticks and building a fire."

The boy looked thoughtful for a moment. He shook his head. "I feel very groggy."

"I think you were doped."

He looked at Cassie for a long moment. "Have you tried to find a way out?"

"Yes," she said, but the entrance is blocked with a heavy grate." She looked at him for a moment and then realized there were now two of them. "Maybe together we can lift it," she cried.

Then she realized he might still be weak from what happened to him, "But if you want to rest first?"

"No," he said. He rose unsteadily to his feet. "We may as well try."

She rose and pointed the flashlight in the direction of the way to the entrance. "Come on, follow me."

Cassie had already rounded the curve in the passage before she realized the boy was not right behind her. She walked back a few paces and called out. "Hey, are you coming?"

"Yeah," he cried back. "I can't see where I'm going."

Cassie pointed the light into the passage. A moment later the boy came up, moving slowly.

"I stubbed my toe."

"Sorry," Cassie said. "By the way, what should I call you?"

"Billy," the boy said. "My name's Billy."

"Well, this way, Billy." She turned back to him a moment later. "I'm Cassie by the way, Cassie Carew."

Billy stopped, held out his hand, "Billy Wesley,"

Cassie took his hand. His hand was ice cold. He gave her hand a weak shake then let go.

Twenty-two seconds later they both emerged in the entrance. There was enough light to see so Cassie turned off the headlight. "That big grate is too heavy for me to lift. Maybe together we can lift it."

Billy looked up at the snow-covered grate, then down at his feet. He lifted one bare foot then the other.

"God, the snow here is cold."

"Snow is usually cold," Cassie said. "Come on, let's try to lift the grate, okay?"

Billy looked up at the grate and then at Cassie. "Okay, where do you want to try this?"

"Lets try here first," Cassie said, pointing to the part of the rectangular gate furthest from them. "I think it hinges up that way," she said, pointing behind her."

"Okay," Billy said, stepping up next to her. Taking his hint from her he put his hands on the bottom of the grate.

"And lift," Cassie said. She pushed with all her might. She looked at the Billy and he seemed to be pushing as hard as he could, too.

The grate did not budge. Finally, her hands began to hurt too much from the cold. She stopped.

She looked at Billy and he seemed to be still pushing. "Stop. You can stop now."

Billy stopped. He shook his hands and put each one under the opposite armpit.

"That hurt," he cried. "But I think I could do better."

Cassie nodded. "Come on let's get back inside. I can build a fire."

"How much wood does this packrat's nest have?"

"I don't know. I've been using it since I've been here. It seems to go back quite a ways."

Minutes later, as Cassie began gathering sticks from the packrat's nest, Billy suddenly began dry heaving. Cassie rushed over and guided him to the wall away from the fire and sleeping area. He

266

seemed to stop but then began again. What he brought up was mostly saliva.

When he finally seemed to be done Cassie offered him a newly opened water bottle.

"Sorry," Billy said in a hoarse whisper, before lifting the bottle to his lips and taking a tentative drink.

"Come over here and lie down," Cassie said. "Whatever they gave you must still be in your system."

She led him to the sleeping bag and helped him into it.

She soon heard him begin to snore.

# In The Morning

## Halloween: 8:31 am

My mind rose reluctantly from sleep, slipping away from a dream in which I held Lo close to me, to the scent of lilacs. In my own bed the view of my ceiling is that of smooth, lacquered log rafters, that Lo had peeled the bark from after I had cut them, and we had put in place together. Now I was looking at a white stucco type ceiling with cracks. I tried to turn, and realized I was twisted up, alone, on a couch too small for me.

My phone began to ring and I knew I had to take it. As I turned to the phone, which was on the floor a longhaired, white cat jumped up on top of me. It shook itself, and I was sprayed with ice-cold droplets.

"Persia!" Rylee cried. She stood in the doorway to her bedroom in a fuchsia bathrobe. Pajama pants the same color extended below the robe.

"Were you out in the snow?" she said coming over. As she picked up the cat it got one claw in me. "Your phone's rang a few times," she said to me. "But I didn't know if I should wake you?"

The call was from Goldstone. He had a number of things to say.

Bobby Wesley had suffered a bite to his penis that had caused a great deal of damage. In addition to the receipt for the electric winch found in the bathroom wastebasket, they'd found a laptop computer in a burn barrel out in back of the trailer. The entire thing had very recently been erased, before someone tried to burn it. Falling snow had put the fire out. The techs might be able to recover what was on it, but it would take time.

Hanassey had not been to his home the night before. Bedder was already out looking for him, and Goldstone wanted me out there, too.

"Does Billy have a vehicle?" I asked.

"Just a second," Goldstone said, then a moment later, read from his computer screen, "1999 green Ford Explorer, license number…"

When I hung up Rylee was petting the rather large cat, which had a very loud purr. As I turned back to her the cat growled.

"He's very possessive," Rylee said.

I just smiled. "I have to go."

"Thank you for staying," Rylee said.

"You may not have told me about the bad guys seeing you. But you did take Yash's keys. They brought what happened on themselves."

A sad looked crossed her face. I noticed she had a light smattering of freckles around her nose. Lomahongva had freckles like hers.

Rylee nodded.

# Tenderness

## October 28: 10:03 am

Billy Wesley woke to someone wiping his face with a wet cloth. Before he was completely awake, before he opened his eyes, he imagined it to be his mother who died when he was five. He could taste vomit in his mouth. Tiny pieces hung behind his teeth. He opened his eyes and the girl stopped wiping.

"How do you feel now?" She asked.

Billy thought for a second, "A little better, but not too great."

The small fire flickered beside them.

"Do you have any idea what you were poisoned with, or who poisoned you?"

What surprised Billy was that she really seemed to care. When he first saw her, saw how pretty she was, he thought she'd be stuck up. But here she was being nice. And she had actually cleaned him up. She wasn't at all what he'd imagined.

He had anticipated this question.

"It had to be this hunter I ran into. I was hunting by myself, and this guy with a long fuzzy dark beard appeared ahead of me on the trail carrying a case

270

of water. He was a big guy, over six feet tall and heavy but more muscular than fat," Billy figured he might as well use Nate, who was probably more likely than anyone he knew to kidnap someone. "I asked if he'd seen anything, and he said he got a deer and was looking for help to haul it to his truck. I was a little surprised because I've hauled deer for a few miles by myself, and this guy looked a lot stronger than me. I asked him where he was taking the water. He put the water down and said 'Look' and pointed behind me. I turned and something hit me. I woke up lying on my back. He was looking down at me.

"He pulled out this canteen. 'You fainted,' he said. Then goes, "Drink!' He tossed some pills into my mouth and started pouring water in. I had to swallow or choke. I looked around; we were on this snowy path. I'm a mail carrier. I'm no weakling, but I had to wonder if I ran, could I get away from him, and if he'd try to shoot me? I was just about ready to start running, when I began feeling dizzy. I woke up here."

The girl just looked at him for a moment then nodded. So he tricked you." She looked at his eyes for a moment. "I hope whatever he gave you doesn't do any permanent damage."

Billy studied her face carefully, looking for any sign she was putting him on, and that she did not believe him. But he saw no sign of it.

"Do you remember much about the accident you mentioned?"

271

"No. I was hunting with my Dad. We were on the way home and a truck came barreling toward us. It was going to hit us, and my dad swerved. I think the truck did hit us, but we were already going off the road and we crashed. I woke up here."

"Did you get a good look at the truck, or the driver?"

Cassie shook her head. "It happened so fast that I didn't see much of anything. She didn't want to cry but couldn't help herself. "I don't know what happened to my Dad."

"I'm sorry," Billy said.

They were both silent for a time. Finally Cassie turned toward Billy after pulling herself together. "I have no idea how long we're going to be here. Do you have anything useful in your pockets?"

Billy put his hand in his front right pocket, fished around for a second, then pulled out a penlight. "You mean like this?" he asked.

"That's good to have, but I meant something to help us escape!"

"But we couldn't budge the grate?"

"Think about it. Why would this guy, and I'm assuming its a guy now because of what you said, take our boots and shoes unless he didn't want us to be able to hike out if we got out of this mine?"

She was smart as well as pretty and nice. If he had to kill her he'd have to hit her from behind when she wasn't expecting it. The terrible things he'd imagined doing, he knew he couldn't do now.

272

For now he had to pretend he really was a prisoner, too, and act like it.

"Maybe the grate is just frozen in place," he said. "Maybe if we built a fire in the entrance we could melt any ice and lift the grate?"

Her face seemed to light up. She thought a moment and then said, "Let's try it." She was up and gathering sticks before he could even get up.

More snow had accumulated on the grate. The holes Cassie had widened were still there but had partly closed in. She grabbed the stick she had used before and began clearing snow from the lower side of the grate. Billy, seeing what she was doing, took out his penlight and went back into the mine. Minutes later he emerged with a stick of his own. He came back and began poking the grate on the higher side.

"Just do this side," Cassie said. "The fire should take care of that side for us. The melting snow should run down the slope away from the fire."

Billy joined her at the low end of the grate.

When they had cleared almost all the snow from the lower half of the grate she stopped. "Let's get more firewood," Cassie said, gesturing to the small pile she had already brought in. "We are going to need more than that."

About ten minutes later they had a pile of sticks a foot high and two feet wide at the point closest to the wall under the lower end of the grate. As Cassie lit the pile with a burning twig from the fire in the chamber he thought of them escaping together. His

Explorer was parked far enough away that there was no reason for her to be suspicious if they found their way to it, together. What would happen after that he didn't want to think about now.

The flames were licking the bottom of the grate now. Melting snow from the high side of the grate dripped onto the floor but as the floor sloped down toward the tunnel entrance the water ran away from the fire. Suddenly with a hissing sound, a block of snow slid downward from the back of the grate to the front. As it hit the hot iron at the front globs of slush fell through the grate and onto the fire. Steam mixed with smoke rose as they watched their fire get smothered.

Billy looked to Cassie to see how she'd react. She stood with a shocked look upon her face.

"To build a fire," she said.

"What?" Billy asked.

"The Jack London story. Guy keeps trying to build a fire to stay alive in the Yukon during the gold rush. He finally gets one going with like his last match. But he built it under a tree limb covered with snow. The snow melts enough to fall off the branches and puts the fire out."

"What happened to him?" Billy asked.

"He dies. The thing is I read that story and told myself that would never happen to me."

"I remember now. We read it in sophomore English. Didn't he shoot a moose, and get inside it somehow?"

"We don't have a moose. But we have more wood and more fire."

Later, after they'd brought all the wet burnt pieces of wood back into the chamber to dry off, they ate jerky together by the fire.

Billy wanted to know more about her. "What school do you go to?" he asked.

She just looked at him a moment then said, "Can we do this some other time?"

At first he thought it was him, but then she said, "I really thought that would work,"

And he realized she was just upset that the plan had failed.

"We should do an inventory of the things you have with you," she said. "You started to look, but didn't finish."

He nodded. He took out his penlight and a mesh game bag from his front pockets and placed them between him and the fire. In an inside pocket he found a penknife and a small metal film can that contained strike anywhere matches. In another similar can he found fish hooks and a small needle with a similarly small spool of thread. Further searching produced two small candles.

Cassie was watching as he finished pulling the empty pocket linings of his jacket out to make sure they were completely empty.

275

"The candles could come in handy," she said. "Do you have extra batteries for the penlight?"

Billy felt his pant pockets and then shook his head, "No." He picked up one of the candles. "Do you want one of them?" He asked, offering it with his left hand.

As she took the candle from his hand, she caught a glint of light from his wrist. "You have a watch!" She cried. His arm had extended out of the coat sleeve revealing the watch.

He looked at her.

"You can use it as a light if you need to," she said. She lifted her watch and pressed the illumination button. The watch lit up the space between them for a second and she turned it off.

Billy nodded. "Good to know," he said.

"Here," she said. Taking the single sleeping bag and opening it she rose and came toward him. "It isn't big enough for both of us, but if we sit close it can cover us both."

"Why don't you take these?" Billy asked, offering the film tin of strike anywhere matches. "It will be easier than using your fire starter."

She took the film tin from his outstretched hand. There was an implication there that she was in charge of the fire. And as far as he was concerned, that was fine with him.


Later he awoke from a dream in which he and the girl were running across open snow. They were not

276

barefoot, but they were trying to get away from something or someone. He remembered looking at her, and she smiled back at him.

When he woke it was dark. Just embers glowed in the fire. He could hear her snoring next to him. He was tempted to put his arm around her. Instead he turned and faced the other way.


# Two Guns


## Halloween: 10:18 am

As I drove up to the complex of assorted old trailers, one old school bus, a few very aged sheds, an outhouse and the one log cabin that had been built in the 1800's, I kept my eyes on the chimneys. Smoke curled from a one-time bread truck parked across the road from the log cabin. That indicated that Denny was staying in the truck he'd converted to a trailer. Inside, I knew, a skinny wood stove fed from the top sat by the door and could be seen through the large glass panel in the door. Firewood was always piled against the wall separating the front from the cargo area where Denny had set up a cot.

Of late this converted bread truck had been Denny's favorite abode. He could even drive it to Missoula if he wanted, though it did not do that well in snow. If he went to town by other means, you could usually see through the front window a rabbit-eared shotgun wired to the steering wheel pointing at the glass part of the door. The first time I'd seen it, I'd been reaching to open that door. I don't know if it was actually set up to fire, but I would not want to find out.

Denny's hearing was poor and he probably didn't have his hearing aid in, as he didn't hear me drive up. I hammered the door with my fist a few times then waited and listened. I heard movement in the back of the van and pretty soon he appeared. As he is in his eighties, he's somewhat stooped over, and wears a brace on his right knee over blue bib overalls. As always he was wearing an old green shirt and a confederate army style hat that was almost charcoal in color. Around his waist his thick black belt, holding a few tools and two black pistols, one on either side, was already on. He had to have been wearing it because he couldn't have put it on that fast. A curl of tobacco smoke rose from an old black pipe clamped between his teeth.

Denny saw it was me through the glass of the door and smiled. With shaded glasses on his heart-shaped pale face, now in old age, resembled something in the weasel family. I'd seen photos of him when he was younger and he had been quite handsome.

He opened the door, put his pipe down on the truck's dashboard, and stepped out saying, "Haven't seen you around."

I smiled. I lifted my deputy's badge and showed it to him. He looked up at me puzzled.

"I'm looking for that missing girl. Did you hear about her?"

Denny nodded. "Heard it on the radio. Can't trust people these days." Someone else would ask why I was talking to them, but not Denny. He knew I knew him well enough not to suspect him. He just waited for me to speak.

"I found something that made me think the girl might be in a mine somewhere around here."

Denny nodded his understanding.

"Do you know of a mine in this area that someone would need a winch to get into? To lower themselves in or to lift something out of the way?"

Denny considered this for only a moment. "The Cat-trap Mine," he said. "Young fellow came here ten years ago from the university. He wanted to study an old mine and do a paper on it. I helped him.

"When his paper was done, a lot of people went looking for that mine. One fella fell down a winze and almost died. So they put a big grate on top of the portal."

I knew a bit of mining terminology. When miners dug a level tunnel in following ore, the closed end tunnel was called a drift. If became a tunnel only if there was an opening at the other end into something else. A winze is a shaft dug somewhere inside a drift to access ore or another drift below. The portal was the entryway.

"You could lift the grate with a heavy winch?" I asked.

Denny nodded. "I used to use an old car jack."

I realized then that Denny was looking at me funny. I guessed he was debating whether to say something. If he had one rule, it was to not butt into other folks' business. He prided himself on not being a gossip.

"There's a young girl's life at stake here. If you know something please tell me?"

Denny was a confirmed misogynist. Even though there was a rumor that he shot a guy in the foot with his shotgun who was bothering a woman under his protection, he didn't much like the fair sex. But I was hoping that because it was a teenage girl missing and not a woman, it would appeal to his compassionate side, if he had one.

Denny looked me right in the eye and asked, "Sheriff's business?"

I didn't know if confirming this was sheriff's business would help or hurt, but one thing Denny couldn't tolerate was a liar.

"Yes," I said as I nodded in agreement.

He hesitated just a moment longer. "Gnat Hanassey was here yesterday asking the same thing," he said.

Denny wasn't senile. He hadn't gotten the name wrong. I believed for some reason he was labeling Nate a pest, "Nathanial Hanassey?" I asked just to be clear.

Denny nodded. "No good the whole family. I caught that Gnat here one day when he was around 12 trying to steal gold I washed. I chased him off. Told him never to come back."

"He is my #1 suspect," I said.

Denny looked over toward his cabin. "He came by yesterday knocking on the cabin door. There was a fellow in his truck with him who didn't get out of the truck. I saw that fella sucking on a bottle like he couldn't get enough. Gnat asked if I knew of a mine that had a big grate on the portal."

"I told him the only one I knew of was the Cattrap. And he says 'tell me how to get there.'" Denny had imitated Hanassey's tone when he said the words and made it clear Hanassey had been demanding not asking.

"And you told him?" I asked.

"I made like this," Denny said and pulled the short nosed black pistol from his right side. He drew his gun so quickly, I barely registered what he was doing until he held it up to point at an imaginary Nate. "I told him to get going, and, if he came back he'd better bring help." He smiled as he said it and I had to smile thinking of the look that must have crossed Nate's face.

"Then he told me he thought his little brother might be up there lost. And asked could I please help him."

"So you did?" I asked.

Denny shook his head, no. "No, I didn't believe him. Called him a liar to his face and he drove off."

"Which way?" I asked.

Denny nodded in the direction that lead to the highway and Missoula.

"But I think he drove by this morning. I was in the outhouse and somebody drove by fast. Didn't get to see him. Sounded like the Gnat's truck. He had a bad muffler when he came yesterday."

"How long ago?" I asked.

"Maybe an hour," Denny said.

I took out my iPhone to call Goldstone to let him know I'd be headed to the Cat-trap mine. But Denny lived in a valley between high peaks. There was no signal.

I considered asking Denny to come with me. But bringing civilians, especially after what happened to the two graduate students, was something Goldstone would never approve. "Can you draw me a map?"

Denny smiled. "I have the paper the fellow from the university wrote. He gave me a copy." He started toward the log cabin.

"Does it have a map?" I asked, wondering if Denny understood what I needed.

"A good map to both the outside and inside," Denny said.

The outside of Denny's cabin was covered with old traps and dried out beaver tails. It was dark inside. The dark smoke-stained logs forming the inner walls, held traps, and more animal tails. The air smelled of wood smoke, animal musk and tobacco. Gun parts littered workbenches covered in old newspapers. He began digging in a rusty gray cabinet. I watched him move stacks of old National Geographics to uncover a pile of papers that gave off a musty smell when moved. He put the papers on a clear spot on what I knew was his breakfast nook. He pushed away an empty coffee cup and a plate with a film of congealing egg-yolk and began sorting. After a few minutes he handed me a stack of bound paper about 30 sheets thick.

The top sheet read: 'An Analysis of the Dangers in a Typical Abandoned Montana Mine: The Cattrap.'

"Do you mind if I read some of this quick in case I have some questions?"

"You can borrow it," he said.

It was impossible to read the small print in Denny's cabin. I went outside and leaned against my truck.

Denny came out and stood next to me. I read the first page, and when I was done, I looked up at him. "This is very helpful," I said.

"Do you need backup?" he asked. I thought about it a long time. I was losing time reading the paper. He knew where the mine was. From the map I knew that anyone trying to reach it would have to walk the last part of the trail. If we found Nate's truck, Denny could watch it. Or wait to see if Nate showed up.

But the problem was Denny was a civilian. And then Lo whispered in my ear. "You know Nate will have to kill him."

It took me only a moment to figure out what she meant. That was the solution! I couldn't leave two-guns behind because Nate wasn't leaving any witnesses. Nate probably wouldn't be a match for Denny if Denny knew he was coming. But Denny had seen Nate and Bobby together after they'd killed Yash and Ken, and before Nate killed Bobby. Nate could not afford to let Denny live.

"Yes," I said, "I'd like backup. But here is something you should know before coming with me. That guy you saw with him was most likely Bobby Wesley. I found Bobby with his throat cut last night after I found the bodies of two university students I believe Bobby and Nate murdered."

"You have chains?" he asked.

I keep good tire chains and heavy duty bungee cords in the Jeep in winter and often put them on whether I need them or not. But if Denny thought we'd need chains where we were going I was going to listen. Together we put them on.

A few minutes later Denny sat in the driver's seat of my Jeep wearing a headlamp. He'd brought his rabbit-eared, double-barrel shotgun, and a thick copper-colored flashlight/lantern with a handle. Both sat between us as we drove toward the Cat-trap. I let Denny drive so I could read as much about the Cat-Trap as I could before we got there. Denny drove somewhat slowly and I was glad of that. I wouldn't have been able to read driving over the wilderness roads at a break-neck speed.

Parts of the paper where about general abandoned mine dangers that I was a little familiar with having rescued two boys from a mine while Lo was still alive. They'd gotten lost not too far in and had been easy to find. But I read up on the subject just in case it ever happened again. Len Polisky, the author, however had mapped the interior of the Cat-trap mine and had included a topographic map to the mine itself.

As we drove it came to me why the laptop had been in the burn barrel at Bobby Wesley's. Nate had done an Internet or Google Earth search for the Cat-Trap. For all I knew he might even have found Len Polisky's paper.

I looked out the window. It was beginning to snow again. We were climbing higher into the mountains and right into the oncoming snow. I just hoped we got there in time.

# A Breeze

## October 29: 7.59 am

Cassie Carew woke with new hope. Even the stone that had worked its way under her and dug into her back did not deter her hope. She took a quick inventory of her surroundings. There was only a tiny red speck of a coal in the fire, which was on her side of their sleeping bag cover. Billy snored just a few inches away from her, and it may have been his snoring that woke her. But she had to admit, she actually felt warmer with him under the sleeping bag with her.

But if what she was feeling was right, they would not have to sleep under that sleeping bag another night. Her thoughts were clear. Sure the snow had caved in and put out the fire they'd started yesterday. But they could do it again. This time she would make sure there was no snow above the fire. If it had snowed again, she'd use a stick to get it off before starting the fire. She'd use her stick to get all the snow off the grate before they started the fire whether it had snowed again or not. Her intuition told her it had not snowed again. When she was a

286

sure as she was about this she was usually right. She would get the fire going hot enough to melt any ice holding the grate in place, and together they'd lift the grate off.

Using her headlight she hurried through the tunnel to the opening. There was no new snow on the grate. Since the snow had slid off the back of the grate the entire grate was clear of snow. She hurried back to the chamber and checked the slightly burnt wood they'd brought back in after the snow landed on it. She touched a few of the charcoaled burnt pieces and they all felt coldly damp. It didn't matter. They could just use new wood.

She thought about waking Billy up to help gather wood from the packrat nest to build the fire. But she decided to get started without him. She needed him at his strongest to lift the grate. She could gather sticks easily enough by herself.

Sometime later she had a three-foot high almost five foot around pyramid of wood beneath the grate. Cassie decided to get one more bundle of wood before she lit the fire. She was so positive they'd escape she began humming to herself.

Billy was still sleeping, but she had no reason to wake him yet. Once she'd melted the ice around the edge of the grate would be soon enough. Besides she was a little worried he'd worry that if they used up all the wood from the packrat nest, they'd have no more for a fire. It was a risk, but one she was willing to take. Her mom always said it was easier to ask forgiveness than permission.

The crevice she had been mining wood from now extended back almost 9 feet. She had had no idea it extended that far back when she'd first seen the stick pile in the crevice. The area was narrow but she was small enough that getting to the far end was not difficult. As she reached into the stick pile that was the packrat's home, she grabbed another large armload and began pulling the sticks out. It was then it dawned on her. The fire would, most likely, melt any ice holding the grate down, but where would they stand? They had no boots and the coals could be hot for hours. They didn't have gloves so how could they lift the hot grate? Just as she began to despair the sticks behind those that she had been pulling on fell down and away from her. To her surprise a breeze began to blow in her face, coming out of the black hole the sticks had left behind.

Back in the chamber she quickly gathered water and food, filling her jacket pockets.

A moment later she was vigorously shaking Billy. "Wake up. Wake up. Wake up!"

"Huh!" Billy moaned.

She realized the beam of her headlight was in his eyes. She took the headlight off, held it beneath her chin, and pointed it up so her face was visible.

"It's me," she cried. "I think I found a way out."

"What," he said, rising now. "Through the grate?"

"No," she said, barely able to contain her enthusiasm. "Behind the packrat nest, there's a tunnel. Air is coming out. It's got to be a way out."

From the relative safety of the chamber they'd been sleeping in, Billy pointed his penlight down into the space that had been filled with the packrat's accumulated nesting material. At the far end the light illuminated a narrow area with a pile of broken rock on the left and the tunnel wall on the right. It stretched like a lopsided V just wide enough to crawl through. For some reason the packrat had not built here. Beyond where the tiny penlight penetrated there was a dark hole.

"It looks like this area caved in a long time ago. The packrat used it to make a nest."

"But," Cassie said, slapping Billy on the back, "can't you feel the breeze?"

"Yeah, I can feel it," Billy said.

"It could be a way out," Cassie said. She waited, but Billy said nothing. He just kept looking into the hole.

"Well, if you're not going, I am," she pushed past Billy and got down on her hands and knees. She quickly covered the ground she'd been through time and again collecting sticks, and reached the new section opening into the dark interior of the mine. Here the passage was narrower than the previous stretch. Crumbled rock on her left side seemed to be in an infinitely slow slide toward the wall on the right. Cassie found she fit through easily enough and soon emerged in a much wider tunnel.

In front of her two logs had been set in the tunnel on either side of what appeared to be the main passageway. Someone had dug into the upper corners of the tunnel's roof so that she stood at the apex of a small inverted pyramid. The walls next to her rose at a slant widening as they ascended.

A noise behind her startled her and she swung around. Billy was pulling himself through the small passage she had just entered from.

"You made it," she said.

Billy shook his head. "I don't know about this,"

Cassie turned her head toward the darkness ahead. "Can't you feel that breeze?"

"I can feel it," Billy said. "But is that a way out?"

"We'll find out," Cassie said.

"What about the food and water we left back there?"

"I have two bottles of water, and lots of jerky," Cassie said holding up one of the bottles. "If we have to, we can go back and get more."

Billy turned and looked back in the direction of the chamber they had come from. "Did you notice there aren't any packrats nesting in the last part of the tunnel we just came through?"

"I wondered about that."

"I wonder if it's because the packrats realized, maybe instinctively, that that part of the tunnel is unstable." He pointed his penlight at the rubble in the passage.

Cassie was quiet while she thought about what Billy had said. She pointed her headlight up at the

290

ceiling of the passage they'd just come through. It did not look at all secure. She didn't want to think about what would happen if the ceiling came down while they were going back for more supplies.

"Let's just see if we can find a way out," she said quietly. With that she moved forward between the two log supports. As she passed through them, she realized they were very old. She resisted the temptation to touch them. She was afraid they'd crumble at her touch. Ahead an almost round tunnel opening offered the only way to go.

She started forward into the tunnel. Billy's penlight flicking around her let her know Billy was close behind. She stopped.

"Can you see well enough with my headlight to not use yours? It might be a good idea to save your batteries as you don't have extras."

She watched the ball of light cast from the penlight that reached past her go out.

"Good idea," Billy said.

They had been following the tunnel for what seemed like a long time, when the tunnel opened up on Cassie's right-hand side. The ceiling here was a bit higher. Two old six-by-six timbers propped up against the ceiling seemed to hold it up. Against the wall in front and to the right head-sized stones seemed to be piled up in a wall-like way.

"What is this about," Cassie asked pointing to the wall of piled stones when Billy came up.

"I think that's waste rock," Billy said. "They piled it up rather than carry it out." He paused and looked at her. "How much longer do you want to do this? I'm getting hungry."

Cassie turned toward the tunnel. She could still feel the breeze hitting her face. She reached into her pocket and pulled out some jerky and handed it to Billy. Then took another piece out for herself.

As she ate Cassie realized she was exhausted. "Maybe we should go back and get more food and water and start again tomorrow," Cassie said. "Get as much as we can carry with us. Then keep going until we find a way out."

# Finding The Cat-trap Mine

## Halloween: Mid-day

We were following a set of ruts left about an hour or so before that were filling with snow. The Jeep hit some high drifts that would have slowed it down or even stopped it, but Denny gunned the engine before we hit them and bulled us through. Chains are great for traction on slippery ice or snow, and they're necessary if you drift into a snow bank, but if the snow gets deeper than the bottom of your vehicle, you bottom out. I carried a shovel in the Jeep just for that reason.

We came around a bend high atop a mountain I had not been on in a while. Visibility with the snow wasn't more than 25 yards. But I could make out a dark shape stopped off on the side the road. As we neared it, it took on color. It was Nate Hanassey's red truck. It had slid off the road into a snow-covered ditch, and it was stuck far enough over that Denny would be able to drive by it by driving partially up on the bank on the opposite side of the road. I couldn't see anyone in the truck. Denny pulled to a stop behind it.

I jumped out pulling my gun and quickly, cautiously moved forward, and covered the alkyd driver's side of the vehicle. I stepped closer and assured myself there was no one in the vehicle.

I walked to the front of the jeep. I could see where the rear driver's side tire had dug down to the dirt of the road. Nate's truck did not have chains. A quick check in front of the red truck revealed boot tracks walking up the road.

I walked back to the driver's side door, opened it, and spotted a bread-box-sized, open, cardboard box on the floor on the passenger side. Around the box on the floor were black Styrofoam pieces. Since I

293

was already wearing gloves, I climbed in, and slid across the seat until I could reach the box. Nate had picked up a parabolic microphone. He was smarter than I had given him credit for.

After taking in as much as I could of Polisky's paper on the mine, I knew there were miles of tunnel and multiple branching ways to go. With a parabolic microphone Hanassey could listen for anyone in the mine, if anyone in the mine was still alive.

I put the box on the seat next to me. Beneath the box a box of 12-gauge, double-ought shotgun shells sat empty. Two more cardboard and plastic packages sat next to the ammo box. I picked both up. One had contained two 400-lumen headlights with a 17-hour rating. One of the headlights was missing. The other package was a 16-count Duracell AA battery pack. The battery pack was half empty and there were no batteries on the floor. The passenger side door opened, and Denny peered in. How he managed to get there I don't know. I pointed to the parabolic microphone box. He gave me a puzzled look. "It can pick up sounds from far away. He'll be able to find them," I said.

"How much farther?" I asked when we were back in the Jeep.

"Mile, mile and a half," Denny said.

I kept my eyes peeled and gun ready searching for a sign of Hanassey walking along the road. But by the time Denny pulled to a stop in a snow-cov-

294

ered dead end in a tunnel of trees there had been no sign of him but for glimpses of footprints filling with snow.

The first thing I did on getting out of the Jeep was recheck the tracks in the snow. They continued on what must be a path through an opening in the trees.

There was no sign of Billy Wesley's vehicle. Had he been here? Could he be parked somewhere else? Was the girl still even alive?

I tried my iPhone and got a signal. I alerted Goldstone and gave him my coordinates. He'd get me backup as soon as he was able. I deliberately forgot to mention Denny.

Together Denny and I moved up the trail following the quickly filling boot prints. Not wanting to wait for Denny, I pulled ahead. Denny could move pretty fast for a man his age on level ground but not uphill. A good ten-minute climb from where the Jeep was parked took me to the top of the trail.

I rounded a bend and saw the large, rectangular, snow-covered, metal grate. It had been pulled up to a 45° angle by a cable attached to a winch. A tarp that had protected the winch was turned aside and both it and the top of the winch were white with snow. There was no sign of a battery. Electric cables from the winch lay loose. I assumed Nate had used the winch to open the grate and then had hidden the battery someplace, so the grate could not be lowered. The tracks we had been following covered the area.

Denny came up behind me. Even though he smoked almost constantly, he didn't even seem fazed.

I saw hunter's orange on the ground near where the far end of the cable was secured to a tree and followed Nate's boot tracks up to examine it. The blaze orange turned out to be a pair of gloves small enough for a young woman. Next to the gloves were two pairs of boots, another set of black gloves, and a farm-style jack. Were there two prisoners in the mine?

I mulled it over. One set of boots would fit Cassie. The other set were men's boots. Back at the grate I studied the winch and saw that a wire hanger had been attached to the control. My best guess was that Billy Wesley had used the farm jack to first put the girl in the mine. Later, he decided to set up the winch. The only thing that made sense out of the wire on the winch control was if Billy intended to go into the mine, lower the grate after him, and still get himself out. The two sets of boots might indicate that Billy had gone in pretending to be a prisoner.

As I turned back to the mine opening Denny was climbing down inside. A huge pile of snow-covered sticks made getting down easier. There was no time to waste. I hurried to join him.

# Three Forks

## October 30: 8:03 am

Cassie shook Billy Wesley's shoulder minutes after she, herself, woke up. Billy groaned, and slowly turned over, opening his eyes reluctantly.

"Come on," she urged. "We have to get going."

Billy didn't say anything. It seemed to Cassie he was deep in thought, though what he could be thinking that was more important than escaping, she didn't know.

"Look," she said holding up a leg by the knee with green-gloved hands. She had something wrapped around her foot. It took him a moment to realize it was part of the sleeping bag he'd left her.

"I made a pair for you too." She said holding two pieces of sleeping bag out along with some strips of cloth.

After he put on the makeshift boots, he rose and began picking up the bottles of water and bags of jerky she had laid out for him. Cassie's own pockets bulged with water bottles, cans of sardines, and jerky packs. She had taken as much as she felt she could reasonably carry. Once Billy was similarly loaded up, she turned toward the packrat tunnel.

"Just a second," he said.

He headed toward the opening grate and Cassie assumed he needed to go before they left. When he came back a few minutes later he followed her as she made her way down the packrat tunnel into the mine. Again they used her headlight only, and Billy had to stay close enough to be able to see by her light.

Cassie moved quickly through the part of the tunnel they had traveled the day before and soon came to the area with the log supports and piled up stones along the wall.

Cassie was relieved to feel the breeze coming from the darkness of the tunnel ahead. She turned to Billy who had a blank expression upon his face. "Here's to getting out today," she said, went over next to him and gave him a quick hug.

At the hug Billy smiled. She didn't wait for him to talk. She turned and continued down the tunnel. She hadn't gone 60 feet when an opening appeared in the floor ahead seemingly crossed by two, 8-inch-wide, old planks set two inches apart. Moving cautiously she examined the area with her headlight as she neared it.

When she reached the edge of the drop-off she turned back to Billy. "What do you think?"

"I think we shouldn't stand so close together," he said, backing away from her. "The ledge could be undercut beneath the boards."

Cassie looked down. Without getting dangerously close to the edge, she couldn't tell if she was on a cliff face with solid rock beneath her or an extended ledge. All she knew was that she had to go forward. Summoning up her courage, she put a foot on one of the two old boards that spanned the drop beneath her. Below, about twenty feet down, she saw the remains of an old ladder leaning against the sloping wall. Without thinking about it more she willed her other foot to move along the board next to the one her foot was already on. As her weight came down on that board the board gave up a loud creaking sound. The far side was only ten feet away. She sprinted, willing her feet to barely touch the wood. In seconds she stood hunched over on the far side gasping for breath.

Billy just stared at her. When she caught her breath she pointed the headlight down at the two boards. "Now you," she said.

As Billy moved toward the boards, Cassie could see the stone floor the far edge of the board rested on was only inches thick and a wide and deep opening lay beneath it.

"Hurry," she said, as she saw some dirt fall from the underside of the ledge as Billy crossed it. As if sensing the danger that she saw, Billy picked up his pace. In an instant he was across, too.

"Look," she said and pointed her headlight back at the undercut beneath the tunnel floor they had just left.

"Wow," was all Billy could say.

They traveled slowly for more than an hour before they came to a large diamond shaped archway beyond which were three openings spreading out like a three-fingered hand.

"Crap," Cassie said.

"Which way do you want to go?" Billy asked.

Cassie thought for a moment then licked the index finger of her right hand.

She stepped over to the left hand tunnel and held the finger up. "There's air coming out here," she said.

"So we go that way?" Billy asked.

"Let me check the other two," Cassie said. She licked her finger again and checked the middle tunnel. "There's air coming out of this one too," Cassie said.

Billy said nothing.

As she moved toward the right hand tunnel her headlight revealed two reddish colored sticks on the floor by the opening.

"Are those flares?" she asked out loud walking toward them. To her surprise Billy's hand grabbed her shoulder hard and held her back.

"What are you doing?" she demanded angrily.

"Those aren't flares that's dynamite!" Billy said. "I saw a whole box of it in the first area where the logs were holding up the ceiling."

"You didn't say anything."

"It's dangerous. The nitroglycerin can leak out, and it can explode if you even touch it."

300

"How do you know so much about mines?" Cassie asked just a hint of suspicion in her question.

"I got that from old westerns. Best to just stay away from it."

Cassie nodded. "But I better check this tunnel for air." She licked her finger and held it in front of the tunnel, and then she shook her head. "No air moving here. The way out has to be one of the other tunnels."

"Good, there could be more dynamite in this one."

They went back and stood between the left hand and center tunnel.

"Flip a coin?" Billy asked.

Cassie thought for a moment. "Why don't you take the left one and I'll take the center one. That way we can cover more ground quicker."

"Separate?" Billy asked, his voice showing skepticism.

"I want to get out of here," Cassie said, the fear and tension escaping into her voice, giving away how insecure she really felt. She had been telling Billy what to do, taking charge because it gave her a sense of control. But she didn't really have any control here at all.

Billy looked at her with a doubtful expression on his face. "Okay. We can do that." He hesitated a moment then asked, "But why do you think splitting up will help us?"

"The breeze is about the same coming from both of them." Cassie explained. "There could be two separate entrances, but if so I think it's unlikely air would be blowing at the same rate from each. So I think it's more likely the two tunnels join up. We need to figure out which one is the better way to go, and separating would be the fastest way to do that."

Billy nodded his understanding. "How far do you think we should go before we check back with each other?"

Cassie had already thought about this. "Why don't we each count 500 paces. If you come to a place where the breeze stops, then just come back. If you come to a fork always go left, unless there's no breeze coming from the left-hand fork. When either of us get to 500 paces head back. If either of us reach a spot where there is a breeze but for some reason we can't move forward, that person will come back and look for the other."

"Okay," Billy said.

"Put your pen-light on," Cassie said.

"Oh, yeah," Billy said with a laugh. He took his penlight from his pocket and turned it on. It cast a small bright circle on the floor of the archway.

"Good luck," Cassie said turning, and walked into the middle tunnel. She heard Billy moving off behind her.

Cassie had been walking slowly. The narrow walls of the tunnel she was following were beginning to get to her. A steady breeze still blew in her face but it almost seemed as if the sides of the tunnel were very slowly closing in. She had just reached 234 steps when she saw that the darkness in front of her light expanded in width about ten feet ahead. A steady drip of water could be heard ahead.

Carefully she moved forward approaching this wider darkness with caution. When she reached it she saw a huge cavern open up on her left. The tunnel she had been following was now a ledge on the side of this cavern that extended both down below her and up above. Pointing her headlight upward, revealed a rough stone ceiling 40 feet above. When she pointed her headlight down she could see stone outcroppings, but her headlight could not penetrate the darkness at the bottom. She had just turned and pointed her headlight ahead along the ledge she was following when she caught a glimpse of light at the corner of her left eye.

She turned her headlight off without even thinking about it and held her breath. The light was faint but it danced on a stonewall across the cavern. Moments later, apparently on a ledge on the far side of the cavern similar to the one she was on, the source of the light appeared--someone holding a small flashlight.

Her first thought was that it was their captor. But the light was too feeble she realized. Their captor would be better prepared. Billy?

Without turning on her light she sidled slowly to her right until she could feel the wall on her right side. There she turned and keeping the wall in the darkness against her left fingertips, moved back until she sensed that she was back in the entryway to the tunnel she had just emerged from.

She turned and looked across the cavern. She watched the light play around going to the roof of the cavern, which it barely illuminated and then to the depths, which it barely penetrated at all. Ready to dart back into the tunnel she had come from if anyone else but Billy answered, she called out, "Billy! Is that you?"

She held her breath for what seemed like an eternity.

"Cassie?" Billy called back loudly. "Is that you?"

Cassie stepped out from the tunnel entrance took the headlight off her head, and pointed the beam towards her face. "Yes. Have you found any branches in the tunnel you're following?" she called out.

"No," Billy said.

"What count are you at in foot steps?"

"203," Billy said.

That made sense to Carrie. Billy was taller and would have a longer stride.

"Do you have a way to go up ahead?" she asked.

Billy pointed his penlight down along the ledge he was following. A small opening was faintly visible on the far end. "Yes," he replied.

"Let's start our count over from where we are now," Cassie called out. "And go to 500 from here."

"Okay," Billy said after a few seconds. And began moving toward the opening ahead of him.

Cassie pointed her headlight to the floor of the ledge. The ledge stretched about four feet wide, but she still stayed close to the right hand wall as she made her way to an opening at the far end. Just as

Cassie reached the opening on her side of the cavern she saw Billy bend and crawl into a much smaller hole across the way.

She hadn't gone ten feet when she heard, echoing through the cavern, a blood-curdling scream.

She rushed back out the tunnel and, standing a foot back from the ledge of the cavern focused her headlight on the hole she'd seen Billy climb into. A moment later she heard a muffled cry.

"Cassie! Help me!" she knew it was Billy and he sounded terrified.

# Falling in Darkness

## October 30: 10:46 am

Billy only glanced at Cassie as her light vanished into the tunnel on the other side of the chasm. He knelt down and glanced into the narrower tunnel in front of him. It would be tight, but he could make it. After a few feet of crawling the tunnel opened up. He had barely stood when his light revealed the floor of the tunnel ahead had caved in. Right in front of him the floor slanted down to an opening into the chasm.

Billy could see an opening where the tunnel continued on about twenty feet ahead. By pointing the penlight at the collapsed floor, he also saw, about two feet down, a small ledge jutting about six inches out, that with just a few breaks extended to the tunnel on the far side.

Billy had been considering his options all morning. He did not believe there was any other way out of the mine but the grated opening. The least complicated thing he could do was go back the way they had come, let himself out of the mine via the grate, remove any evidence that he'd been here at all, and go home. If Nate Hanassey or his brother asked, he'd say he trapped the girl in the mine. If they didn't believe she was dead, they could look for her themselves and take care of her themselves. Of course, if she somehow got out alive, things could go badly for him.

But the idea of escaping with Cassie and just letting her get away kept coming back to him. He knew it was an almost impossible idea. The reality that he'd probably end up in prison if he tried it kept rearing its ugly head. But almost involuntarily he found himself going along with the impossible plan.

What would he do if he were a prisoner just like Cassie? It was a question he'd been asking himself, and a question that had been modifying his actions. Now as he looked at the ledge he knew as a fellow prisoner he'd climb down to the ledge, work his way across to the tunnel, and see if the air he felt moving past him was coming from the tunnel or the chasm below. If it was not coming from the tunnel, the tunnel was a dead end and he could go and rejoin Cassie.

He decided, since he'd be climbing, to take the makeshift boots off.

Putting the homemade boots in his jacket and the penlight in his mouth he lowered himself to the ledge. Then taking a handhold on the rough rock just above his eye level, he began to move sideways out along the six-inch ledge. He soon came to the first of the breaks in it. By stretching his leg out he was able to secure is footing on the section past the break. It was as he tried to step across a second break that a number of unexpected things happened.

First he was stretched out between the two sections of ledge when the ledge below his right foot gave way. The entire rest of the ledge from where his right foot had been to the opening he was heading for fell away. As he grabbed tighter with his hands, putting more weight on his right hand to offset the loss of balance caused by losing the support of his right leg, his body moved awkwardly, his face bumped into the wall and knocked the penlight out of his mouth.

Billy watched in horror as the light fell, illuminating the chasm for at least two hundred feet before landing with a splash, dimming for a moment, then winking out. The darkness crowded in around him.

"Cassie!" Billy cried as loudly as he could. "Cassie!"

He kept crying her name realizing that now she was his only hope.

His hands were growing numb. His left foot was growing numb. His right foot went from hanging in the air to trying to get purchase on the ledge where his left foot rested. But to actually get up on that ledge, he would need to move his hands. But without light to see where he needed to grab he could not. He had tried to find something to grip with his left hand. But as he stretched that arm out, searching for purchase, his right arm hurting so badly he felt he might lose his grip, he found nothing.

He had no idea how much time had passed.

"Cassie," he cried but his voice was now hoarse from calling for so long. He caught a glimpse of her light just before he heard her moving toward him.

He turned his head. She stood at the opening of the tunnel with her flashlight on him.

"What do you want me to do?" she asked, shaken.

"Just hold the light," he said. With her light on the ledge he could now see the one place he'd need to grab with his right hand in order to be able to move back in the direction of the tunnel. He swung himself sideways, getting lift from his left foot and grabbed the protruding stone. A minute later he was at the edge of the tunnel with Cassie trying to catch his breath.

"Are you alright?" she asked.

"Yeah," he said more harshly then he intended. He had been terrified. Now he felt embarrassed.

"Maybe we should stick together from now on?" Cassie said.

"You think?" Billy said sarcastically. He didn't understand his emotions. She had saved him. And he was feeling angry.

"Here," she said, handing him the extra candle and tin of matches. "Just so you have it."

Billy took the candle and match tin but said nothing. He sat down and began putting the makeshift boots back on.

"Didn't your watch light work?" she asked.

"Shit," Billy said. "I was holding on with both hands, so it didn't matter, but I didn't remember either. A moment later his watch light glowed illuminating his face.

"You'll remember next time," she said.

She led the way out of the small hole Billy had crawled through when she last saw him, and along the path at the edge of the chasm where she'd seen his light.

It wasn't until they had gone back to the area where the tunnels forked and started together into the middle one that it occurred to Billy he could have just pushed her into the chasm as they went past. She would never be able to testify against him that way. And they would be passing the same chasm again shortly on the other side.

But as they passed the chasm on the other side, with the wall on their right this time, Billy did nothing. She had the headlight. He imagined himself taking it from her and then pushing her. And the idea that she would know he was doing that to her just made him feel sick.

# Fatal Choice

## October 30: 2:37 pm

They walked along following the tunnel for some-time. There were times when the tunnel dipped a bit as if going deeper but for the most part the tunnel was level. The sound of running water could be heard, faint, but steady, as they walked, but it seemed to always be far away.

They were rounding a curve in the tunnel when Cassie's headlight suddenly blinked off.

"What's the matter?" Billy asked, thinking she had turned it off for some reason.

"Batteries ran out. I'll have to put in new ones."

Billy felt in his pockets. He pulled out one of the candles and the tin of matches. As he struck the match, Cassie looked up in surprise.

"Thank you," she said. "I was going to try and change the batteries in the dark." As she said it, one of the new batteries in her hand fell to the floor and rolled. By the light of the candle, which Billy moved to better see the battery, she picked it up.

As she snapped the headlight shut and turned it on, Billy blew out the candle.

"We make a good team," she said.

"Yeah," Billy said.

"Look! There's something ahead in the tunnel," Cassie said.

Billy followed her headlight beam. The tunnel ahead appeared to widen and something was built up in the center of the widened area. As they neared it the sound of running water grew louder.

"It's some kind of wooden frame," Cassie said. She rushed ahead leaving Billy behind.

The timbers were old but looked solid to Billy from a dozen feet back. Cassie stepped up on the lip of the frame and looked down.

"There's water running below. It is going in the same direction as this tunnel," she said, and then turned to step off the lip of the frame.

Just then the wood beneath Cassie's feet gave off a loud sound like many sticks breaking at once. And the thick-looking timber that formed the lip frame caved inward. To Billy it seemed like Cassie hung in the air for a second and then sank instantly.

"Cassie!" Billy cried, and rushed forward.

Light now came from a hole in the floor of the tunnel. Billy looked down. The portion of the frame Cassie had been standing on had collapsed. Cassie was just below the lip of the 4 x 4 foot hole hanging on by a jutting rock where the lip had been with her right hand and part of a beam with her left.

Cassie looked up, and the light from her headlight shone directly in his eyes blinding him. "Help me," she cried.

The sound of rushing water was very clear beneath her and the sound was so loud it almost drowned out her second, "Help me."

The headlight was blinding him. He reached out and took it from her head.

"What are you doing," she cried.

"I need to see what I'm doing," Billy said as he slipped the head light on his own head. He looked down. Cassie's situation did not look good. Far below, almost 40 feet Billy guessed, the water was running at a fast pace in the direction they had been headed.

Cassie looked down. She saw the water and an even more fearful look crossed her face. "I can't swim very well. Billy, don't let me fall down there.

Billy realized he could just not do anything. At any moment Cassie would fall. She'd never know he'd hesitated to help her.

"Billy!" she cried.

Billy, without even completely realizing what he was doing, lay down on the floor of the tunnel with only his shoulders over the hole. He reached in and with his left hand grabbed the wrist of the hand she was holding the rock with.

"Don't let go until I tell you," he said.

Cassie looked down again. Then she looked back up at the blinding headlight, her voice pleading. "Billy, I'm afraid. Please don't let me fall."

Billy reached out and grabbed Cassie's left wrist. He was adjusting his grip when her right hand slipped off the rock. With the sudden movement, gravity pulled Cassie out of his hands. He watched as she fell. A scream escaped her lips before she hit the water. She was screaming his name.

Billy watched the water envelope Cassie and sweep her away. He didn't even think about it. He swung his body around and dropped down the shaft feet first.

# Swimming in Darkness

## October 30: 2:38 pm

As Billy fell he threw his hands up over the head-light to protect it. As he hit the water the headlight flew off his head, but his hands still held the straps. His feet never touched bottom as his head went under. He came up quickly in the fast moving water. He set the headlamp back on his head while fighting to stay above the surface, and glanced at a much wider tunnel than the one he fell from, paralleling the one above. He saw a form that seemed to be thrashing about 30 feet ahead of him. It had to be Cassie. She seemed to be moving at the same pace he was. He began swimming, keeping his head above water, lifeguard style, with everything he had.

Billy reached Cassie in less than a minute, but the instant he grabbed her she turned and in her panic grabbed his arms and pulled him under. He could see her face in the light from the headlight. Her eyes were wide with fear.

314

His lifeguard training came back to him, and he broke her hold on him by making a church steeple with his arms and thrusting them up between hers. He immediately swung her around, put an arm across her chest and lifted her head from the water while he swam on his side.

Cassie was choking, and Billy knew she could drown from inhaled water. He had to get her out. But the dark water of the tunnel kept swinging around slow curves with no sign of stopping.

Then, to his joy she started breathing rather than choking. It seemed like he'd been carrying her for a long time when the stone roof ahead opened up into darkness.

A moment later Billy saw they were entering the bottom of another large chasm like chamber. The tunnel widened and the floor came up as the water spread out across a wider area. Billy's feet found purchase and putting his other arm around her, he carried Cassie to higher ground.

"Are you alright?" he asked.

"I think so," she said. She looked at him. "You saved me." Almost instantly she started choking again.

"Get it all out," Billy said, patting her on the back. He knew patting her back wasn't going to help, but at least he could show concern.

When she finally was breathing normally again, he sat down next to her and emptied the sticks he'd gathered from the entryway before he left from his pockets. The sticks were too wet now to burn, but they might be okay by morning.

Of the sleeping bag boots she had made them, one of his was still on his foot. It was soaked and cold and he slipped it off. Both of her's were missing.

"I think we should take a well earned rest for now," he said.

When she didn't answer he turned to her. She was snoring.

# A Parabolic Advantage

## Halloween: 11 am

Nate Hanassey reached a spot in the mine where the three tunnels branched. He was out of breath and very angry. He'd seen no sign of Billy Wesley's Ford Explorer outside. Although the winch was by the entrance, he had no idea if Billy was somewhere in the mine.

Finding the grate closed and Billy's winch working gave Nate hope that he'd find at least the girl and possibly Billy, too, inside the mine.

A dead end passage he explored off the main entry showed definite sign that at least two people had been using it as a latrine area for a few days.

The chamber he discovered next had looked like a damn picnic area. There were empty water bottles, full water bottles, the remains of a campfire, and a cut-up sleeping bag.

He'd put his bare hand in the ashes of the campfire. Not only were the ashes still warm but he'd burned his finger on a still hot coal. A minute later Nate discovered the narrow passage way. After assuring himself that that was the only way someone could have gone, he pointed the parabolic microphone at the tunnel. He was already wearing the earphones that came with it. The only thing he could make out was the sound of air moving through the tunnel.

Until Nate reached the three forks, there had been no other way for anyone to go. He was glad he had the headlight as he could keep his hands free while he adjusted the parabolic microphone. His shotgun was propped against the tunnel wall. Starting at the right hand side tunnel he pointed the microphone

317

inside. He listened for a full minute. All he heard this time was the sound of far off distant water.

He moved to the center tunnel and aimed the microphone. He had only been listening a second when her heard the distinct sound of a young woman's voice. He couldn't make out what was being said but a moment later he heard what sounded like a male reply.

Rather than head down this tunnel immediately, he moved over to the far left tunnel. Again he adjusted the microphone and listened. Again he heard snippets of both the female and male voices.

Nate did not know much about mines, but he did know that tunnels often connected. He was in front of the far left hand side tunnel and decided to search it first. Reattaching the parabolic microphone to his belt, he raised the twelve-gauge sawed-off shotgun he'd stolen in a burglary a month before. Following the light from his headlight, he entered the far left-hand tunnel.

Because he was moving slowly: turning off his headlamp before every turn, allowing his eyes to adjust to the dark, and looking for light ahead, his progress along the tunnel to the open cavern took a half hour.

When Nate perceived the opening ahead he'd turned off his headlight, grabbed the parabolic microphone and listened. He caught faint traces of someone speaking. They were far away.

Nate emerged from the tunnel. A solid wall was on his left. A deep chasm hung open on his right.

318

He moved the earphones off his ears and listened to hear what he could without them. He could hear a faint drip of water far off but nothing else.

Nate reached into his pocket and pulled out a plastic tube. He bent it between his hands and it began to glow green. He tossed the tube into the chasm. It fell a long ways before he heard a muffled splash far below. Why couldn't the two of them have fallen into this pit? Nate's luck was never that good.

With the beam of his headlight, he explored the area at the end of the ledge he was on. A small opening indicated the tunnel went on that way, but as he looked into the opening, he saw that a narrow ledge, the only path between the opening where he was and a another opening further down, had sheared off about halfway along its length into the open chasm. The stone where the ledge was missing sparkled like a new cut. He swung his headlight beam to the far side and saw a much wider tunnel opening at the end of a ledge on that side.

Patiently, Nate unhooked the parabolic microphone again and pointed it first into the opening to the sheared-off ledge. The break looked recent. It was possible they had caused the ledge to beak. It was possible they had gone that way and survived. He heard nothing. He moved the microphone toward the chasm. All he heard was a steady sound of water moving.

When he pointed the parabolic microphone at the opening across the chasm he was soon rewarded with the faint sound of voices.

As he turned back he thought to himself that if he'd been lucky, he'd have chosen the middle tunnel in the first place. But he wasn't, then he laughed to himself thinking, neither were the two he was chasing.

Nate didn't know now long it had taken him to reach the ledge on the far side of the chasm and the opening where he'd head faint voices. He'd been going slowly, afraid a drop-off might open beneath his feet at any time. Once there, he pointed the parabolic microphone into the tunnel and was rewarded with a clear conversation going on somewhere inside marred only by the sound of rushing water.

"How old are you?" a male voice Nate assumed was Billy asked.

" Why?" a female voice replied.

"I'm guessing you're 15 or 16."

"Almost 16. Why do you ask?" she said.

"People frown on someone my age dating a 15 year old."

"How old are you?"

"I'm figuring today is Halloween. I'll be 22 tomorrow."

"I'm old for my age," Cassie said.

"Not old enough."

"You could wait for me," the female voice said, with a teasing note to her tone, as Nate turned off the parabolic microphone.

320

"Nobody is going to be waiting for either of you past today," Nate said to himself.

# An Old Miner's Eyes

## Halloween: 12:23 pm

Denny and I stood before an archway beyond which three tunnels opened up. Denny was already examining the floor. Over the years rock and rock dust had fallen from the ceiling. There were tracks in this dust. I was pretty good at reading tracks. Denny was a grand master.

"They went into both of these tunnels," Denny said pointing to the left and middle tunnel. "Gnat followed them. Don't know which one they went in first and therefore which one we need to go in. Gnat messed up their tracks when he went in."

"There are two of them, besides Nate?"

"Big one and a smaller one. Both wearing what I guess is some of that cut-up sleeping bag we saw," Denny said.

So Cassie was probably still alive. What was Billy, if the person with her was Billy, doing with her? "Is there a way out in either of these tunnels?" I asked.

Denny shook his head. "The right tunnel's the only way out. If it hasn't caved in. But it's maybe a good thing they didn't go that way."

"Why," I asked.

Denny turned his head and pointed. In his headlight I could see two sticks of dynamite. "Dynamite and caps all over that tunnel."

I nodded and looked at the two tunnels. "But they could still be ahead of Hanassey?" I asked.

Denny nodded.

"We need to split up. You take the left tunnel and I'll take the middle," I said.

"Makes sense," Denny said. He looked at me. "Shoot to kill?"

"Only if you have to," I said. "How far behind Nate do you think we are?"

"Not long," Denny said.

"Then lets move quietly," I said.

Despite being old, Denny could make good time in the mine. We reached an open area; each of us emerging on ledges, separated by a chasm, not long after we'd each entered our separate tunnels. We gave each other a thumbs up but didn't call out.

Moments later I entered a tunnel on my side of the chasm and lost sight of Denny.

# Check Your Back Trail

## Halloween: 1:53 pm

Nate Hanassey sat in a short but widened chamber in the mine. He'd been listening to the sounds from the tunnel ahead. The voices of a man and a woman were very distinct. He was sure he was only a few hundred yards away from them. He'd discovered the spot where it seemed they'd fallen into a winze and landed in deep water. Somehow they were still alive. It was time to remedy that situation.

Suddenly. he thought he heard something behind him. Or had he? Nate always felt he had a sixth sense about things. He'd escaped on numerous times from homes he was burglarizing, because he sensed rather than heard someone coming. The only reason he had ended up in prison was because a partner had ratted him out when the cops put pressure on him.

That partner was now in a 55-gallon drum at the bottom of Rainbow Lake.

Nate realized it could be his imagination. But he didn't have to rely on his gut this time. He pointed the parabolic microphone at the opening behind him and listened. He was rewarded. Men were speaking far back in the mine. They were coming.

Nate thought for a long time. The best thing to do he decided was lie in wait for them.

# Corners in the Dark

## Halloween: 2:46 pm

When I saw the collapsed collar my heart sank. That there was water down below rather than a hard floor did not give me solace. My first thought was that one or both of them had fallen to their deaths.

Had I started imagining that Billy Wesley wasn't as bad as I had originally imagined him to be?

There was no sign in the chamber where the two had obviously spent some time that Cassie had been assaulted. And I reasoned, perhaps naively, that a girl that young would most likely be a virgin, and there would have been some sign her virginity had been taken.

There had been some blood in the chamber, but there had been no sign of violence there. Someone had been brought in bleeding. That may well have been Cassie after her accident. Whatever Billy Wesley was doing was not right, but I was beginning to think he was not the monster I had originally imagined.

I got as close to the winze as I dared. The drop was at least 13 yards and the water below was moving swiftly. Billy Wesley, I had read, had been a lifeguard. But I didn't even know if Cassie Carew could swim.

An examination of the tunnel past the winze revealed that someone, most likely Nate Hanassey, had continued on. My choices were to follow the way Hanassey had gone or drop down into the water. Both the tunnel and water were going in the same direction and it was likely they'd come together at some point. Hanassey had probably figured that out, too.

I chose to follow Hanassey. I pointed my flashlight down the tunnel in the direction Hanassey had gone. The tunnel seemed solid and fairly straight. I turned my flashlight off and peered into the darkness. I saw no sign of light. I moved forward in the dark for about 40 paces then turned my flashlight on again. Then I repeated the process. There was no point in alerting Hanassey with my light.

About five minutes later I came across a small alcove that had been dug into the tunnel wall. I kept my flashlight on and pointed at the floor as I passed it. A crude table had been built there. Across the table were spread sticks of dynamite in varying degrees of decay. I saw at least one blasting cap on the floor near the table.

Until I was well clear of the table and any stray blasting caps, I kept my light on the floor. When I came to another straight section of tunnel, I began my on and off flashlight procedure.

As I walked I strained my ears for any sound of voices or movement. But I heard nothing. A few hundred yards further, I came to a spot where a quick peek with my light revealed a long stretch that ended in a corner where a huge unpeeled log held back a wooden-beam-braced wall of stacked, slightly leaning, bowling-ball sized waste rock. These I knew were called gobbing by miners. This gobbing rested on the right side of the passage. With my flashlight off I moved as quietly as I could toward the corner checking for any light at all peeking around the edge, listening intently for any sound.

I'd learned to be very careful rounding a corner when I didn't know what lay beyond it, not as an MP or sniper but as a child. At my cousin's house a bunch of us were playing war with cap guns. A neighbor kid I was with, named Joey, ran gung-ho around a corner of my cousin's house where an alley ran to the back. Not anticipating that anyone would be lying in wait, he had been cut down in a volley of cap-fire. My cousin, who had just waylaid my erstwhile companion, taught me the second lesson I learned that day. He assumed my companion had been the only enemy coming around the corner. My cousin had turned about-face and was walking down the alley with his back toward me. He was boasting to his team how he had just gotten Joey, as I turned that corner and shot him in the back.

I stopped just before the corner in the dark. From behind the unpeeled log I leaned out just enough for one eye to peek around its edge.

I saw nothing. I heard nothing. I waited a full minute, then another, then a third. It seemed clear. I started to step out around the log post, but then, instead, moved the flashlight to my left hand and extended my left arm around the corner. I leaned over just far enough to peek with my left eye as I turned the flashlight on.

# An Ambush

## Halloween: 3:01 pm

Nate Hanassey waited for whoever was behind him in a stope that was about as large as large barn. The carved out cavern resembled half a ball that sat at a slant in the earth. The tunnel path here was like a ledge on the edge of a steep slope to Nate's left as he faced the tunnel the voices were coming from.

Ever since he'd heard the voices behind him he'd known he'd have to deal with whoever was following first. The kid and the girl were not expecting him. Whoever was following was.

He had an advantage in that whoever was coming after him had to round the corner he was watching to follow the tunnel into the stope. It was a blind corner where gobbing was held up by one thick log post and an old wooden wall.

He'd had a long wait. He'd had to use the parabolic microphone to assure himself that someone was still coming. At first he thought there where at least two people coming. But now all he heard was one. Whoever was coming was coming very slowly and very cautiously.

328

Finally, he could tell that the person was very close. He put the parabolic microphone down and readied his sawed-off shotgun. When a flashlight showed around the corner he'd let go with both barrels.

# Buried

## Halloween 3:02 pm

With the loud blast that rang out my flashlight was torn from my hand. Pain shot up my forearm. I caught a glimpse of flame in the distance as the beam of the flashlight winked and died. A loud wrenching sound filled the air, a tearing of wood, and I realized too late that the log timber holding back the wall of waste rock had taken most of what I guessed was Nate's shotgun's blast and was now collapsing.

With both legs I kicked backward as hard as I could as rock began to push against me on my right side. Dust filled the air and I began to choke as I fell. I landed hard on my right side and heavy blows began to pound my legs.

When the movement of rocks subsided I lay a moment in the darkness and discovered I could move both my arms as I grabbed my bleeding left forearm with my right hand. I assumed I'd been hit by at least one double-ought buck shot round. My legs would not move. Using my hands, I found that my legs were partly buried in stones that had tumbled into the tunnel as the barrier the log supported collapsed.

One rock was digging into the top of my thigh. I grabbed it and lifted it off and bent forward to remove the next, when a light appeared behind me down the tunnel. Not long after later, Denny appeared. He bandaged my arm then and began helping lift the rocks off me.

Six minutes later I as able to stand on aching legs and view the damage the collapse had caused. One .33 caliber buckshot ball had grazed the fleshy part of my forearm. Now, bandaged, it hurt like nothing I'd felt since I'd had a kidney stone years before. I was very lucky I had jumped backward when I did. Where the corner had been was now a pile of stones head high. The passage was completely blocked. Had I remained a few feet further in, I would have been buried alive and it was doubtful Denny could have dug me out in time.

"What now? Swim?," Denny asked as he handed me a new looking headlight.

"Where did you get this?" I asked, as I put the headlight on.

"Gnat's truck," he said.

The water seemed the only way to go, but when we got back to the winze through which I suspected Billy and/or Cassie had fallen, water no longer rushed by forty feet below. Instead, the water now filled the lower portion of the shaft, and the drop was only thirty feet to a pool of water that seemed to be rising.

"Must have caused a cave-in below in the lower tunnel," Denny said.

"We have to get to those kids before Nate does," I said.

"I have an idea," Denny said. He led me back to the alcove with the makeshift table.

Denny examined the pieces of dynamite on the old bench very carefully. "Old dynamite sweats nitro. It can go off if you even bump it," he said.

He had found an old empty cardboard box beneath the table and now lifted an intact looking stick of dynamite into it. Next to the one he lifted sat another stick, partly corroded, which had a few yellow beads of liquid on the outer skin.

Denny pointed at the corroded dynamite stick I had been looking at and said, "Got to avoid ones like that."

My heart was in my throat as he chose three more sticks and carefully placed them in the box. When he was done I took a deep breath. Then he gently picked up the box and held it out to me.

He must have registered the surprise on my face. "Just walk slowly and don't jostle the box. The caps are the dangerous part."

Instead of going I watched him turn away and bend down. He'd found an old Prince Albert tobacco tin, which he now stepped on and flattened. Next, still bent over, he carefully pushed two of the rifle-cartridge-like, cylindrical blasting caps onto the flattened can.

He turned and looked at me, perhaps surprised I had not gone ahead as told. "You go ahead of me. You don't want to be anywhere close to these."

At the cave-in Denny placed the four sticks of dynamite in a crevice between stones at about waist height. With his pocket knife he cut the sides of the cardboard box I'd carried the dynamite in away from the bottom, cut the rectangular section into one long strip by cutting it at a corner, and stuck an edge under the four dynamite sticks. He then very carefully placed the two blasting caps on top of this long paper fuse.

He pulled out his lighter, and handed it to me. "Wait until I've gotten quite a ways down the tunnel. Then light the fuse and run!"

When Denny's headlight was just a small spot down the tunnel I lit the base of the cardboard fuse.

I thought with my height and longer legs I could run pretty fast. Yet, I seemed to be moving down the tunnel in slow motion.

332

Thankfully, we were both far down the tunnel, when, with a sound like being inside a thunderclap, the dynamite blew. I turned back to see a red ball of fire like a dragon's breath rushing toward us, it closed half the distance to us, and then the flame died, but its heat washed over us like a pounding, scalding wave.

Where the flames had been now hung clouds of dust. Through the dust it was hard to see if the blast had cleared the passageway. Then, sudden and un-expected, like an aftershock to an earthquake, with a deafening roar, the stone around us seemed to rumble as if the entire mine were caving in.

# All Hallows Eve

## Morning

When Cassie, lying on her back, opened her eyes a vast expanse of roof stretched high above her in flickering light. The cavern they were now in was so vast all she could see was darkness at the far end. The sound of rushing water filled her ears. She turned on her side. Billy was feeding sticks from a small pile spread out across a stone floor into a very small fire.

She turned toward the water and saw it came from a tunnel from which she assumed they had come. The stream spread widely out and ran across the floor just a few feet below her. It seemed to vanish into a rock wall too far away to see clearly in the fire's light.

"You saved me?" she said.

Billy looked at her and gave a bright smile. "Good morning, at least I think it's morning." He paused a second and then added, "My watch seems to have stopped. And, it appears we are now 'even' in the saving department."

She looked at him for a long time. "All I did for you was show up with a light. You had to jump down a deep hole and swim after me."

"You said you don't swim well."

Cassie just shook her head. She didn't know what to say. Billy looked into her eyes. She'd never had any boy look at her that way.

"How old are you?" Billy asked a moment later.

" Why?" Cassie asked.

"I'm guessing you're 15 or 16," Billy said, he seemed almost sad when he said it.

"Almost 16. Why do you ask?" she asked.

"People frown on someone my age dating a 15 year old."

At his words Cassie felt something she had never felt before. But whatever it was felt very, very good.

"How old are you?" she asked back.

"I'm figuring today is Halloween. I'll be 22 tomorrow."

"I'm old for my age." Cassie said.

"Not old enough," he said, reaching out and touching her cheek gently with his fingertip. She wanted him to keep touching her but he took his hand away.

"You could wait for me," Cassie said, hopefully.

"We have to get out of here first," Billy said. "Did you see the size of this place? He'd had the headlight off but now he turned it on and moved it about the chamber they were in. It appeared to be a gigantic ballroom sized cavern. Old wooden scaffolds climbed the far walls. Small tunnels seemed to go off in every direction.

"I guess I lost my boots," she said, lifting her feet and wiggling her toes.

"I have one left," he said listing the still soggy piece of sleeping bag with his hand. "Do you want it?"

Cassie shook her head no.

"Then neither do I," he said and tossed the wet 'boot' into the stream. "Maybe we should start looking around for a way out."

Cassie nodded. She got up and followed him toward an opening to the side of the spot where the water ran.

"So today is Halloween?" Cassie said after a bit. "If it weren't for the accident I'd be trick or treating with my little brother sometime today."

# A Hunter and His Prey

## Halloween 3:02 pm

The double shotgun blast rang out in the cavern. As expected the flashlight vanished in the darkness, but he did not expect the whole wall on the far side of the stope to give way. Rock crashed down and then one giant slab fell from the ceiling, flew down the side of the stope and punched a hole in the floor below. When the crashing was done he saw water welling up out of that hole.

He quickly reloaded the sawed-off. With his shotgun ready he went as close as he dared to the now caved in opening. A quick glance told him no one would be coming that way.

He went back and picked up his parabolic microphone and pointed it toward the open tunnel at the other end of the stope. Before long he heard faint voices. He was headed in the right direction.

# A Sound in the Dark

## Halloween 3:02 pm

Cassie and Billy both looked back in the direction of the tunnel on the far side of the cavern they were making their way across. A muffled explosion followed by the sounds of a cave-in came from that direction. They had assumed that tunnel, as it was in the direction from which the water was flowing, was the same one they had been following before they entered the water.

They were not far from the right hand wall of the cavern. They had followed the water to see how it might exit on the far side. The water vanished into a tunnel so low they couldn't have entered it if they wanted to. So they had followed the wall, hoping the tunnel they had been walking through earlier continued on up ahead. The sounds of the explosion and cave-in sent both their hearts racing.

"Do you think someone's coming?" Cassie asked.

"No body knows we're here but the person or persons who put us here," Billy said. They had been moving slowly as the floor of the cavern they were in was uneven and littered with boulders of varying size.

"So we need to find a place to hide or a way out," Cassie said.

"I think, if we don't find a way out with the very next tunnel we check, we should find a place to hide and turn off this headlight. That didn't sound that far away."

Cassie looked across the floor of the cavern to the glowing coals of their little fire, now, quite some distance away. "Do you think we should go back and put that out?"

"I think they'll smell the smoke even if we do," Billy said.

Suddenly, sounding far away, a voice came echoing out of the tunnel. "Billy! Cassie! Where are you?"

"Maybe it's help," Cassie said, her rising hope obvious in her voice.

Billy's stomach clenched. He felt sick. He recognized the voice. It was Nate Hanassey's voice.

"That sounds like the guy I met carrying the water—the guy who has to be the one who put me in here. I think we really need to find a place to hide," Billy said in a whisper. He took Cassie's hand, and they both began running toward a dark hole that opened in the wall just fifteen feet ahead of them. As soon as they entered they saw that it was just a tiny L-shaped alcove that went nowhere. They both crowded into the L, and Billy turned off the headlight.

# A Final Stalk

## Halloween: 3:21 pm

Nate Hanassey proceeded very cautiously down the tunnel he was following. He'd learned in the prison yard that you should never underestimate an opponent. The one time he'd not followed that rule he'd taken a pencil to the groin before he split the man's skull.

He hadn't walked for long before he saw in the distance ahead that the tunnel opened into a much vaster darkness. When he was near the opening into this new cavern, he aimed the parabolic microphone into the black void, and then, called out to Billy and Cassie. He did not expect a reply. He heard what he expected: a whispered voice very clearly saying they should hide. It would not be long before he had them.

Moments later, standing in the gigantic open area, a light, off to his right, caught his eye. He turned his headlight off and looked toward the light. It looked like the dying coals of a fire.

"Billy! Cassie! Where are you?" He called out, trying to make his voice sound concerned.

He kept his eyes focused in the direction of the dying fire.

There was no reply. He now doubted they were by it, but he would have to check it out. It might take awhile to find their hiding place, but he would find it.

He scanned the area he could see with his headlight very carefully. He could see no immediate danger to himself. He had a ploy that just might work.

"Billy!" he called loudly. "Billy Wesley! The cops are on our tail. They shot your brother. Bobby's dead. We have to get rid of the girl and get out of here. Do you hear me?"

His voice echoed through the cavern. For a few moments all he heard was the sound of water.

"Bobby?" He heard Billy whisper on the parabolic microphone. Nate could tell he'd gotten to him.

A moment later he hear the girl say, "Look at me." Nate could tell she was losing it. "Did you have anything to do with this?"

"There was an accident. Your Dad died. They would have killed you." Billy whispered.

Nate grinned sensing Billy's desperation.

The girl began screaming, "Let go of me." And Nate didn't even need the parabolic microphone to hear her. The sound was coming off to his right from a point in the darkness. He had just taken a step in that direction when the whole mine seemed to heave. A hot wind blew out of the tunnel behind him and he heard the ear wrenching sound of cracking stone.

# Point of View of The Prey

## Halloween 3:44 pm

When Nate had called to him that Bobby was dead, Billy lost it. "Bobby?" he said out loud in shock. Cassie had been pressed against him in the darkness. When he said "Bobby?" she stiffened. He could feel her body pulling away from his. She turned and looked right at him.

"Look at me. Did you have anything to do with this?"

Billy could tell she was about to lose it. He realized he had wanted to tell her the truth as soon as he had gotten to know her.

"There was an accident. Your Dad died. They would have killed you," he whispered.

He sensed she was about to run off blindly into the dark. He somehow managed to grab her coat. He had to explain. Q

"Let go of me," she'd cried sounding so terrified he couldn't believe it. He tried to hold onto her coat

342

sleeve, to talk to her, to calm her. But instead with a burst of energy that amazed him she shook him off.

He took another step after her but stumbled and fell.

Lying on the floor of the cavern he reached up and touched the headlight. If he turned it on, Nate would see her. He'd see both of them. He'd have a gun. They might both be dead in seconds.

Then the floor of the mine heaved as if from an earthquake and he fell to the floor with a thunderous crashing about him.

# Confluence

## Halloween 3:48 pm

"What the hell?" I cried when the mine stopped moving around us.

"Let's hope we didn't kill them all," Denny said.

We both rushed to the corner where we'd set the explosives. There was a hole through the stones about four feet around. I dove through and Denny followed.

I saw as I emerged on the far side of the hole where a huge slab had slid downhill and punched through the floor. With a glance I saw that water was pooling around the hole.

We hurried ahead, while being careful at every corner, at every step across the tunnel floors least the explosion had weakened the floor over another tunnel, or Nate Hanassey was lying in wait for us. Finally, we rounded a curve and were greeted by bright light ahead. This was light that could only be sunlight.

"This's the big stope," Denny said. "It came very close to the surface. The explosion must have caved it in."

Fearful that Cassie might have been under the ceiling of the stope when it caved, I rushed ahead. Denny followed.

Large slabs of stone littered the path through the center of the stope and blocked our view of the slope up to the opening. So it wasn't until I came almost to the center of the now roofless cavern that I saw Nate Hanassey directly ahead of me. Nate stood above me on a rising slope that seemed to lead right out of the mine. His thick arm was wrapped around Cassie Carew's neck, and he had a sawed-off shotgun pointed at her temple. He was looking off to my right.

"Let her go, Nate," a desperate unseen voice cried out from behind some rocks.

Nate was focused on the area where the voice was coming from. I had my revolver out but Nate was at least 50 yards away. Denny and I both moved forward as quietly as we could

"You come out now, Billy, or I start cutting her," Nate called back. Billy, obviously, couldn't see that Nate wasn't holding a knife.

Cassie suddenly screamed as Nate pushed the muzzle of his gun painfully into her temple. "I'm starting to carve on her right now and in just a little bit she ain't going be so fucking pretty if you don't come out."

He dug the muzzle in harder and Cassie screamed again. Billy stepped out from behind a boulder not ten feet from Nate.

Nate pointed the shotgun at Billy and pulled one of the triggers before Billy had closed half the distance between them.

Nate still held his gun toward Billy who was falling. Cassie was twisting in Nate's grasp, and screaming. I knew in another instant he'd shoot her, and telling him to drop his gun would just give him a chance to turn and use her as a shield while he shot at me.

The distance was 25 yards now. It was a long shot for a pistol but I had no choice. I squeezed off my shot holding the sights on Nate's right ear. Nate Hanassey's head exploded.

I moved as the girl broke from Hanassey's grip and Hanassey began to fall. I reached Hanassey seconds after he hit the ground and kicked his gun away from his hand. As I looked at his misshapen head I knew kicking the gun away hadn't been necessary, but you can never tell.

Cassie Carew ran to where Billy Wesley lay on his back on the ground. There was blood in Billy's mouth. I could see that most of Nate's buckshot had hit him in his abdomen.

I watched Cassie get down on her knees and take Billy's right hand.

"Will you forgive me?" Billy whispered.

Cassie just cried.

I walked over. By the time I got there Billy was dead.

Cassie looked up at me with tears flowing from her eyes. "Is my Dad really dead?" she asked, her eyes pleading with me to say that Nate had been lying.

I nodded. "And it was an accident," I said.


Surprising to me was that my cell worked from the top of the open stope. Goldstone wanted to find a helicopter to fly out to the mine to us. But it wasn't necessary. My iPhone had GPS, and we were not that far from a main road.

Goldstone did commandeer a snowplow, and, within an hour and a half of Billy's passing, Cassie was on her way to the hospital to be checked out.

# Epilogue

## November 1:

When Adahy came by my cabin the next evening for belated trick or treating with his mother, Rylee was there. That afternoon, after getting up at noon, I had gone to talk to Cassie and Callie Carew and then to tell Rylee personally that Cassie had been rescued.

When Callie opened the door she grabbed and hugged me, like I don't think I was ever hugged before. Cassie filled in the details for me, of how she'd discovered a tied, bleeding and unconscious Billy. I couldn't blame her for believing he was also a prisoner. There appeared to be much more to Billy than I had ever imagined. The thing that Cassie said, that would always stick with me was, "I can understand, now, how he'd feel he had to protect his brother. I guess I'm just lucky he didn't hurt me."

Rylee seem to still be blaming herself over Yash and Ken, and I, perhaps because she looked so much like my late wife, feeling sorry for her and having to feed the animals, had invited her to my home for an early dinner to try some elk steak. On the way to my cabin I think I was at least partly successful in convincing her how important the part she and her friends played in finding Cassie, actually, was. I found out she was 22, as I guessed. Before she came in I asked that she wait until I cleaned up a bit. What I actually did was put the photos I had of Lo away. I told myself it was because I did not want to make Rylee uncomfortable.

I had just started cooking two elk steaks and was finding, once I'd distracted her, that I enjoyed Rylee's exuberance, which was refreshing, when a soft knock came at the door, and I heard Adahy's voice cry, "Trick or Treat!"

"Just a second," I called.

I found a smiling Adahy in an obviously home-made costume and his mother when I opened the door.

I introduced Rylee.

"Adahy didn't want you to miss out being trick or treated," Yona said. "Next, we are going to Two-Guns. We missed him yesterday, too, on our way to the mall.

"How did you make out at the mall?" I asked the boy.

He nodded and spread his hands wide.

"He's been eating it so fast he is going to be sick," his mother said.

As I fetched an apple for Adahy's treat, I couldn't quite place Adahy's costume, so I asked.

"I am medicine man, braver than Batman, stronger than Superman. I see with magic eyes," he said.

"What magic do you see?" I asked.

He pointed right at Rylee and said, "This sister that looks like Aunty Lo does not like spiders."

I turned and looked at Rylee. She was staring in horror at a spider descending the log rafters above her head. Even in winter you could always find spiders in wilderness cabins. I grabbed the spider off its thread, opened the front door and threw it onto the pile of stacked firewood by the door where it rushed to hide between the logs.

"Won't it freeze?" Rylee asked, anxiously.

"It will hibernate," I said, "under the pile most likely."

Adahy took the apple I gave him with a stoic expression. But I knew he'd gotten enough candy trick or treating in Missoula.

"Adahy! Would you like to come by Saturday and go on a hunt with me?" I asked.

His eyes brightened. "But I'm not old enough to hunt elk. Am I?" he asked testing me.

"We can hunt rabbits. If it is okay with your mother?" I said.

He looked at his mother and she nodded.

"His father had an old single shot .22 he hunted with as a boy," Yona said. "May we bring it?"

"I have some .22 shells, I believe," I said.

Adahy left a very happy boy, but Rylee kept looking for spiders while we ate. I took her home early. On the way she asked if I didn't get lonely up in my cabin all alone. I couldn't tell her I had a ghost that looked like her for company, and so, said, "There are lots of friendly spiders." She shook her head. I walked her to her door. Luckily her room mates were back. I asked if she thought she'd be alright. When she said, "yes," I simply said goodnight and left.

# November 4:

On Saturday, November 4, 2017 Yona dropped off Adahy in the morning. We spent the morning target shooting and were going to try our luck hunting rabbits after lunch. We were just finishing a hearty meal of peanut butter and jelly sandwiches, Adahy's favorite, when a knock came at the door.

Shawna Edwards looked gorgeous in her uniform and gave me a warm smile.

"I wanted to congratulate you. You found her."

"Yes," I said. "Thanks in part to you and Tim. I hope Tim isn't upset with you? "

"Tim and I are fine. And he will be pleased when I tell him what you said. Listen…" she said, and paused.

"I hate to keep doing this to you, but I just got the afternoon off, and I thought we might be able to hang out?" Then she gave me this funny look. "Although Tim said you seemed to have hit it off with someone named Pumpkin at his club. So it that's the case...."

I felt my face redden.

Adahy stepped up behind me at the door. "We are hunting today," Adahy said.

I turned to Adahy, "Can my friend Shawna join us?"

"I like hunting. I've been hunting since I was a little girl."

"This hunt is only for warriors," Adahy said. "Perhaps you can hunt with us another time."

Shawna smiled and stepped back. "Well, if that's the case," she said, looking up at me, "Can I please get a rain check?"

"This white lady isn't afraid of spiders," Adahy said. How he figured that out I don't know.

I didn't hesitate. There were always spiders in my cabin. "Sure," I said. "A rain check."

# The End

# Acknowledgments

No book gets done without the help of readers. I want to thank David Braden, John Curran, Keilani Curran, Jim Allen, and Tom Curran for readings in progress.

## Author's Note:

A great deal of effort was put into trying to make this manuscript error free. But no one is perfect. If you find an error or typo, please let us know at editor@winslowdoyle.com

Made in the USA
Columbia, SC
20 December 2017